Her Only Desire

Her Only Desire

DELILAH DEVLIN

New York Boston

Copyright © 2014 by Delilah Devlin
Excerpt from *His Every Fantasy* copyright © 2014 by Delilah Devlin
Cover design by Elizabeth Turner
Cover copyright © 2014 by Hachette Book Group, Inc.

Forever Yours
Hachette Book Group
237 Park Avenue
New York, NY 10017
hachettebookgroup.com
twitter.com/foreverromance

First published as an ebook and as a print on demand: May 2014

Forever Yours is an imprint of Grand Central Publishing.
The Forever Yours name and logo are trademarks of Hachette Book Group, Inc.

The publisher is not responsible for websites (or their content) that are not owned by the publisher.

The Hachette Speakers Bureau provides a wide range of authors for speaking events. To find out more, go to www.hachettespeakersbureau.com or call (866) 376-6591.

ISBN: 978-1-4555-2835-6 (ebook edition)
ISBN: 978-1-4555-4649-7 (print on demand edition)

To my daughter, Kelly, and my sister, Elle James, who dared to take a wild airboat ride with me in the bayou and shared an even wilder time in New Orleans. If only I could remember the details…

Her Only Desire

Chapter One

The sound was faint and haunting, entering his dreams like a distant echo. A metallic tinkling drifting closer, coming and going, like tiny golden bells worn on a waving arm.

Boone Benoit awoke in a sweat. He lay still for a moment, searching the darkness around him, remembering the layout of the furniture in his bedroom, but finding no new shadows to cause alarm.

But he heard the tinkling in the distance and slipped out of bed. Opening the French doors that led onto the balcony, he stepped out into the humid night air and listened.

Nothing. He must have imagined the sound. Or maybe the gardeners had installed wind chimes, and they'd stirred in a breeze. Although, right this moment, the thick bayou air was perfectly still.

Another door opened farther down the balcony. From the corner of his eye, Boone saw his right-hand man, Sergei Gun, step outside.

"You okay, boss?"

"I'm fine, Serge. Just thought I heard something."

"Want me to have the guards take a look around the grounds?"

He began to shake his head. His unease at being back was clearly playing with his head, and he wasn't happy about it. He'd only been back a day, but in Bayou Vert, news traveled faster than CNN across backyard fences. For all he knew, someone might be there in the dark, staring down the barrel of a rifle. "Yeah, have them make a round. And find out if someone put up wind chimes."

Serge's head canted.

He probably wanted to ask why, but knew Boone well enough to refrain. Boone and those closest to him had secrets they all kept close to the chest. For good reason.

"What do you want them to do if they find chimes?"

"Shoot 'em," Boone said with a grim smile.

Serge's teeth gleamed in the shadows. "Get some sleep, boss."

"You too."

Boone stepped back inside and lay down on the bed, closing his eyes and trying to relax, but he strained to hear the telltale sound—golden bells on a bracelet, tinkling at the end of a pale arm.

Dragging in a deep breath, he wondered if he was ready for this. Ready to return to his childhood home. Ready to face his past and the terrible thing that had happened here.

Likely, the sound had been only a dream, dredged up by his own feelings of guilt. A blood-soaked memory. Boone acknowledged the guilt. Accepted it. But now was the time to face the part he'd played. Dead calm settled around him and he drifted off into an uneasy sleep.

* * *

Clotille Floret waved a lazy hand at a fly buzzing, although even that felt like too much effort in the stifling heat. She went back to washing down small bistro tables and chairs outside the restaurant, not that anyone in their right mind would want to sit outside on a day like today.

Still, Mae insisted. Didn't matter what the season was, things had to be done in a certain order. And since she was the one signing Tilly's paychecks, Tilly didn't bother arguing. It wasn't like Tilly had anything better to do. Life in the bayou was unchanging—summers even more so. There was no Walmart, no movie theater, no entertainments to speak of other than the restaurant and Tater Cribb's tiny bar, which boasted four concrete-block walls, AC that worked most of the time, and a jukebox that played hits from the eighties since he'd never bothered updating the selection. Tilly knew every tune by heart.

Like a Southern-fried Brigadoon, this seedy little bayou town had been stuck on a single track. Unmoving and morose. After her mother had died and her aunt and uncle had moved away, Tilly had been marooned here, trying to make ends meet to set things right for her brother. Only her efforts were too little and too late.

Sweat trickled from her brow into her eye, and she swiped it away with the back of her hand. She'd dawdled outside long enough. A string of chores awaited her inside.

The sound of an automobile approaching drew her attention, and she watched a dark limo slide down Main Street, dark windows hiding the passenger, the engine a low, contained rumble. Unease shivered through her, tightening her belly. The day everyone in town had sworn would never come had arrived.

As the vehicle drew near, she couldn't help but pull down the edges of her Daisy Dukes. Somehow, the thought of flashing her ass cheeks to the man who rode by in that impossibly luxurious black Bentley seemed a little too stereotypically trashy. Never mind that was how she earned her best tips.

The car's appearance in Bayou Vert was noteworthy enough that LeRoy Duhon stepped out of his bait shop. And Cletus Guidry wiped a greasy rag as he strode from the bay of his auto repair shop to watch. He was likely drooling. Fat chance he'd even get to change the oil on the sleek beauty. Up and down the short block, townsfolk gathered on the sidewalk. A presidential candidate on a baby-kissing campaign tour couldn't have gotten more attention.

The only person who didn't come outside was Tilly's boss, Mae Baillio. Mae stood inside the restaurant, watching through the screened windows. Her dark hands folded over her middle, and her gaze followed the car like it was a hearse, leading the way to the graveyard.

Boone Benoit's return might have felt like that to her. Tante Mae had known the young Boone, remembered the scandal all too well. She'd been working for Tilly's aunt at the time.

Even for Tilly, the slow procession felt…ominous. She'd been a tween when the tragedy struck, and although she'd cried buckets of tears in the days after, she'd recovered, showing the resilience of a child. Not so, the rest of her family. They'd worn the pain like open wounds, never letting them heal. Something she hadn't understood until she'd found the little treasure box.

She turned her back and walked into the restaurant, striding up beside Mae as the car slid out of sight.

"Man's got brass balls," Mae whispered, her voice hoarse.

Tilly shivered, wondering if everyone felt like she did. Like the ground would begin to shiver and shake before opening up a huge jagged gash to swallow the entire town.

Change was coming. Wasn't something anyone in the bayou was likely to embrace. Hurricanes came and went, flattening buildings then sweeping them out on rising tides. The town took

Nature's violence all in stride. But this was different. Darker. A reminder of the scar left on their collective souls.

"Thought for sure he was only prettyin' up his house to sell it," Tilly said softly, placing a hand on Mae's tense shoulder.

"Saw it in the cups. He be here to stir up trouble."

Although Tilly didn't believe in the portents the older woman read in her tea leaves, she couldn't shake the thought Boone Benoit was back for justice. Not something she could voice aloud, because most folks thought he'd escaped a rightful lynching.

Mae shook off her hand and crossed stiff-legged to the corkboard, where yet another list of jobs opening at the plantation had been tacked just that morning. As often as Boone Benoit's foreman put up the notice, Mae tore it down and wadded it in her fist. The crisp page crackled as her brown fingers balled it tight.

Not that Tilly had needed more than a quick glance when the large, muscled foreman sauntered inside day after day to post yet another notice. The position that made her uneasy was still there. Still open.

She didn't dare apply. Not just because everyone she knew would be appalled. The secret she'd kept bottled inside was too near the surface of her emotions to risk being anywhere near Boone Benoit.

And yet, how could she not? The money from her cashed-in 401(k) was gone. Her house sold. The only way she could rescue Denny from the group home that so frightened him was a better-paying job. Shaking her ass for the male customers at Mae's Cafe wouldn't get her what she needed, and that left her with only one alternative.

"Saw you lookin' at da board," Mae said, her dark eyes cold and narrowed. "You know you're only buyin' trouble. You should go back to da city. Can't take care of Denny if you don' take care of yourself first."

"Denny could never live in the city." The thought saddened her. Denny wasn't quite right. Moving him with her to the city simply wasn't an option.

"Maybe you should just let him go."

Tilly shook her head. It was something she had considered, although she was too ashamed to admit it.

The bell above the restaurant's door tinkled.

Tilly gave Mae a quick, tight smile, and then pasted on a bigger one as she turned. Her lips froze. "Oh. Hey there, Leon."

Sheriff Leon Fournier tilted his head, and his gaze skimmed quickly over her thin tank only to linger on her long, bare legs. "Nice to see you, Tilly."

Tilly rolled her eyes. "Answer's still no. Want your coffee with cream?"

"Ain't everything better with cream?"

She ignored his amused drawl, skirting past him without touching. Once behind the counter, she breathed easier and busied herself pouring coffee into a Styrofoam cup, hoping he'd take the hint he should take the coffee with him as he left.

Leon leaned a hip against the counter and pointed toward the window. "You see Benoit skate through town like he owned it?"

Tilly arched a brow. "Doesn't he? Half the men not out shrimpin' are workin' on his place."

"Thought he was gonna sell it."

"Maybe he's gonna meet a Realtor there," Tilly mused, hoping her statement was true.

Leon's lips pursed. "Haven't seen it go up on any of the real estate websites."

She arched a taunting brow. "You know how to use the Internet?"

His eyes narrowed. "Girl, what you got against me?"

"Not a girl, Leon." Her fingers wrapped around the edge of the counter. "And maybe I don't like bein' stripped every time you look at me."

"Cain't help it," he said, smiling. "I'm a man. Somethin' sweet as you comes back to town...Mmm-mm..." He shook his head and gave her another look.

A leering look that made her annoyed. There was no denying he was a handsome man with his thick chestnut hair, broad chest, and dark uniform. Too bad he knew it. "Here's your coffee," she said, plunking it down on the counter. "You have a nice day, Sheriff."

But Leon didn't take the hint and instead settled on a stool. He opened the lid and silently reached out his hand to Mae, who handed him two sugar packets with a stern look.

"Didn't think you liked sweet. Just spicy," Tilly said. "Isn't that what you told me yesterday when you came by for a cup of Mae's shrimp gumbo?"

"I can like both, sweetheart. 'Specially when it's served just right."

She leaned over the counter, moving into his space.

His eyelids dipped, and by the flare of his nostrils, he drew in her scent.

"When are you gonna give up?" she said, dropping her voice. "I'm not interested."

He laughed. "Sugar, I'm the best you're gonna get in this town."

Fingers tense, she rubbed her rag near his cup, pushing it toward the edge of the counter.

But he caught the cup before it toppled into his lap. "If you'd burned me, I might have had to arrest you for assaultin' an officer of the law." His eyebrows waggled up and down and a grin stretched. "You want a little time in lockup? That make things easier for you?"

This time, she laughed and shook her head. "Leon, were you always such a lech?"

He chuckled and slid off the stool.

The bell tinkled again.

The large-muscled construction foreman from Maison Plaisir strode in, his glance going to the sheriff, to whom he gave a nod. Then his gaze casually slid to Tilly.

"The best I'm gonna get, huh?" she murmured, straightening from the counter. To the foreman, she said, "Can I get you somethin', Mr. Jones?"

The foreman drew a paper from his back pocket, folded once. Without glancing down, she knew the paper was another notice. "When are you gonna give up?" she chided in a friendly tone. "Mae's just gonna put it in the trash again."

His mouth twitched. "Position's still open, Miss Floret." He handed the paper directly to Tilly, gave a nod to Leon, then left.

Her mind went blank. He wanted her to apply?

"What's he talkin' about, Tilly?" Leon stared.

Ignoring the suspicion in his voice, she looked down at the sheet and the job highlighted in yellow at the top.

Hospitality Executive.

The salary listed right below was higher than the amount had been yesterday. Too high to ignore. With that much extra cash, she could afford to rent a place for her and Denny in no time.

"You're not thinkin' about workin' out there," Leon whispered. "It's different with the men. No female in her right mind would go there. Especially not someone like you."

"Someone like me?" she said, her back stiffening.

"Well, pretty. Young. Especially if *he's* back for a while."

"Doesn't appear there's been any more trouble around Boone Benoit. He's more than redeemed himself."

The sheriff's lips turned into a sneer. "Spendin' time in the navy as a SEAL only means he's learned more efficient ways to kill."

"He was never prosecuted," she said, feeling stubbornness tighten her grip on the paper.

"Only 'cause his daddy made everything disappear and my daddy was willin' to help."

Tilly jutted her chin. "Both your daddies should have let the law run its course. He might have been acquitted." Her gaze met his and held.

Leon's doubtful expression only echoed the prevailing sentiment. Boone Benoit had beaten a murder rap.

"Don't do it, Tilly."

"You're not the boss of me. Think I want to work here forever?"

"You're a smart girl. Got yourself an education." His hand waved at the folded paper. "You can do more than this."

Her pulse pounded. "Think I haven't tried? I can't work on a boat. This town doesn't have any other jobs I can get hired for besides waitin' tables. Who around here runnin' a family business wants to hire me? No one's wife or mother would stand for it."

"Mae's gettin' on in age. Maybe you could take over someday."

"And in the meantime..." She glanced down at her frayed shorts, and a pang shot through her gut. "I used to wear Donna Karan and Jimmy Choos."

"No need to get snooty."

"I'm not. Just makin' a point. If this," she said, waving the sheet, "is my only opportunity, I have to take it."

A muscle flexed alongside his jaw. "Don't say you weren't warned."

Tilly sighed. "I appreciate your concern. I do."

His eyelids dropped a fraction. "Might help if he knew you were datin' the sheriff…"

She laughed, and then punched his shoulder. "Not even if you were the last man on earth."

"You're a hard woman." He shook his head.

"I've had to be." And she'd have to stiffen her spine one more time. Boone Benoit's posting was just too tempting to ignore, especially for a woman who couldn't help but flirt with disaster.

Chapter Two

The next morning, Tilly let herself out of her car in a wide gravel parking area and walked slowly toward the imposing iron gates. She ignored the deputy in the squad car parked in the shade of a sycamore, knowing he'd probably radioed Leon the moment she'd arrived. Through the wrought iron she noted the gravel drive framed by tall oaks—a view she hadn't seen since she was a child. The last time she'd been there, she'd held tight to her mama's and Denny's hands as they'd brought a picnic basket to join the Fourth of July festivities going on at the plantation that had been a long-standing tradition in Bayou Vert.

She'd been excited, wanting to skip ahead, but her mother had held her back. If she'd gone skipping, so would her brother, and her mama hadn't wanted Denny to draw any more attention than he already did. Although nearly a grown man in body, he'd been her best friend and cohort in many of her adventures. He didn't mind baiting her fishing hooks with worms, didn't mind climbing to the roof of the schoolhouse to see the stars. As wonderful as she'd believed he was, she'd been aware from a very young age that most people didn't look at him the same way she did.

That day, even their cousin Celeste had turned up her nose at the sight of him, pretending she didn't know him. However, Celeste's boyfriend, Boone, had been kind, offering to let them sit near the fireworks platform. Denny had sworn it was the best day ever. But it had been the last time either one of them had set foot inside the estate.

And here she was today. Her stomach clenching so tight she felt a little nauseous. Trying not to think about the thing that screamed inside her mind, aching to be released.

A secret so profound it could alter the path of one man's life and destroy what was left of her family forever. That secret was one she could never tell.

Some nights, she awoke drenched with sweat, sure she'd blurted aloud the words. But she only dreamed she revealed the truth that had left such an ugly scar upon her community.

How she wished she'd never found the bracelet. Never seen the photograph. But that photograph was part of her small town's legacy. A dark chapter with murky underpinnings, coloring everything after it with dismal tones, dark suspicions, and angry frustration for a justice that would never be served. Her damnable curiosity had led her to the discovery.

Her secret had consequences. Karmic ones. She had proof. From the moment three years ago when she'd plucked the golden charm bracelet, so pretty and delicate, from among the odd assorted treasures she'd found, nothing but bad luck had followed. Her mother succumbed to cancer months later. The only home she'd ever known was lost to foreclosure. She'd been forced to live underneath her uncle's roof for several months until she'd saved enough to rent a cheap apartment, eager to escape the Thibodaux house, where an atmosphere of desolation and endless sorrow smothered the inhabitants in their never-ending mourning. Arrangements were made for her brother, who needed specialized care. The day social services loaded him into a van and drove away, he'd been so confused, he'd cried big fat tears.

Dark days had followed. Even with the bracelet safely hidden, Tilly couldn't brush off the lingering fear that somehow someone would find it. In this town, darkness was impossible to escape. Even on cloudless days, the thick canopy formed by interlocking oaks, dripping with Spanish moss, cast an eerie pall, smothering the light, muffling the sounds of the wind blowing across the marshes from Barataria Bay to Bayou Vert.

Darkness had always been a part of the town's psyche. When you add the isolation of living in a bayou more accessible by boat than it is by the thin ribbon of state highway, especially when the seasonal rains hit, it was easy to understand. Folks believed themselves alone. Forgotten. Free to mete out their own justice, live by their own rules.

In one unforgettable instance, they'd been robbed. A bright light extinguished with no one to bear the blame. The helpless rage festered, then faded, covered by a thin skin. But when prodded, it erupted like an angry boil.

Boone Benoit's return to the bayou was just the nasty jab the town needed to awaken from its slumber. Tilly felt the stirrings of a coming disaster. One she was helpless to avoid. She'd find herself at the center anyway. She might as well be close enough to make a difference if things went sideways.

She drew a deep breath, clearing the cobwebs of the past, and stiffened her backbone.

The panel for the automatic keypad controlling the massive gate in the estate's stone wall was missing, wires hanging. Tilly unwrapped the fencing wire that held the gates closed and slipped through, heading down the long empty lane, catching glimpses of the big house through the foliage.

Maison Plaisir had been the grand dam of the bayou until ferocious hurricanes and the owner's neglect decimated the old plantation house and gardens. No good could come of the current refurbishing. Everyone said so. Better to leave the old house to rot, they said.

She marched up the long drive, shaded by tall oaks. The branches were carefully pruned, forming a dark tunnel that led to the marble steps of the estate house.

As she approached, the sounds of chainsaws and hammers and shouts from workers in the garden and on the gabled roof became clearer, louder. Perspiration dotted her forehead and upper lip, and she quickly wiped them with her sweaty palms.

Damn. She'd wanted to appear cool, collected. The position she applied for was important enough that she'd overcome her fear of being in his house. She'd never been one to keep her emotions or her words inside. One careless misstep could spell disaster.

She felt as though fate was clearing her path to enter Boone Benoit's world. A job tailor-made for her credentials. Who else possessed a degree in hospitality or had her experience? If fate wanted her here, then there must be a reason. She didn't believe in coincidence.

Besides, how often would he be there? The CEO of Black Spear, Limited had offices on every continent, as well as a headquarters in New Orleans. His interest in his family's ancestral home couldn't be all that deep. He hadn't set foot inside this section of Jefferson Parish in over fifteen years. More likely, the recent activities were in preparation for selling the estate, or a symbolic gesture—like shooting the bird at the folks who'd turned their backs on him.

No, Boone Benoit couldn't be considering returning to Bayou Vert. Not with a murder charge still hanging over his head.

Her footsteps crunched on fine pea gravel. One heel twisted, sinking, but she quickly pulled it free. She'd decided to dress the part. Complete with a professionally tailored gray suit and pearl pumps. Her clothes may have been chosen off the rack, but she knew she looked good.

Her long blonde hair was pulled back from her face in a pony-tail, after working long and hard with the straightener to remove every bump and curl. Not a lock out of place. Not a single thread hanging from her clothing. Due to the heat, she'd foregone panty hose, but her skin tone was an even creamy tan from waiting on the diner's outdoor tables in shorts.

No one would find fault with her appearance. Competent, pretty, but not too sexy. All in the attitude. Or so she reminded herself.

She drew near the edge of the gardens, although calling them that seemed like a stretch. Leggy, overgrown rosebushes sur-rounded by creeping vines managed a few valiant blossoms. Aza-lea bushes, grown wild, smothered the annuals popping from bulbs in the ground. Hedgerows were in dire need of shaping.

The growling whine of a revving chainsaw pulled her glance to the side, where two workers, their chests bare and gleaming with sweat, worked with ropes and pulleys to cut the limbs from an oak tree that threatened a trellised gazebo.

In the distance the sound of barking and paws scattering gravel filled her ears. Tilly shot a glance around the yard and watched as a small pug rounded the corner of the big house.

"Max, here, boy! Max!" someone yelled.

But the dog made a beeline for her, yipping and barking.

An animal lover, Tilly stepped back and bent down to greet

the dog. "Here, Max," she said, reaching out a hand as the dog came nearer.

"I wouldn't do that," came a warning from a large man dressed in coveralls, who jogged behind the dog.

The dog halted two feet away, growling and spinning in circles.

At the sight, Tilly didn't know whether to laugh or curse. She took another step backward and her heel sank into the ground. She tried to take another step, sure she'd pull free, but the mud beneath the gravel held firm and her foot slipped out of her pump. She tumbled to the side, gasping, hands outstretched to break her fall, her bag sliding away.

The dog leapt into her lap, nipping at her skirt and sleeve.

"Dammit," she muttered, forcing the dog from her lap and trying to rise. He caught the hem of her skirt and she went down again, this time on her hands and knees. Kneeling in her skirt, her right knee stinging from abrasions, she glared at the little yipping dog.

The large man in coveralls scooped up the dog. "Bad Max, bad dog." He turned away without an apology.

Of all the nerve. Her mouth gaped and she glared.

"Let me help you."

Startled, her gaze shot upward. Her breath caught on a shocked inhalation as a face hovered over hers—dark, short-cropped hair with a hint of unruly curl, dark lashes framing ice-blue eyes. A prominent, masculine nose and square jaw saved his face from being too perfect.

She'd known he was handsome—her memory and the Internet had prepared her for that. What she wasn't ready for was his sheer physicality. But then she remembered he'd spent time in the navy. Perhaps he'd kept to the discipline. He wore dark dress slacks and a crisp white shirt, the sleeves casually rolled up to reveal tanned forearms that were thickly muscled. His shoulders were broad, his hips trim, his thighs big as tree trunks…

Her blood pounded in her ears. Good Lord, how long had she been staring?

Boone Benoit held out his hand. "Come. I promise I only murder pretty girls on their birthdays."

What might have been a joke coming from any other man sounded bitter. As bitter as the twist of his firm lips.

She reached tentatively to accept his hand and found herself dragged up and pressed against his body. Immediately she stepped back and nearly fell again, forgetting she'd lost three inches of height on one foot.

His hands grasped her waist to steady her, and then quickly let her go. He knelt and plucked her heel from where it was lodged in the ground and tapped his thigh, commanding her to rest her foot on his body.

The act was unthinkable, what he suggested… with so many gazes upon them. Her pulse raced.

The chainsaw had stopped. The gardeners straightened and stared.

A blush suffused her face, and she held out her hand. "I can manage on my own."

His head tilted to the side, blue eyes narrowing. "Would you deprive me of the pleasure?"

His tone was unexpected, startling in its rumbling sensuality. Already flushed with humiliation, now her skin tingled for an entirely different reason. His words conjured images of other pleasures. Sensual pleasures. And she had no doubt he'd done it deliberately.

Without another thought for their audience, she placed a hand on his muscled shoulder and raised her foot, toes pointing downward. Thank goodness she'd treated herself to a pedicure. The soft shell-pink polish and smooth heels were far more presentable now than they'd been the day before.

His hand turned and cupped her heel. He slowly slid on the shoe, tilting it at the last moment to set it firmly in place. The moment stretched, his hand slid up the back of her calf, a subtle movement that anyone watching might have missed. "Are you a runner?"

Shock made her shiver. All he'd needed was a single gliding touch to know that? "I was."

"Your calves are very nicely defined."

"Thank you," she murmured breathlessly, pleased although the comment was completely inappropriate.

"I'm sorry Max startled you."

"I'm fine," she bit out, too off-kilter to censor her stiff tone.

Before she could gather the nerve to move her heel from his thigh, he folded up the hem of her skirt. "You're bleeding."

"It's nothing," she said, embarrassed by the attention and her clumsiness.

With a slow move, he set her foot on the ground and rose.

Good Lord, he's tall, she thought as she followed his movements. Her gaze was in line with the top of his shoulder.

Bending, he swiped her leather bag from the ground and held it in his hand, then bent his other arm, his gaze steady on her.

The directness of it challenged her in a way she didn't understand.

She slipped her hand into the corner of his elbow.

"Can't have you falling again."

"I should have worn more sensible shoes. The dog surprised me."

"You look appropriately...businesslike." An eyebrow quirked. "Are you applying for the hospitality manager position?"

She was tempted to deny it, sure she hadn't made the best first impression, but couldn't think of another excuse for her presence. "I had hoped to speak to whoever's doin' the hiring."

"Then you're in luck. That's me."

"You?" Her startled glance shot up to his face.

"As this will be my home, I want to personally interview everyone I employ."

Home? Dismay tightened her stomach. He wasn't fixing up the place to sell or to hand off to someone else to manage? He planned to live here?

While her mind whirled, she followed Boone Benoit as he led her up the stairs to the wide porch that surrounded the house and opened one of a pair of dark teak doors at the entrance. He stood aside while allowing her to enter.

She brushed past, aware of the narrow space he made, acutely conscious of the heat radiating from his body and his appealing scent, a mixture of cinnamon and musk.

After he closed the door, he touched her elbow, guiding her to the left of the large tiled foyer, through an empty dining area and into the kitchen.

Renovation had already been completed there. She glanced upward at a copper punched-tile ceiling. The cabinets were mahogany, the counters a charcoal-gray marble infused with hints of copper. Black and white tiles covered the floors. "It's lovely."

"Not much was changed from the original design, other than adding two Sub-Zeros and enlarging the pantry."

"Will you be doing a lot of entertainin', then?"

His lips twitched, and then settled back into a straight line. His expression was neutral as he said, "I will be entertaining, yes."

She had the feeling he was laughing at her but wondered what he found so funny. Had she sounded too provincial?

He stopped beside a sink. "No stools as yet." Without warning, he reached for her waist.

Alarmed, she stepped back.

Again he gripped her and lifted her easily to the cool countertop. "Your knee," he said, his voice softer, his gaze probing.

Tilly swallowed to wet her dry mouth. "I'm Clotille Floret."

"I know."

Then he must also know Celeste had been her cousin. The thought that he'd flirted, knowing that, disturbed her.

"I'm Boone Benoit."

"I know," she said, just as softly.

"And that's enough to know for now, don't you think? No need to share our secrets just yet."

The blood drained from her face and she bit her lower lip.

His gaze narrowed, but he turned, opening a cabinet and pulling down a plastic box. From it he took wet wipes, antiseptic spray, and a large bandage.

She held out her hand. "I can manage on my own," she said, injecting more strength into her voice than she felt. What she wanted was for him to leave her before she gave away any more clues about how much he unnerved her.

Ignoring her hand, he peeled open the wipes, and then pushed up the hem of her skirt.

Her body stilled. She resisted the urge to push it back into place, but only just. He didn't expose any more than her knee.

Boone wiped away the grit, dirt, and a small amount of blood from her skin. "You're applying for the position of hospitality manager…" His hand lingered on her knee while he waited for her answer.

"Yes," she said, although she shook her head.

He set aside the wipe and sprayed her knee with antiseptic. "You have experience?"

The spray burned, and she crimped her lips to keep from gasping. "My degree was in hotel management, and I've been the assistant manager at two major hotels in Houston, the Sorella and the Saint Regis. A copy of my résumé is in my bag."

"The position's filled."

Her shoulders dropped an inch. "Oh." She should have felt relief. She wouldn't have to deal with him on a frequent basis.

He squirted more antiseptic, and then bent toward her.

She was tempted to push him back because she was embarrassed. Instead she watched, fascinated, as he blew a stream of warm air over the wound, cooling the fierce sting. Then he tore the paper wrapping from the bandage and pressed it against her knee, his large hand flattening over it to seal it. Through the tape she felt each finger like a caress. Which it wasn't. She gave herself a mental shake.

"I have another opening." This time, his voice was even, void of any undertones. "One I believe will suit you."

At this point, all she wanted was to leave. He confused her with his touches, his velvet voice. She was in over her head. "What position would that be?" she asked, an embarrassing quaver in her voice.

"I have need of a personal assistant."

Her brows rose, affronted at his offer. With her credentials, was that the best he thought she could do? "A secretary?"

He shook his head. "So much more than that. You'd be my liaison with the staff here and at my offices in New Orleans."

"I'm sure you can find someone much better suited. Someone who actually knows your business."

"I want someone from Bayou Vert. Someone who can walk in both worlds."

Both worlds? Like this backwoods town was an alien planet? "I don't take dictation."

"Are you sure?"

Again, he used that velvet voice. The one that made her insides quiver. She lifted a finger to point behind her, the way they'd come. "I should leave." Then she hopped from the counter and smoothed down her skirt.

"Wait."

She craned her head to meet his gaze.

He lifted his hand, index finger pointed down, and swirled it. "Turn around. You have dirt on your skirt."

With her free hand, she reached back to brush it off.

"Don't be stubborn." He gripped her elbow and gently forced her to spin around.

Cheeks on fire, she stood stiffly while he swept her backside with swift brushes of a hard hand. When he stopped, she held her breath, waiting for him to release her.

"Think about it," he said, leaning near her ear. "I'll add another fifteen thousand to the annual salary. I'm sure at your first review you can wrangle for even more. You'll become indispensible to me."

Her mind reeled. The amount he proposed was ridiculous. And tempting, despite the fact she knew she'd have to refuse. "Why me?"

"Why not?" His gaze crawled down her body slowly, and then flicked back to meet hers. He gave a careless shrug, but the hand still cupping her elbow squeezed. "You'll do."

Her gaze narrowed. She was glad he'd done that. Sized her up like a meal. Anger flushed through her, replacing the tingling awareness and sickening fear with something sturdier. She jerked away her arm. "I'll need a day." She could take forever. The answer would still be no.

"Take two. I'll be leaving shortly for a platform on the gulf. When I return, I'll send around a car."

"You'll need my number. My address."

"I'll find you." At her widened glance, he shrugged. "It's a small town." He gave her a smile, and then bowed his head and turned.

Tilly watched his tall, straight back saunter away, and wondered if there was any possibility he knew what she'd found.

If he'd come back to avenge Celeste's death, he'd picked the perfect person to begin with.

Chapter Three

So, we're going to The Platform?" Serge's wry voice came from the doorway.

Boone stood at the window, a hand gripping the frame as he watched Clotille Floret make her way slowly down the drive. Her lush figure swayed with unintentional allure. Small breasts, a narrow waist, lovely wide hips. No doubt the pretty gray suit had required extensive alterations so it wouldn't hang from her straight shoulders and mask her feminine frame. Every bit as pert and uptight as the suit, she'd radiated a cautious interest, unable to resist the sensual thrill building between them from the first moment their glances met.

Although tentative, she'd obeyed his command to set her foot on his thigh. She'd gasped as he'd swatted at her backside, but he'd bet money that gasp wasn't out of outrage. Every time he'd touched her, felt her hesitate then take a deeper breath and concede, he'd felt his interest ratchet up another notch. Her reactions felt like a fist closing around his balls.

Boone had no intention of fighting the overpowering desire to draw her into his web. Especially now that he'd met her face-to-face. He went with his instincts. Always.

Everything about her drew his interest—her shape, her pale blonde hair, her wide cornflower-blue eyes. Her voice, with its cultured Cajun drawl. Her resistance. She was the mirror image of her cousin, but with a hint of innocence Celeste had never managed to exude.

His fingers tightened around the edge of the window frame. "Send a car after her. I don't want any more accidents."

"Already handled."

The moment the foreman's mule pulled up beside the stubborn woman, Boone turned away. He smiled thinking of the argument she'd give Jonesy, but then glanced at his next-in-command.

Serge shook his head, his expression stony.

He disapproved of Boone's plan. They'd moved from BUD/S to SEAL Qualification Training to SEAL Team 5, and served together on three deployments in the Middle East. No one knew him better. "Doesn't seem your type," Serge drawled.

"Perhaps not at first glance. First touch, now…" He'd noted the arousal in her widening pupils, the flare of her nostrils, the trembling of her foot on his thigh. Being told what to do had stiffened her spine, but still she'd complied.

"She'll be a distraction," Serge said, his voice neutral but his expression hardening.

Boone arched a brow. "Haven't you been urging me to seek distractions?"

"She's young."

Not too young. But Boone knew what he meant. He'd never pursued someone so inexperienced and unschooled. "Are you getting scruples this late in the game?"

With a shake of his head, Serge sighed. "Maybe it's the fact this is a game."

Boone sent him a silent warning.

It was just a glance, but Serge grunted in agreement to drop the conversation. "Shall I muster the pilot?"

"Wouldn't want Ms. Floret to view me as a liar as well as a murderer."

He'd seen the way she'd first looked at him. Eyes wide and frightened. She was Celeste Thibodaux's cousin, so she'd likely been raised on the sensational story. And since she worked at Mae's restaurant, he had no doubt the crotchety woman had filled her in on the sordid details concerning his relationship with Celeste.

Serge tapped the Bluetooth in his ear. "Lincoln, find Bear. Mr. Benoit's decided to visit The Platform." When his gaze returned to the window, he pointed toward Jonesy's vehicle as it continued down the long drive. "So, that's the cousin?"

"Yes, second cousin. Her mother was Celeste's older cousin."

Serge whistled softly. "She's a looker."

Boone stiffened against Serge's appreciation. "And to answer the question you aren't asking, yes, she's very much like Celie. Except in disposition."

Serge lifted an eyebrow. "And persuasion?"

"Light-years apart." Which shouldn't have filled him with satisfaction, but did.

"You're treading in dangerous waters."

"Have before."

"Yeah, but she's not a hostile."

Boone dropped his gaze and began rolling down his sleeves, irritation making his moves jerky. "She was born and raised here. They're all hostile. Don't believe otherwise for a second. But someone here knows something. Just a matter of time before my presence here forces his hand." He shot Serge a glance. "The sheriff still have a squad car parked at the gates?"

Serge snorted. "Hasn't budged. Damn incestuous bunch."

"It's a small community. Closed. Even when my father was the main employer, we were the outsiders." He shrugged. "No buccaneers in our pedigree."

"You don't have to do this." Serge waved a hand at the window. "No charges were ever filed. Won't ever be. They had no proof then. Still don't."

"And that's the problem. Whoever tampered with the evidence knows what really happened. My life was…changed. Irrevocably. Celeste's ended." Boone drew a deep breath to tamp down the anger that was always there, simmering deep inside him. But anger was a luxury he couldn't afford. It blinded. "I want justice. Not for me. For her. Celie didn't deserve to die that way. I'll understand if you want to step away. It's not your fight."

Serge shrugged his rugged shoulders. "We've fought wars for lesser reasons. I'm not hesitating because I don't have the stomach. But I see what it's doing to you. This place…" He shook his head. "This town's dead, but no one here seems to know it."

"What about the others?"

"We're all in, Lieutenant."

"Boone," he reminded him, but caught Serge's sly smile. He'd called him by his old rank to irk him. "Tell Jonesy to get the foreman's house ready."

"You so sure she'll accept the offer?"

"She won't be able to resist. Her dossier is thin, but every decision she's made over the past two years indicates family is her first priority. Her mother's gone. She's motivated to save the only family she has left—her brother." He rested his hands on his hips. "This position is her only hope."

"Sure you want her living here on the estate?"

"I want her close. Her presence on the estate is sure to stir up something. Leon's interested in her. Mae hired her. Someone's going to get nervous, see the parallel, and make a mistake." His jaw clenched and he forced it to loosen. "When it all goes down, I want her here and protected."

Serge nodded. "Do you want the house wired?"

Boone drew in a deep breath, and then nodded. "For her own safety," he murmured, although his mind leapt ahead to sexier reasons.

His friend's mouth twitched. "Does she have any idea the sort of entertaining you expect to do here?"

"Not a clue." An answering grin stretched across his face. "Showing her the ropes will present a challenge."

A rich chuckle burst from his friend. "You're really hiring her to be your secretary?"

"No. I have a perfectly competent staff. She'll be my shadow, learn to anticipate my needs."

Serge shook his head. "Like I said. A distraction."

"A sweet distraction with the right connections."

Again, Serge chuckled. "I almost feel sorry for her."

"Don't. No harm will come to her." Boone arched a brow. "None she won't enjoy, anyway."

Serge touched his ear again, and his gaze flashed to Boone. "The Agusta is ready. Need to pack?"

"We're only going for a day." Boone shook his head. "What I need is in my locker at the club."

Serge led the way through the foyer and out the door.

Boone's gaze swept the front porch, newly reconstructed, and skimmed over the ravaged gardens. He made a mental note to hire more gardeners to begin clearing the planting beds. Everything would be as it was, down to the last azalea bush.

The whomp-whomp of the helicopter sounded from just

beyond the stand of tall oaks framing the walkway. *Leon is likely having a conniption with it landing so close to the cruiser in the parking lot.*

Boone smiled and buttoned his cuffs. He'd have to arrange for a jacket and tie to be brought to the limo that picked them up from the landing field in New Orleans. A mere detail, but paying attention to everything, even the seemingly unimportant things, had gotten him to where he was now: CEO of his own international security corporation. Friends in all the highest places. A senator or two in his pocket. No one connected to his late father.

Following on Serge's brisk heels, he left the main walkway to enter a garden gate and the wide green field where the helo waited. The blades fanned the air, whipping at his clothing and hair. He bent his head, climbed the accordion steps, and waited impatiently as Serge pulled them up, closed the door, and handed him a set of headphones.

Ignoring the chatter between Serge and Bear, his pilot, he glanced out the window as they lifted. Flying along the ribbon of narrow highway that lead back into town, Boone caught a glimpse of a dark cherry-red Corolla.

Must be Ms. Floret's car. He smiled. It fit her somehow. Clotille Floret. He liked her name, the way it rolled off his tongue. Liked her smooth tanned skin and the silky feel of his fingers gliding along it. Liked her big blue eyes—so guileless but also so deceiving. The woman was a tempting package. Innocent… but not.

An excellent judge of character, he could read most anyone in a glance. He was certain she was hiding something. But what? She wasn't frightened of him, he was sure of it. But she seemed terrified of something related to him. He didn't believe she was afraid of any backlash from her friends or family for coming to him for a job. The tilt of her firm, round chin had been too proud, too self-assured for her to worry for more than a minute about any ruffled feathers. She'd do whatever it took to help her brother and to satisfy her own curiosity about Boone.

Sitting back, he gave Serge a small, tight smile, knowing his friend knew exactly where his thoughts had roamed, and how he planned to purge the irksome scruples that arose when he thought of how he must seduce Tilly Floret.

Perhaps fate had driven him back here at this precise moment in time to seek the answers that had haunted him all these years. Fate had given him a gift—Celeste's sweet young cousin, a woman who was completely unskilled at the game he was about to play.

* * *

Tilly pulled into the gravel drive in front of her small apartment. It was really just a finished detached garage, converted by Mrs. Nolan after her husband had passed in order to earn income to supplement her social security. Nothing fancy, but comfortable and clean.

Mrs. Nolan didn't rent to men, considering them somewhat inept at housekeeping. Tilly kept her place neat on the off chance her landlord wanted to take a look inside. Not something that bothered her, and she'd been well aware the old woman kept a key so that she could nose around. Her mother had often complained about the woman, who sat in her recliner with the blinds open, watching the comings and goings of the town so she'd have plenty to gossip about at Mass on Sunday.

Glancing toward the house, Tilly gave the tiny white-haired woman a small wave and suppressed a grin. Then she unlocked the door, hung her keys on one of the small hooks on the Sacred Heart plaque beside the door, and rushed to the thermostat on the opposite wall of the postage-stamp-sized living room.

No matter that Tilly paid her own electricity bill, Mrs. Nolan considered running the AC when she wasn't at home a waste. Tilly had given up on trying to appease her landlady by turning the thermostat low when she left for the day. Whenever she had, the old woman had let herself in with her key and turned it off. So Tilly turned the dial on the old-fashioned round thermostat and waited for the blessed sound of the AC to kick on. It would be a while before she would feel any relief. She kicked off her shoes, unbuttoned her jacket, draped it over the armchair, and kept walking toward her bedroom, unzipping her skirt as she went. She'd wait in her underwear for the air to cool.

Her knee stung as the material slid down, an unwanted reminder of how the bandage been applied. The image of Boone Benoit, his lips pursed as he blew against her raw skin, entered her mind. For just a second, while she'd stared down at him this afternoon, her heart had stopped beating. She'd imagined his mouth pursed above another, sweeter spot on her body and desire had flooded her, just as it did now. Once again, her skin flushed and her breaths hitched.

"Stop it," she said to herself, and then let out a groan. At the time, she'd convinced herself that he couldn't tell what his breath on her body had done to her. But she'd only been lying to herself.

His sharp, dark gaze hadn't missed anything. And the fact he had aroused such feelings in her probably made him laugh inside. She'd blushed like a virgin. Good Lord, had he guessed just how inexperienced she was?

He'd been toying with her. Every practiced touch igniting a hunger she didn't realize she possessed. Every glide of his hand, the spread of his strong fingers, had filled her mind with licentious images of his hands running beneath her skirt and touching her. Even now, at just the memory, her panties were damp.

She would have to tell him no. No matter what the ridiculous salary. Working in close proximity to a man like Boone would be too uncomfortable. Too tempting. He was way out of her league, and they both knew it. What had he been thinking offering her the job in the first place?

The phone rang and Tilly sighed in relief, glad to have something to take her mind off Boone Benoit. She picked up her cell and tapped ANSWER. "Hello?"

"Tilly? That you?"

The voice, at once deeply masculine and yet filled with a childish yearning, cut through her self-absorption. "Denny! Are you all right?"

"Tilly, when can I come home?"

Her throat tightened, and she closed her eyes. "I told you, sweetie. Home was sold. It's not there anymore."

"But I miss you."

"I miss you too." She swallowed hard.

"When can I come home?"

Tears filled her eyes. No matter how many times she told him, he would never understand. The house where they'd been raised had been the only home he'd ever known. "Soon, Denny. I'll come for you soon."

"Tilly, I can't find my treasure."

Tilly's chest tightened. Her glance went guiltily to the photo on the counter. The one of her and Celeste. "I have it, hon. I didn't want the others finding it and stealing it from you," she said, squeezing shut her eyes. She'd buried it where no one would ever find it. "Denny, I have to go. See you soon."

"Oh, okay. I'll see you tomorrow."

Muffled sounds came from the receiver, followed by a female voice. "This Miss Floret?"

Tilly sniffed, swallowing the lump in her throat. "Yes, Ms. Parham."

"Sorry, he was a little agitated today. Insisted on callin' again."

"I don't mind if he calls. I don't get to Thibodaux often enough to see him."

"Sorry about this. He thinks you and your mama are comin' for him. Now that he's talked with you, he should be good for a while."

"I really don't mind," she said again, her stomach knotting.

The group home supervisor stayed on the line for another minute. Tilly must have made appropriate responses, but she was surprised when she heard the click as the call disconnected.

"Oh hell," she whispered. There had to be another way. Something that wouldn't entail her selling her soul to the devil in order to afford to bring Denny home. Or at least to Bayou Vert, since the town was familiar and Denny didn't do well with change.

Tilly glanced again at the photo—of Celeste dressed in her pretty blue prom dress, her face radiant, and her arm around Tilly's shoulder, her hand cupping her shoulder. The bracelet glinted in the flash of the camera.

This was how she remembered her cousin. In that one shining, happy moment. She'd overheard mutterings from her aunt when she'd been drinking, about the horrible state of Celeste's body. Her aunt had seen it because she'd pushed through the line of officers who'd ringed the little shoddy cabin where Celeste had died.

Bathed in blood. Nude. Knife slashes and deep gouges had ripped her face and belly. Tilly was fiercely glad she had this last memory of her cousin, looking beautiful and entitled. So beautiful there'd never been any doubt who'd be crowned prom queen.

She'd worshiped her cousin, but from afar, since Celeste's world was all filled up with people much more exciting than a gangly little girl. They'd never been close and never spent much time together, other than the few times Celeste had tolerated her presence when family gathered.

Tilly had mourned her passing, but only because that was what family did. She felt guilty over the fact she didn't care more. Or maybe her empathy had been driven from her when she'd suffered living with her uncle and aunt very briefly after her mother's death. The looks her aunt had given her were filled with bitterness. She was alive. Her precious daughter wasn't.

Turning abruptly away, Tilly walked to the Naugahyde armchair and settled in, drawing her knees close to her chest. Suddenly cold, she wrapped her arms around them and hugged herself. A shiver shook her frame. The past was the past, and she needed to make sure it stayed buried.

Everything was so complicated. Getting more so every day. If she went to work for Boone, she'd still have to wait to bring Denny back. He needed constant supervision, and Bayou Vert didn't have an adult day-care facility. The longing in his voice as he'd asked when he could come home tugged at her heart. Made her feel guilty because she hadn't worked out his return yet. He'd been there nearly a year. A part of her had hoped he'd adjust well and that maybe she could return to Houston and her old life. Of course, the gap in her résumé would mean she'd have to take a less prestigious position than the one she'd left when her mother fell ill.

Guilt burned in her stomach like acid. Denny wasn't an inconvenience. He was her brother. Although he was seven years older, she'd been looking after Denny since she was a child. She hadn't minded that other kids looked at her funny when she'd led him around by the hand. When he'd been teased, she'd fought his battles. Nursed his scrapes. Read him stories when he couldn't sleep. He'd been her cuddly, fuzzy bear. She'd been his princess.

When she thought about the fact that she'd grown up and he hadn't, her chest hurt. But over time, she'd learned to cope with the disappointment, believing something innocent and beautiful was preserved forever inside him—until she'd found his treasure box.

Try as she might, she couldn't look at him and not think about the significance of the pretty gold bracelet she'd found nestled there. Maybe there was an explanation, one that didn't lead to a horrible conclusion. Still, she'd never asked him how he'd come by the bracelet. She didn't want to know. Because if she knew for certain, she might have to tell someone else, and her promise to her mother to protect him always would be broken.

Feeling as though a noose was slowly tightening around her neck, she could no longer avoid the truth. She had only one choice. With tears slipping down her cheeks, she acknowledged she'd have to accept Boone Benoit's offer. She'd have to enter his world and hope that once he'd won this little battle of manipulation, he'd turn his attention to someone else.

Wealthy and handsome, he no doubt had women falling from the sky to be with him. His flirting today had to have been because, as far as she could tell, she'd been the only woman on the estate. And perhaps because he was willing to use whatever talent he possessed to get what he wanted.

But *why her*? Did he know she was Celeste's cousin? Did he get some sick thrill from knowing he held her fate in his hands?

She hoped that wasn't the reason. Because if it was, she shouldn't be feeling the way she did—trapped, but deep down thrilled by the fact. One look into his eyes, and she'd drowned in the sensual promise she saw there. He'd only had to pat his knee, and she'd followed his silent command.

What on earth would she do if he wanted more?

Chapter Four

Boone rattled the ice in his glass, and then set it on the bar.

"Another, Mr. Benoit?"

At the bartender's question, Boone shook his head. If he accepted another, he wouldn't be permitted past the secret door at the back of The Platform's busy lounge. He'd downed a single scotch on the rocks—just enough alcohol to soften the rough edges the day had left. Any more than that and he'd be banned from playing. The club's strict code of conduct was the reason he'd joined in the first place. Boone didn't like messy.

He straightened his tie and walked to the floor-to-ceiling windows overlooking the Port of New Orleans, barely registering the tinkling of piano keys and the soft croon of a blues singer everyone else in the crowded upscale lounge ignored. Beneath him, barges with blinking lights slid into the dock while dockhands worked around the clock to unload their cargo. Moonlight glinted on the crests of the large boats' wakes.

The Platform had been built in the sixties to accommodate the exclusive tastes of oil executives and transportation scions.

As a businessman who served the security needs of both those industries, he'd earned an invitation several years ago.

"Your room's ready," Serge said as he stepped close to Boone's elbow.

Without shifting his gaze from the window, Boone asked, "Did you find something special for me?"

"She's new. Blonde. Says she likes a little pain." Serge grunted. "Nothing heavy, but enjoys a flogging and some pinching."

Boone's lips curved in a smile he didn't really feel. Still, his cock stirred and filled. The image of another young blonde's wide blue eyes sent his libido into a pleasant state of arousal. He drew in a sharp breath and met Serge's dark gaze. "What's her name?"

"Mandy," he drawled, then smirked.

Likely a pseudonym. Many prospective subs assumed girl-next-door names to imply an innocence they didn't possess. Then again, few of the wealthy clientele who played here ever gave their true names either. Since he didn't have any political aspirations, or a family who might be shamed if his proclivities ever came to light, he never bothered to build a fictional persona. "Would you like to join me?"

"Seeing as how I don't have any other plans…" Serge shrugged, his lips twitching.

The two men strode through the main salon, past the bar to the guarded door hidden behind it. After a nod, a heavily built guard buzzed the door to allow them through.

Inside was another lounge, similarly decorated, with plush seating areas and a juice bar. While the two lounges shared physical similarities, here the atmosphere was heavier, scented with sex and sweat. His heartbeat kicked up a notch, an automatic response whenever he entered a club designed to cater to his particular needs. His body moved more fluidly through the room, and his glance noted the platforms sitting in the four corners of the large room and the players performing scenes for those gathered around the stages.

Muted techno played in the background, the bass a deep throbbing beat that pulled at his groin. Lights dimmed around pockets of plush seating, an invitation to leave behind any inhibitions and make use of the chaises, chairs, and sofas.

Boone's gaze flicked over a threesome—a naked redhead seated in the center of a red velvet sofa, sandwiched between two businessmen whose shirts and pants lay open. The woman's hands pumped on both their cocks as she kissed one then the other, her legs splayed to allow one to fondle her bare pussy while the other massaged her plump breasts. His mouth twisted in a snarling smile when the woman glanced at him, licking her lips.

Boone skirted a platform where a blindfolded woman, whose manacled wrists were attached to chains extending from the ceiling, bent over a padded sawhorse. Her bottom was plugged, and the Dom standing behind flicked her with the end of a short whip. One of her thighs gleamed with the fluid dripping from her swollen cunt as her reedy voice warbled with delight. He slowed, studying the careful strokes the Dom delivered, approval curving his mouth.

He veered toward the hallway and the long line of private rooms. At one door, he stopped, punched in the key code, waited for the lock to gleam green, and then pushed open the door.

When he stepped inside, he scanned the room. All was in order. The walls were painted a soothing sage. All the furnishings were dark teak; upholstery was black leather. Recessed lighting added an air of intimacy. The glassed-in shower had a stack of clean towels waiting on the bench beside it. The platform bed against one wall was covered in a fresh Egyptian cotton sheet. Cabinets that held his implements gleamed from a fresh application of polish.

The woman kneeling on the pad in the center of the room was nude, hands on her thighs, her head bent, gaze cast dutifully toward the floor.

Serge had done well. Boone scanned her with a practiced eye. She was cute, not too slender, with large, pink-tipped breasts. Her skin was creamy pale—not a tan line in sight—and her hair a silky blonde. Her triangular-shaped face gave her a kittenish look. His gaze halted on her hands—short, bare nails. Nice. He hated polish on fingernails.

Boone drew in a breath and began to disrobe, hanging his jacket and his shirt on a coat tree next to the cabinets. Behind him, he heard the sounds of Serge washing his hands in the sink set in a bureau, and then sliding open drawers.

Boone toed off his shoes, slipped off his socks, and then padded barefoot toward the woman. He bent and tucked a finger under her chin to lift her face.

She tilted her head, her blue eyes blinking.

He studied her. Midtwenties. Dark brows. Not a natural blonde, but her hair hung just past her shoulders, and the length pleased him. Her expression, however, did not.

Her eyes glittered with excitement; her lush, painted-red mouth pouted.

He had no doubts she'd try to top him at least once during their session. He didn't have the patience to deal with any brattiness tonight. Any attempt by the woman to direct the outcome of their session was doomed for failure. "Serge tells me you like nominal pain. Flogging, pinching. Any prohibitions?"

"I told him no vaginal intercourse," she said huskily, then bit her bottom lip as her gaze swept his frame. "Although I could make an exception."

"I'll keep that in mind." His mouth curved, and he dropped his hand. "Get up now."

"Yes, sir." She moaned a little as she pushed up from the ground.

He wondered how long she'd been waiting like that and whether her muscles were prickling as blood circulated back into her long legs. Glancing at Serge, he tipped his chin toward the chains dangling from the ceiling. She wouldn't have to kneel again any time soon.

Serge had stripped as well, retaining only his trousers. He stepped toward the woman and led her, a hand politely cupping her elbow, toward the chains. With his expression neutral, he lifted her slender wrists one at a time and secured them in leather-padded cuffs. Then he walked to the wall and turned the wheel that drew up the chains. He didn't stop until Mandy stood on tiptoe, her arms stretched toward the ceiling.

Boone admired the arch of her back, the thrust of her round buttocks, and the curve of her large, uptilted breasts. He strode toward her, cupped one fleshy cheek, pleased with the firmness of her bottom. "A spreader bar between her knees, I think."

"Yes, boss," Serge said, his voice quiet and tight.

His friend's tension was unusual, almost disapproving. He seemed to like the girl, and that surprised Boone. Serge had always thought of women as mere conveniences and nothing more. And because Boone wasn't all that interested in Mandy, he decided Serge would take a more active role than usual.

Boone circled her, studying her body—her toned legs, her tight abdomen, her freshly waxed pussy.

Serge walked behind her, nudged her feet farther apart with

his toes, and then bent to attach a spreader bar, wrapping leather bands around her knees that closed with the crisp crunch of Velcro. His hands lingered on her knees, and then slid up her inner thighs.

The woman's breath hitched. The position couldn't have been comfortable, because she hung now by her wrists, her body contorting to stretch higher on her toes to relieve the pull.

But Boone didn't want her comfortable. He wanted to see whether she'd complain.

He touched her between her legs and found her dry, her lips cool, showing no sign of arousal. But that was changing.

Mandy's breasts quivered with her quickening breaths. Her nipples beaded prettily.

He flicked one with his thumbnail.

Without a word, Serge stepped beside him and offered him a set of feathered clamps.

Ignoring her widening glance, Boone teased her nipples with brushes of the feathers, waiting patiently as her breasts tightened and her nipples extended. Then he pressed open one clamp and attached it to a red tip, using the screw on the side of the clamp to tighten it. He attached the second clamp and tightened it too.

"How's that feel? Is it too much?" he asked softly, glancing at her face to gauge her expression.

Her mouth opened, jaw sagging just a bit with pleasure, but she shook her head. "Tighten it a little more."

Disgusted at her lack of manners, Boone dropped his hands and walked away, listening for her reaction, knowing she wouldn't be able to control her temper.

Sure enough, her breath huffed out. Her feet shifted. A thin, gritted groan sounded.

With slow strides, he walked to an armchair and settled in, facing her, his expression perfectly blank.

Her eyes shot daggers at him. Her bottom lip stuck out like a stoop.

Behind her, Serge lifted a brow.

With a slight lift of his chin, Boone gave the signal.

Serge raised his arm and swung a bare wooden paddle at her backside. The oak paddle with its drilled holes made a satisfying whack.

Mandy gasped at the stroke and tried to turn her head toward Serge, but her arms were extended too high for her to do anything but dangle as he landed more slaps on her backside.

Boone suppressed a smile as her eyes grew wider and wider, the pout wiped off her face as swats from the paddle warmed her bottom. As Serge continued, she twisted her body slightly to the right and left now, trying to avoid his steady strokes.

Boone didn't doubt her distress, but since she didn't ask for Serge to stop, he allowed his friend to continue dishing swats, watching Mandy with growing approval as her body shivered and soft hiccuping sobs sounded, while at the same time, her breasts hardened, and her pussy pulsed with the tensing of her thighs. Mandy was thoroughly aroused.

Serge paused and patted her bottom with his palm. "Skin's nice and red." He slipped his hand lower and cupped her pussy from behind. "Not dry anymore either."

"Huh?" Mandy twisted, her toes balancing comically beneath her spread knees. "Bastard!"

Boone watched his friend dip a finger inside her cunt and swirl it. "But not nearly ready for you, sir."

Serge glanced toward Boone, who gave him a nod to continue.

Her pussy made a wet clasping sound as it clenched around

Serge's fingers, and he plunged them deeper. Her body sagged. Her next indrawn breath was edged with a cry and her pussy clenched moistly again and again.

Boone cleared his throat.

Serge withdrew his fingers and gave her hip an approving pat.

"Release her," Boone said, keeping his voice uninflected.

While Serge lowered her hands and unwrapped the cuffs from her wrists, Boone opened his pants, pushed them down just far enough to free his cock, and waited, keeping his breaths even and his cock *uninterested*. His concern was for whether she'd give him what he wanted most right now: complete, utter submission.

Freed, Mandy swayed on her feet for a moment, rubbing her wrists, her gaze falling to Boone's soft shaft. Her cheeks reddened, nostrils flaring with desire, as she slid her tongue across her lower lip. She didn't lift her gaze to lock with his, something he was glad of because if she did, no doubt her pride would demand she preen just a bit.

Boone placed both hands on the chair arms. "Come to me on your knees," he said softly.

Mandy glanced back at Serge.

At the narrowing of his friend's eyes, Boone's belly tightened. Had she given him a smug smile?

Her expression didn't give away her true mood as she dropped to her hands and knees and crawled slowly toward Boone. For now, she behaved.

Serge's gaze dropped to her bottom and pussy. His eyelids dipped and a smile played on his mouth. He was likely enjoying the results of his efforts. The sight of a reddened bottom and lush, wet pussy were their own rewards.

Mandy's breasts swayed beneath her, her head dipped, more lioness than kitten, because her eyes were narrowing as she drew closer. When she reached Boone, she bent lower to rest her head on his bare foot.

Boone held his breath, waiting. A test he was sure she'd fail.

When he didn't immediately acknowledge her presence, her tongue licked the top of his foot tentatively. When he still failed to respond, she drew his big toe into her mouth.

What the hell? Boone's eyebrows shot up.

Serge grinned and shrugged his shoulders.

"Give me a plug," Boone mouthed, as he frowned down at the girl who was doing everything she could to tempt him into letting her have her way with him. Each pull on his toe caused an answering throb in his dick. He nearly laughed at his predicament, but because he meant to retain control of this session, he tamped down his sudden pleasure, concentrating instead on his growing irritation.

He sighed. He'd wanted her to suck his cock, but her blatant teasing called for more punishment. No wonder she'd been available for play, unclaimed. Mandy didn't understand the nuances of the game they played. Didn't have a true sub's heart.

Serge padded close, a tube and a thick black plug in his hands.

"Take her to the bench," Boone said, his tone sharp.

Her head bobbed up, a hint of anger in her eyes. The pout returned to her lips.

When she stood and walked woodenly to the spanking bench, Boone stripped off his pants. His nudity would make her think he was more interested than he actually was, and he liked the feel of the air-conditioned air wafting over his steamy sex. His interest in her needs and pleasure was quickly fading.

With a hand resting at her back to guide her down, Serge bent her over the bench and secured her hands and ankles.

Boone accepted the lube, spread her buttocks with his fingers, and then squeezed the tube to lay a stripe atop her tiny hole. He rubbed the gel into her with his thumb, his motions quick and clinical. Then he accepted the plug, coated it with more lube, and slowly tried to insert it inside her.

Her asshole clenched, resisting the intrusion.

Boone grunted. Perhaps she wasn't as experienced as she pretended. His irritation softened. "Breathe, Mandy. Unless you want this to stop now."

Her indrawn breath was a little more ragged this time, but she took another deep breath, and her bottom relaxed.

He slid the plug inside her, the narrowing at the base ensuring she couldn't easily expel it. Then he stood back, admiring the view. The ugly black plug stretched her hole—something she obviously enjoyed, because her pretty sex swelled even more. Moisture was beginning to trickle from between her folds. He dipped his fingers inside her and swirled, satisfied with the fluid slicking his fingers.

Her body was primed. Her feminine heat softening, and the thought of how snug and tight she'd be surrounding him, tugged at his cock.

Standing back, he caressed the pinkened skin of her ass, enjoying the feverish heat. The state of her bottom was symbolic of their exchange. Mandy hoped for a firm partner, someone who would push her beyond herself, fulfilling needs deeper than the transitory pleasure of release, something she likely didn't yet understand. For him, he needed the focus this session brought. For their time together, he craved control—over her body, over his, but especially over his mind. Here, he could concentrate on the raw emotions he produced, guiding Mandy through the power exchange—taking hers, but giving her pleasure and fulfilling her deeper need to surrender her trust. The moment a partner gave that trust, a rush like no other, a deeply satisfying pleasure eased the grip of his tightly held pain. He wasn't Boone, the boy who'd fled his home in shame. He was a man in charge of his own fate. However, he doubted he'd achieve that state of nirvana this night.

Sighing, he raised his hand and gave each pink globe a stinging clap that rocked her against the bench.

Mandy groaned, and her head dropped. Her back shivered.

He walked around the bench and knelt in front of her, studying her face.

Gone was her bravado. Her blue eyes were moist.

Boone softened at her tears. "Sweetheart, do you know what you did to displease me?"

Her lower lip trembled. "I sucked your toe when you didn't ask."

"That's not everything, dear. Your expressions give you away. When you really want something, you try to maneuver your Dom into giving it to you. It's called topping. You play at submitting, but you haven't learned any discipline."

"But I want to learn." She bit her lower lip, likely knowing she'd once again broken protocol by speaking out of turn.

He arched a brow. "Do you? Really?"

"Yes, please, sir," she whispered. "Teach me?"

He shook his head. "I'm not taking you on, Mandy. I don't have the time. But I don't want to leave you unfulfilled. The next time you play, watch that mouth," he said, tapping her bottom lip. "No pouting. No glaring. Don't make a move unless you're instructed. How's your bottom feel?"

Her lips twisted. "Burns, sir." Her gaze went to his flagging cock and she sighed. "I don't want to leave you disappointed in me."

His lips quirked at her childish tone. "Then there's hope for you. Will you do whatever I ask? No complaints or pouting?"

She nodded, her expression growing more hopeful.

"I need a bit of a workout."

Her eyes brightened. "I'd enjoy a flogging, sir."

Really? Boone grunted. The lesson had gone completely over her head. He heard Serge's chuckles and shook his head. "Then how about practicing a bit with me. I'll flog you until I think you've had enough. You'll forget all about rules and simply give yourself to me. No holding back. We'll both get what we need for now."

Sniffing, she nodded.

Boone went to the cupboard and opened it, searching among the implements mounted on pegboard backing for just the right flogger. He chose one with long purple strands made of deer hide and another of a stiffer suede.

When Boone returned, Serge stood beside her with his arms crossed over his chest.

Boone leaned toward him and whispered, "Get a bench ready to place in front of her. I want you to fuck her mouth." He tapped Mandy's ass. "Don't you dare bite my friend."

A choked giggle made him smile, and Boone relaxed, forgetting about the problems waiting at Maison Plaisir.

Summoning a pleasant image of Tilly Floret with her clothing askew, her dewy eyes wide, and her mouth begging, he swatted Mandy's sweetly rounded bottom with the deer-hide flogger, striking side to side in a steady rhythm that had her moaning in delight, her pussy drenched. While careful not to strike one spot too often, he worked, warming her backside, her back and thighs, the steady strokes calming his mind.

When she lay limply draped over the bench, her sighs soft and thready, he bent toward her ear, whispering, "Serge will give you his cock. Pleasure him with that pretty red mouth."

He nodded to Serge, who placed a bench in front of Mandy's lowered head and dropped his trousers. Taking a seat, he gripped his cock and slowly fed it into Mandy's waiting mouth.

Boone tossed down the deer-hide flogger and picked up the next one. He slapped the flanges against his palm, liking the sting and the sharper sound it made.

Mandy's bottom lifted, anticipating the first stroke.

The marks he and Serge had left so far would fade quickly. Her skin was warm, but not a single welt had been raised. That was about to change. By the time they left her, she'd have tender stripes and knots she'd feel acutely for days. Then perhaps the point he wanted made would stick.

Mandy had a fiery spirit. Some Dom might treasure it, but she wasn't a true submissive. If someone wanted a woman who begged for punishment but would never truly give herself into another's care, she'd be perfect.

She wasn't for him, though. Before he'd even entered the room, he'd known it. His interest was locked on a different target—Tilly Floret. He wouldn't find true satisfaction until Tilly knelt at his feet and declared her willingness to serve. It would probably be a long seduction, requiring patience on his part, as he introduced her to his world and peeled away her layers to hold her mind and body in thrall.

At the thought of Tilly, a fierce hunger coursed through Boone. His cock stirred, filling and lengthening. He paused in the whipping to stroke his shaft with the suede flanges, root to tip, then gave Mandy's ass straight up-and-down pops with the ends of the flanges.

She gave a muffled cry and her bottom wriggled.

Serge gritted his teach and petted her head. "Watch the teeth, sweetheart."

Boone watched her head as it bobbed over his friend's rigid shaft, and imagined his own being sucked just as eagerly, wet slurps and thick groans accompanying each strong tug of a feminine mouth.

Again, he popped her, choosing a new spot, and then rubbed it, feeling the heat and the slight rounding. She'd have a bruise there. He pushed his thumb at the center of the rising knot and watched as her pussy released a fresh wash of fluid.

She'd said she was willing, liked a little pain. She certainly hadn't been lying.

He dropped the flogger, her lesson forgotten as his own lust deepened. How long would it take to lure Tilly to his bed? How many nights would he sit before the security monitor, watching her bedroom, imagining every faint moan she made in her sleep bore his name?

With quick moves, he rolled a condom onto his dick, lubed up, and knelt on the bench behind her. He pulled the plug from her ass and nudged the widened hole. Then, with a narrowed glance at Serge, whose mouth was smirking, he thrust slowly inside her ass.

The grip of her tiny muscles caused his breath to hiss between his teeth. He palmed both cheeks and pressed them apart to ease the constriction around him as he tunneled deeper.

Her buttocks quivered, her thin moans coming faster as her head continued to move up and down at the same speed.

"Jesus, she's gonna suck me dry," Serge groaned, his eyes squeezing shut.

Boone dug deeper, giving her short, deepening thrusts until his groin was snug against her. He slipped a hand between her body and the bench, curling his fingers to find her clit.

At first contact, her body jerked, and a shiver worked its way down her spine. She was plenty wet, her pussy soaked with silky fluid. He dipped his fingers inside, keeping time with the gentle rocking of his hips, and fingered her tightening little bud.

Mandy's cries became muffled, choking sobs.

Serge wouldn't let her up. He palmed the back of her head and kept her working, even while she quickly flew apart.

Boone leaned over her back and gave her sore bottom a hard pinch. "You can't come until Serge does. Do you hear me?"

She bobbed her head, and then wagged her face side to side, sinking deeper on Serge's shaft.

His friend's body hardened, the muscles of his chest and abdomen bunching, sweat gleaming on his skin. "Close," he gritted out.

Boone leaned away and slipped three fingers in Mandy's pussy while applying pressure to her clit with his thumb, and continued fucking her with ever-sharpening strokes. He'd force her over the edge—see if she could hold back just long enough to first give Serge what he needed.

Serge's head fell back, a low groan sounding. His fists gripped the bench where he sat as he pumped up into her mouth, spending himself inside her.

The moment the tension in Serge's body eased, Mandy sobbed and bounced shallowly on the bench, grinding her ass against Boone, her pussy clenching hard around his fingers. Her orgasm was fierce and hard.

When she peaked, Boone pulled free and bent to release her hands and ankles. He slid off the used condom, and rolled another on. "Push up on your arms."

"Can't," she sobbed. "I'm shaking."

"Do it anyway if you want me to fuck you."

Mandy shook her head in silent protest, but pushed up, changing the angle of his thrusts.

Boone pressed against her engorged lips, and pushed between them, sinking deep. He had a straight shot toward her womb. Her engorged slit cushioned the end of his hard strokes.

Boone gripped her hips. "Serge, flick her nipples."

As Serge leaned forward to play with her clamped breasts, Boone gathered her hips and pulled her down his cock at the same time he thrust upward. Hammering hard, he bounced her against his groin. When her cries grew louder, he slipped a hand around her belly and toggled her clit. His body tightened the moment she screamed and crested again. His balls exploded; cum spurted in steady scalding spurts.

When he could draw a breath, he pulled out and padded toward the shower. He shook out a towel and wrapped it around his waist. As he walked toward the door, Serge rose and lifted an exhausted Mandy in his arms to carry her to the bed and give her the gentle aftercare she'd earned. He gave Boone a wink and then gently removed the clamps from her nipples.

With the sound of her heartfelt groan of appreciation, Boone let himself out the door and headed to the locker room. His body was sated, but his mind was already racing. Making plans for a sexy campaign to bind a woman to him—one who didn't have clue how to handle his darker appetites.

He'd show no remorse. But he would give her gentleness. He'd be merciless, relentless in his pursuit, but she'd be lavishly rewarded.

Smiling to himself, he reached into a stall and turned on the spigot. Tilly Floret might suspect he wanted her, but she didn't know just how far he'd go to possess her.

Chapter Five

The next morning, a knock sounded on Tilly's front door. Having just finished a light breakfast of buttered toast and coffee, she tightened the belt of her bathrobe and headed to her door. A moment later, she wished she'd peeked through the peephole before opening it.

Boone Benoit stood on her porch.

Her throat dried. She touched her hair, groaning inside because she hadn't showered or even combed her hair. Feeling at a distinct disadvantage, she eyed his dress shirt and dark trousers, his neatly combed dark hair, and the gleam in his cool blue eyes.

Forcing some starch into voice, she lifted her chin. "Do you follow up with every prospective employee personally, Mr. Benoit?"

"I couldn't wait for an answer." With a narrowed gaze, he glanced at his watch. "I have a helicopter being fueled now. We leave in forty minutes."

Her mouth gaped. "We? Seriously? I haven't said yes."

"But you planned to, right?" He waved a hand. "Go dress. Wear something casual. We're heading to a conference in a private compound, so don't worry about putting on a suit. Unless it's a bikini," he said, a dark brow arching. "You might get a chance to catch a swim in the pool."

She shook her head. "I can't leave at the drop of a hat. And it would take a sight longer than forty minutes to bathe, dress, and pack."

"No need to pack. Jump in the shower and dress. I'll have everything you need brought to the villa. Hurry up, Tilly." He pushed through the door.

His actions forced her to back away or be pressed against his chest.

His gaze swept the small living area. "Is the furniture yours?"

"No, it's Mrs. Nolan's."

He gave a nod, seeming relieved.

Did her home not meet his higher standards? She straightened her shoulders. "Mr. Benoit—"

"Boone."

"Boone, I'm not going anywhere with you. Not right now."

His gaze swung back. A frown dug a line between his dark brows. "Why not?"

"Because I haven't said I'll work for you, and you haven't given me notice of any travel plans."

Both brows rose. "I told you now."

"Precisely." She stared. "Does everyone jump when you say?"

He shrugged, and then gave her a grin.

That grin surprised her because the gesture seemed almost boyish.

He sighed and raked a hand through his hair. "Look, something's come up. Last-minute business. I'm in a hurry."

Muscles tensing, she folded her arms over her chest. "And I'm not."

His mouth pursed. "If I ask nicely, will you shower and get dressed?"

"I was going to do that anyway before you came. If you leave, I can continue with my plans."

"You're coming with me."

She fisted her hands and glared. "You're impossible."

"Tilly," he said, "I can make anything possible. Was the salary not enough?"

His voice had softened into a seductive rumble. First he bullied, now he was trying to cajole her? She sputtered. "The salary was ridiculous."

"Want me to lower it?"

"No!" Her chin jutted upward.

He shrugged. "Then you've agreed."

"That I will come to work for you, yes. But—"

He raised a finger. "No buts. Get showered." He sat on the arm of her couch. "I'll wait."

She realized her mouth was agape and closed it with a snap. Then, giving him a glare, she retreated to her bedroom and locked the door.

"Fifteen minutes," he called.

Fifteen minutes! Her answer had never been in doubt. Stalling had been a salve to her pride. He likely knew it. His persistence despite her stubborn refusals sent an odd surge of excitement zinging through her veins.

She flew out of her robe and pulled her nightgown over her head. She rushed to her closet and pulled out the first thing that met his specifications—a baby-blue sundress and white sandals. In a flash, she searched her drawers for pretty white underwear and a lacy bra, not something that she wore every day, but which would give her confidence a little boost, and then headed to the shower.

Fifteen minutes later, she skimmed her lips with pink gloss and stood back from the steamed-up mirror. Her hair was still wet, so she'd pulled it into a ponytail. It would have to dry on the trip. Because she hadn't had time for much makeup, she'd brushed blush on her cheeks, dabbed her eyelids with pale gray shimmer, and brushed mascara on her lashes.

So she didn't look sophisticated. He'd just have to deal. Next time, he could give her a little warning.

Picking up a straw handbag, she let herself out of her bedroom, careful not to open the door too wide so he wouldn't see the mess she'd left in her wake.

Boone glanced up from where he still sat, his ankles crossed in front of him, his dark lashes lowering as his gaze swept her.

A blush heated her cheeks, and a secret thrill ran through her body. "I'd have managed better with a little more time."

"You look perfect." He straightened and held out his hand. "Give me your keys."

She shook her head. "Why?"

"I'm having a crew move you while we're away."

"M-move me?" Her heart and mouth stuttered. "Where?"

"To the estate. I'm giving you the old foreman's house. It's newly renovated. You'll be quite comfortable."

Her mind whirled. He wanted her to move to Maison Plaisir? Impossible! The thought of living so close, of never escaping his attention or having time away to fortify her resistance, left her shaking. She shivered, trying to think of a reasonable argument. "But I have six months on this lease."

He waved a hand. "My man will settle with Mrs. Nolan. I'll need you close at hand. Your keys…"

Feeling a little shell-shocked, she went to the key holder beside the door and began to slip off the house key.

A large hand closed around hers and took the entire ring. "Don't worry about a thing. Your car will be moved too." Then he reached around her and turned the doorknob.

A hand settled against the small of her back and guided her out the door and down the steps. She went as docile as a lamb.

Tilly angled her head toward her landlady's window to see Mrs. Nolan with her nose pressed against the window. The whole town would know she'd left with Boone Benoit. Blood pounded in her ears. And, good Lord, she hadn't yet informed Mae she was quitting the restaurant. She drew away from his hand. "I can't go. I have things I have to do. Mae doesn't know I'm quitting."

"Jonesy's already informing Mae Baillio you've left her employ."

Anger flickered inside, warming her. "You had no right—"

Boone stepped closer, sucking away her air. "Don't fight me, Tilly. You were going to say yes. I'm making this easy."

This was happening too fast. She blinked at him—trying to read his expression, the stillness of his features, the rigidity of his posture. It would be easier not to have to face Mae or Leon or anyone else in the town. They'd try to dissuade her. Remind her about family loyalty. To them, she'd be working for the man who murdered her cousin. She was the only one who believed he hadn't—she'd never believed it. She'd remembered his kindness with Denny, his patience over her cousin's mercurial mood changes. Instinctively, she'd known Boone Benoit was no cold-blooded murderer. And now she possessed a clue, something that pointed at another suspect. Although the direction it pointed was one she couldn't think about without being sick.

Boone stayed quiet as she composed herself, and then stepped back and bent his arm, offering it.

Aware Mrs. Nolan watched, she slowly curled her hand into

the crook of his elbow, sucking in a breath at the contact. His skin was warm, the muscle beneath her fingertips hard as steel. Her heart raced; her cheeks flamed. But she lifted her chin and allowed him to lead her to the Bentley parked so absurdly in her driveway.

During the ride to the estate, their seats faced each other, knees nearly touching. Her back was to the driver, who was separated from them by a thick panel of glass to ensure their privacy. The smell of rich leather and masculine cologne reinforced how foreign this felt. How out of her element she was with this man.

She wanted to ask him again, why her? She didn't buy the quick answer he'd given her the day before. Boone didn't act impulsively. He couldn't while running a successful multinational corporation. He'd planned this. So why her? Because she was Celeste's cousin? Was he using her presence at the estate to thumb the noses of the workers, who'd carry word of her every move straight back to Bayou Vert? She hated to think that was the only reason. But she couldn't imagine what else could be motivating him.

"Would you like a cup of coffee?"

"We'll be in a helicopter in a few minutes," she snapped, then widened her eyes because she'd just been rude to her new employer.

"Right, you might have to pee," he said, his expression neutral. "There are no accommodations in a helicopter."

She glared at his crudeness. And predictably, her cheeks flamed. She cleared her throat. "Where are we goin'?"

"To Monterrey."

"California?" she asked, her mouth dropping.

"Mexico."

Her thoughts whirled. "But I don't have a passport."

"You won't need one. We'll be flying from one private airstrip to another. Authorities will be satisfied with your driver's license."

"Will we be gone long?" What about her brother?

"For as long as the negotiations take." He drew his hands together in his lap. "Are we going to play twenty questions?"

"Am I bein' tedious?" she asked, her lips tightening.

"No, you're delightfully stubborn." He sighed. "Let me surprise you. Soon enough, I'll put you to work. For now, relax. Consider this a minivacation."

"A vacation," she said faintly.

"We'll be sharing a villa while I'm working." At her startled stare he tilted his head. "You'll have your own room. Please don't be concerned. I hired your *professional* services."

Her heart had stopped when he'd said they'd be sharing accommodations, but tripped with the gentle emphasis of "professional." Was she disappointed? "You've hired me to work. Why not start me with this trip? I don't need a vacation. It seems…"

"How does it seem?"

"Like you're playin' with me," she whispered, barely able to speak through a tight throat.

"Do you think I intend to seduce you?" A dark eyebrow rose. "I could have called any number of women to accompany me if *all* I'd wanted was a playmate."

And now she felt foolish. Why on earth would he be interested in her that way? "I guess I'm confused. You rushed me— I'm trying to catch my breath."

The corners of his eyes wrinkled. "You'll get used to the pace."

The car slowed, and Tilly glanced out the window, realizing they had arrived at the parking lot outside the estate and the iron gate was open. A large man dressed the same as Boone held open the gate. They continued until the vehicle stopped beside another gate that opened onto a grassy field. The car door opened, and the large man extended his hand to help her out.

Startled, she stared. He was as handsome as Boone but more rugged. His face all angles and hard planes. His dark eyes studied her, but not unkindly. His mouth curved in a slow smile. "I'm Sergei Gun. Vice president in charge of security services. Call me Serge."

Standing between both tall, beefy men, Tilly felt slight and feminine—and completely out of her element.

"Duck when we near the blades, but don't worry," Serge said easily. "We'll get you safely to our destination."

He held her arm as he escorted her through the gate and to the open door of the helicopter. She'd never flown on one and hoped she wouldn't embarrass herself by getting airsick. The sound of the whirring blades was deafening.

Climbing the steps, she was acutely aware of the men climbing in behind her. Two more appeared behind Boone and Serge to join them in the enclosed cabin. A hand pressed to the small of her back guided her to the small row of seats to the left. She didn't bother to look back to see who touched her. The imprints of Boone's fingers burned through the thin material of her dress.

She settled into a seat, placing her purse on her lap. But Boone grabbed the purse and gave it to Serge, who stowed it away in a metal bin. Then Boone knelt in front of her and reached around her body, pulling out shoulder straps and clicking the fasteners together. When he leaned closer and slipped his hand behind her, she drew in a shocked breath because he skimmed her bottom.

But he was only searching for the waist belt, which he clicked into the harness. Then he took a seat across from her, a hint of a smile playing at one corner of his mouth. The two men who had joined them at the helicopter's stairs slid in on either side of her.

Headphones appeared in front of her, but unlike the ones Boone and his men donned, hers didn't have a wire connecting them to anything. Still, she was grateful for the protection they provided her ears, even if she was cut off from the nearby conversations.

When the helicopter lifted, she held her harness, her gaze going to the windows and her stomach dropping to her toes as they rose quickly into the air.

A tap landed on her knee, and she glanced up to find Boone's steady gaze on her.

You okay? he mouthed.

Fine time to ask whether her stomach would stand the journey. But apparently, it could. She nodded.

His eyes blinked slowly, and he smiled. He pointed at his watch. *Four hours.*

So long? Having never traveled any farther than Houston, she hadn't really thought about the distance. Now she had four hours with only her own thoughts to keep her occupied.

Four hours to think about how he'd bulldozed his way into her apartment and into this trip. Four hours to contemplate their destination and the fact she'd be living with him in close quarters. And thank God she hadn't accepted the coffee!

Both Boone and Serge spoke into microphones beside their mouths.

She didn't have to read lips to know they were talking about her. Their gazes touched her...everywhere. Rather than drive herself crazy trying to figure out what they said, Tilly frowned and stared out the window.

Both men wore self-satisfied expressions, lips curved in faint smiles, eyes narrowing as they studied her.

Four hours, he'd said. At this moment, she wished she'd worn something frumpy and thick. Wished she'd ignored the knock at her door. Only now did she wonder to what had she really agreed.

* * *

By the time they'd touched down on a concrete airstrip at their destination, her nerves were raw. The door opened and white-hot air took her breath away. Once she'd moved from the helicopter, she opened her jaws, trying to pop her ears. The roar of the helicopter's engine was still inside her head.

Serge handed Tilly her purse.

Boone touched her elbow and led her to a waiting car, a black Esplanade with tinted windows.

Another two vehicles flanked the car, armed guards standing near the doors.

When she noticed the military-style weapons, her heart skipped a beat. But they were in Mexico now. Trusting Boone to know what was necessary, she allowed him to seat her inside the car between himself and Serge. They sat so close, both men's thighs touched hers. Her skin rose in goose bumps.

Tilly frowned and tugged at her skirt, which was trapped beneath Serge's leg.

"Sorry," he said, lifting so she could free her garment. "You only had to ask, Ms. Floret."

Boone patted her thigh, drawing her attention to where his hand rested on her leg, then up to meet his gaze. Feeling rather like a butterfly beneath a magnifying glass, she kept silent, sure she'd only manage to say something that would make him laugh. She was tired and irritated—and afraid.

Not for her physical safety, but by the fact she was dependent on him here for everything. Other than what she wore, she had no clothing, no toiletries. She didn't speak the language, didn't know what to expect when they arrived at the villa. He'd said he'd hired her for her professional services, but the way he'd spoken those words made her want to shout *those* services couldn't be purchased.

But they could be wooed. From the moment he'd arrived on her doorstep, she'd been hyperaware of every aspect of his appearance and actions. Although he was dressed in a dress shirt and trousers, a typical businessman's attire, his posture and expression were wary, alert to their surroundings, to her every reaction. The breadth of his shoulders, the solid build of his body should have been reassuring, because she had no doubts he could handle any danger that might befall them. But his undeniable masculinity also disconcerted her.

She imagined being at his mercy, bending to his will. The thought didn't frighten her. The possibility thrilled her to her toes. Boone Benoit was a dangerous man in more ways than she'd ever imagined.

The entire trip, while she'd ignored him and his VP of security, she'd imagined him shirtless at poolside, catching him naked coming from his shower. Any number of possible scenarios where she might be caught blushing like a virgin or wiping drool from her chin. She'd never dated a man like him—so powerful or damnably intuitive. Damn, she was going to make a fool of herself. She just knew it.

They drove through mountains sparsely peppered with crooked trees and limestone rock outcroppings. Their caravan followed a narrow road that hugged the side of a mountain, winding downward toward a green valley with a small village nestled at the bottom. They passed crowded streets with rough shanties, and then rose to the opposite side of the valley where large estates dotted the hilltops.

When they turned into an estate enclosed by a tall, stuccoed concrete wall, she couldn't resist gawking as the gates opened quietly by remote, and they drove into a compound with a large cobblestone courtyard. Deep red Hibiscus flowers grew in pots lining an alcove entrance. Purple bougainvillea bloomed in profusion, draping from a red-tiled roof.

Once more, with her hand tucked into the corner of his arm, she allowed Boone to escort her inside. Cool, pine-scented air greeted her. Saltillo tiles clicked beneath her sandals. The walls were creamy beige, the furnishings heavy and dark.

A brunette woman dressed in a crisp sleeveless white blouse and pencil-thin, charcoal-gray skirt approached. Her gray eyes swept Tilly's frame, then she gave Boone a cool nod. "You should find everything ready, Mr. Benoit."

"Thanks, Beatrice. Have Alejandro and the Peterson Group reps arrived?"

"Yes, sir. They're in the conference room."

He drew in a deep breath and dropped his arm, turning to Tilly, his expression, disappointingly, all business. "Beatrice will show you to your room. If our meeting lasts past dinner, help yourself to anything in the kitchen, or pick up any phone. Someone will be there straightaway to see to your needs. If you want to swim, don't worry if you don't see anyone around. Security is discreet. You'll be safe."

He left without a backward glance, Serge following, a finger touching a Bluetooth hooked over his ear. "The Tex-Oil point man's arrived as well, Boone. They're reviewing the kidnappers' demands now."

Kidnappers? That's what this was about? From her online research of his company, she knew this was one aspect of his business, but knowing and *really* knowing were two completely different things. The thought that Boone was the man companies and families turned to in such a horrible crisis left her feeling unsettled, and even a little proud. Boone wasn't what everyone back in Bayou Vert thought. He was a man who'd made saving people his life's work.

When the door shut behind both men, Tilly breathed freely for the first time since Boone had stepped through her doorway. Tension drained slowly away. Oddly, his absence left a hollow feeling.

"Mr. Benoit's staff phoned in your particulars," Beatrice said, her words more clipped than before. "I'll show you to your room. Let me know if anything in the closet doesn't fit."

Her particulars? What did she mean? Tilly turned her head to find Beatrice's hard gaze staring back.

The woman turned on her neat gray heels and led the way through a spacious living room to a long hallway with several closed doors. At the end, she opened a door and stood to the side, allowing Tilly to enter.

Tilly wasn't given to frills and floral, but the pale violet wallpaper with its sprigs of white flowers and green leaves appealed, as quintessentially feminine as the rest of the house was starkly masculine. The furnishings were a dark mahogany—a raised rice bed covered by a sumptuous sage-green duvet; a tall highboy; a vanity bedecked with exotic bottles she couldn't wait to unstopper and sniff. Beneath her feet was a lush, looped wool area rug in a dark sage. Tilly walked to French doors overlooking another, smaller courtyard with a bronze table-and-chair set and wicker chaise. More bougainvillea draped the exterior wall.

Beatrice's heels tapped behind her. "The gate in the far wall leads to the pool." She stepped beside her elbow and pointed to the wall of closets. "There are several bathing suits inside to choose from. Towels are in the bathroom. A pitcher of lemonade is on the table outside. You can take a glass to the pool. Enjoy the sun. But be sure to use plenty of sunscreen. Boone wouldn't like you getting burned."

The quick thrill she'd felt at the thought that Boone might care whether she burned was quickly doused by the other woman's demeanor. Her tone was crisply professional, but she stood so close, Tilly knew she was deliberately trying to intimidate her. The woman's clothing was a much higher quality than the plain sundress she wore. Her skin, hair, and nails were perfectly groomed. The hard stare she gave Tilly spoke volumes of her opinion of the reason for Tilly's presence.

Tilly straightened her shoulders. "Thank you. That will be all," she said quietly, holding herself still until Beatrice's dark eyes snapped with anger.

But the other woman gave her a blunt nod and backed away.

Tilly didn't bother watching her leave, grateful to at last be alone. Good Lord, the woman's antipathy toward her had been palpable. She was clearly jealous. Was she an ex-lover? Would Tilly be tripping over ex-lovers during her stay? Anger at Boone for putting her in this situation flared. For a while, she'd actually felt a little special when he'd turned his attention on her. She walked to the closet and slid back the white doors, surprised to find the closet deeper than she'd expected. Most of the rungs were empty. So no one used this closet on a regular basis. At least, no one now.

But several outfits hung before her—dresses, slacks, blouses, a sari, and all the accessories, shoes, bags, scarves she might need—in colors that would complement her tanned skin and pale hair. When her gaze lit on the bathing suits, she fingered the scantier ones, but passed them up for a tankini with matching bikini bottoms in a dark navy. She stripped where she stood, donning the suit and stepping into a pair of dark flip-flops. Everything fit perfectly—not something she wanted to contemplate right that moment.

He'd said she could treat this little jaunt like a minivacation. So while he worked, she'd explore. Grabbing the sari, she wrapped it around her hips and tied it in a knot. He'd also said she needn't worry about her safety. However, she did wonder about her privacy.

Boone didn't leave anything to chance. He'd had her clothing checked for size, then new items ordered while they were still in the air. During the flight, he'd arranged for her things to be moved to the foreman's house and her lease terminated. A fact that made backing out of their agreement now extremely awkward, almost impossible.

What had seemed like a boast, that he could make anything possible, now appeared to be true. If he decided he wanted her for more than her "professional services," how would she ever say yes and not wonder whether her surrender was something he considered his due? The thought appalled, because a scenario where she said yes was too easy to envision.

Chapter Six

By midafternoon, a payment had been negotiated with the Los Omegas cartel for the release of two Tex-Oil middle-management employees snatched en route to their Mexico City offices the previous morning. The suits overseeing Tex-Oil interests in the negotiations weren't happy with the amount. The Peterson Group reps, the insurance company that supplied kidnapping and ransom coverage to Tex-Oil, indicated their willingness to wire funds to a Cayman Island account to pay for the men's release.

Boone wasn't convinced the deal was solid. The cartel had agreed too readily. Dread settled in his gut. He didn't like feeling this way, didn't like imagining what the families of the missing men must be going through. But he wasn't being paid to worry. His mission was keeping laser focus on the recovery effort. Boone firmed his jaw and glanced at his point man, Alejandro Mata, who sat slumped in his chair, his fingers steepled and his expression hard as granite.

"What more do you want?" one of the insurance company reps asked. "They've given us proof of life."

"Doesn't feel right," Alejandro said, echoing Boone's thoughts. "When they call tonight with the account information, we'll agree to two payments. The first, a quarter of the funds, paid to them now in goodwill. The second payment comes upon the handoff of the men." Although he didn't need Boone's approval, he glanced his way.

Boone nodded, uneasy with the never-ending waiting game. He didn't like the fact the only option they had so far was to play the kidnappers' game and give in to their demands. "They hold all the cards. We haven't been able to find their trail, and have no idea which faction of the cartel is even holding them. The operation was well organized. After the grab, they left so many trails we wasted time following every single lead. Their transmissions are scrambled. If anything happened to the phone they left at the scene, we wouldn't have had a hope of communicating."

"It's pretty damn slick," Alejandro muttered with a flip of a hand. "A grab in broad daylight. A driver in your employ who passed every security check."

"Maybe your background checks aren't that good," the leader of the Tex-Oil team snarled.

Boone refused to show his irritation and met the man's glare with a steely look. "Our screenings are the best in the business. We didn't stop with the driver—we vetted his entire family. And we've been thorough with surveillance ever since the abduction. His nephew doesn't get on the school bus without one of our people watching. But local cops are involved in this. Likely federal troops as well. It's too professional." Without giving the man a chance to rebut, he glanced back to Alejandro. "You'll handle the response?"

Alejandro gave him a solemn nod. "We're moving the response team again. Making sure the cartel can't find us either."

"Good." Boone shot a glance farther down the table at Miguel Torres, an ex–Delta Force soldier who was the response team leader for Tex-Oil. Boone gave the man a steady stare. "Any concerns we haven't addressed?"

"None," Torres said, his tone clipped and professional. "Alejandro and I are in lockstep for the duration. So long as the suits let us handle it," he said, tipping his head toward the executives who glared in frustration, "we'll be fine."

Boone glanced at his watch, and then back to the oil execs. Satisfied they'd done all they could at this point, he moved to end the meeting. "We'll be in touch. Be ready to wire the cash as soon as you hear from us." He pushed away from the table, walked to the door, and entered the code to unlock it.

The conference room was hardened against attack, a panic room with a steel-reinforced skeleton, sensors to test the air coming from its own dedicated air-conditioning unit, and an arsenal of weapons hidden in the base of the long ebony conference table.

His presence hadn't been required for this meeting. Alejandro was his Mexican bureau chief and plenty experienced in K&R coordination. He'd been with Boone since he'd started the company, and was another member of his old SEAL unit whom he'd hired straight after leaving active duty. However, with the continued turbulence in the region, Boone liked to make a show, reassure the executives he still had his finger on the pulse of his company, however far-flung its assets. The security services division operated on trust. He'd earned it over the years for successful, discreet negotiations, and for mounting paramilitary operations for rescues when situations warranted. So far, this one hadn't blown up.

Relocking the door, he headed down the closed-in breezeway to the main house and let himself in.

Beatrice, who'd been monitoring the comings and goings of his guests, waited in the living room. She turned in her swivel chair at the desk where she'd been working. "I assume all's going well."

"I wouldn't be ducking out if it weren't."

She flushed. "Your other guest is at the pool," she said, gesturing toward her computer monitor with the feed in the corner of the screen where she'd been keeping track of Tilly's whereabouts.

He nodded his thanks. "We'll be dining in tonight. Alone."

She gave him a polite smile.

One that didn't reach her eyes.

Boone made a mental note that Beatrice was due a promotion. A position that moved her out of his immediate influence. She'd become a little too familiar. Had overstepped her bounds a couple of times already, assuming a closer relationship than he'd tolerate. "You're free for the rest of the day. Serge is on watch. Take one of the cars and do some shopping. Use the company card if you like."

Her back stiffening, she arched a brow. "Thank you, *sir.*"

The emphasis she placed on the last word, one she rarely used as the staff closest to him always called him Boone, fired anger inside him. She was well aware of his sexual proclivities, having often called to book his room at The Platform and half a dozen exclusive clubs around the world. He'd never invited her. *Would never.* He wondered if her nose was out of joint because she'd assumed Tilly was a submissive he'd brought along for sex play.

He left her standing in the living room and walked down the hallway toward his own bedroom. Taking only a few moments, he donned swimming trunks and let himself out the garden gate.

The sun was intense. He hoped Tilly had made use of one of the beach umbrellas. If she'd let herself burn, he wouldn't be pleased. His lips twitched at the thought of a suitable punishment. Something subtle that she wouldn't recognize as such.

But he needn't have worried. She lay on a hammock beneath an umbrella, sleeping. One cheek was pressed against the knotted ropes. Her skin was flushed, but from heat, not excessive sunning. Not surprising, she'd chosen the most demure of the bathing suits he'd ordered.

He glanced to the table beside her and noted an insulated thermos was on the table, the glass beside it half-filled. So she'd hydrated. Boone stepped close and placed his hand on her bare calf. A light touch, which didn't waken her.

Giving into temptation, he smoothed a hand across her warm skin. Soft and creamy. The sunscreen she'd applied smelled faintly of mangos. He gave her skin another caress.

She gasped and raised her head, her eyes blinking away sleep as she realized who'd touched her. "Boone," she said, her tone husky.

He slid away his hand. "I wondered if you'd like to join me for a swim," he said, smiling because one of her cheeks bore deep indents from the hammock's webbing.

Stretching her arms over her head, she gave a huge yawn. "I wasn't comfortable going in alone. What if I cramped?"

He grinned. "I'll keep you safe." The statement stirred something inside, confusing him for a moment, and he pushed away the feeling before holding out his hand.

Tilly stared for a moment, but then accepted it and swung her legs over the side of the hammock. The moment she stood, she pulled away. They walked to pool's edge, a foot of space between their swinging hands.

Boone shoved to the back of his mind that staff watched them via cameras mounted in trees surrounding the pool. He never really gave the surveillance a second thought, but he knew Tilly would consider it an invasion of her privacy. Given the world he operated in, the loss of privacy was necessary.

Nearing a natural rock outcropping overlapping the pool, he cast a sideways glance. "You'll have to lose the sarong."

"Hell. I showed more of my ass in my Daisy Dukes," she muttered under her breath. Unknotting the garment, she let it fall to the ground, and then stood, her hands balling at her sides.

"You're lovely. You've nothing to worry about."

A snort sounded. "I've seen pictures on the Internet of the size twos you date." She widened her arms. "I'm considerably larger."

"You're a healthy girl. With curves a man appreciates."

"Okay," she said, blowing out a deep breath. "If I wasn't feeling self-conscious before, I am now." She gave a little laugh.

A grin tugged the corners of his mouth. "Let's see if the suit can withstand a little salt water."

"What's it made of?" She grinned. "Do you think it might dissolve?"

"A man's entitled to his own fantasies."

She laughed and climbed down the steps into the pool, deep enough that the water lapped at her smooth thighs. Then she dipped beneath the surface and popped up, glancing down at her suit. "Nope. You're doomed for disappointment."

Feeling lighthearted, he dove into the deep end of the pool. He surfaced, found his footing, and glanced around. She stood in the same place, her gaze locked on his frame. Before she looked away, he noted a sparkle of answering heat in her eyes.

Hiding a smile of satisfaction, Boone waved a beckoning hand. "Don't worry. Join me."

Again, she dunked down and swam toward him, careful to keep her head above the water.

"Not much of a swimmer?" he asked as she stopped in front of him, dog-paddling.

"I live on the bayou." She wrinkled her nose. "Snakes, alligators…"

Boone laughed. "Come deeper. I'll watch out for you. Nothing will nibble at your toes." *Unless it's me.*

They swam, Tilly venturing into deeper water, bobbing beneath and no longer looking apprehensive. When she rolled to her back and floated, he swam closer, enjoying the view. Her nipples were tight little beads against the thin fabric, her breasts gentle curves. More than anything, he wanted to cup one and see if it would fill his palm. Even more than that, he wanted to hear her gasp of pleasure. But because touching her now wasn't the smartest plan, he refrained and glanced at her face.

She'd been watching him watching her, and she dropped her lower body and reached up to smooth back her hair. Tension tightened the sides of her mouth. "You really shouldn't look at me like that. I work for you."

"Am I making you uncomfortable in an unpleasant way?" he drawled.

Her mouth opened, but then she scrunched her nose. "You had to add that last bit? I could have said yes and it wouldn't have been a lie."

"So, in a pleasant way." Heat pulsed in his veins and he flashed a smile, ruefully aware they were both fighting their attraction.

She shook her head. "This is the oddest corporate induction I've ever received."

Boone shrugged, his casual gesture pure pretense. His attention was locked on its target like a heat-seeking missile and patience wasn't winning. "You're rested. You've seen a bit of what my life is like. Mission accomplished."

"Helicopters and secret meetings." She smiled, but her eyes narrowed on his face. "Do female employees always get this rarefied treatment?"

Boone raised both hands in surrender. "You have me there. I was pleasing myself. I wanted your company."

She swam to the far side of the pool and climbed onto a rock, pulling up her knees and wrapping her arms around them as her gaze followed him.

Not liking the fact he couldn't read her expression, he swam closer and hauled himself up beside her. Aware of how close they sat, and how much skin they exposed, he battled with his own body, hoping he wouldn't betray the intensity of his interest in a way that might embarrass her. "I won't lie and tell you I don't hope that we'll become close," he said softly. "How close is up to you, Tilly. No pressure." And as much as it killed him, he meant every word.

She heaved a sigh. Her gaze fell away as her cheeks grew rosy. "Wow, way to put it out there. I think I liked it better just wondering if this was something one-sided." Her head swung back, gaze meeting his, nearly fearless. "I'm confused. I don't understand why you'd be interested in me."

At that moment, Boone felt his age. More than ten years separated them. Life had hardened him, made him sometimes cruel and ruthless. And although he'd begun this seduction as part of his plan to flush out a killer, he wanted none of the bitter ruthlessness to touch her. Tilly was showing an unexpected courage. She was being honest, displaying that innocent curiosity he found so enticing. But how could he answer her in kind? How could he be truthful? "You're beautiful," he said, and then grimaced inside, because while it was true, it wasn't the reason he was interested in her. The answer was becoming very complicated.

"Size twos..." she sang back, her chin lifting higher.

He narrowed his gaze. "You're someone from my home," he said, nearing the truth. "I've been away a long time. You know the circumstances that forced to me to leave, and yet you don't look at me with accusations in your eyes. I find that intriguing."

Her gaze fell again. "You must know who I am."

"Celeste's cousin," he said quietly. "You're similar in appearance, but you couldn't be further apart in personality. I have a type I'm attracted to," he said with a self-mocking smile, "and you're not it." He let his gaze sweep her frame. "However, I approve of the differences, Tilly. There's nothing more important to you than family. You're loyal. Smart. Ambitious too, although your mother's illness interrupted your life before you were able to realize your ambitions. I can offer you another path."

Her breath left in a slow exhale. "And I have to wonder—at what price, Boone Benoit?"

The directness of her question and her unwavering blue gaze took his breath away. How could he tell her he'd give her anything she wanted not to change? Not to learn to despise him? And she worried what her involvement with him might cost her? Boone cleared his throat. "Do you want your brother to join you on the estate?"

Her lips firmed into a straight line. "Would you hold that over me to get what you want?"

"Would that make saying yes easier for you?" Her mouth began to open, but he gave a sharp shake of his head to forestall her argument. "Your brother coming to Maison Plaisir isn't contingent upon anything. It has nothing to do with whether or not you surrender to me."

She shook her head, tears shimmering in her eyes. "Surrender. Contingencies. Is everything a campaign, a military maneuver? Learn your target's weaknesses and strike?"

Her tears tightened his chest. He reached for her hand.

Glaring, she pulled back, and then lowered her legs, preparing to push off into the pool.

He leaned toward her, holding her there with just his gaze. "Are you angry because I'm manipulating you, or because you're tempted? The truth, Tilly."

"Am I tempted?" she asked, her voice husky. "Yes, but in the same way I couldn't resist staring at a cobra."

"So, I'm a snake." His chest pinched. He snorted and looked away. "I'll leave you to your swim."

* * *

As he pushed off the ledge and into the water, Tilly wished she could have taken back that last bit. She'd seen his grimace, and although she couldn't be sure it hadn't been from pure annoyance, she thought she read pain in his expression.

Her mind whirled with everything he'd said. As she'd feared all along, he had ulterior motives for hiring her. He was attracted, that much was obvious, but was the reason because he saw her as a challenge to overcome? Or because he was truly interested... in her... not just the momentary pleasure he might find?

The answer worried her, because he was right—she was tempted. But now that was mitigated by the fact she was mad as hell, knowing just how well he'd planned to get her here. She wasn't the least flattered by the effort. Deep down, she knew his motivation was revenge. How she was supposed to fit into his game plan, she didn't know.

The tops of her shoulders tingled. She needed to get out of the intense sun. She'd take a shower, rummage through the kitchen for food, and do her best to avoid him until their departure.

The sight of him in his swim trunks, his sex perfectly outlined in the thin fabric, had been almost too much to bear. Her nipples had hardened instantly. Her mouth had watered. She'd had the urge to lick the droplets on his chest, to run her fingers through his short wet hair.

They'd both been nearly naked, wet, and steamy hot. She'd been tempted to tell him nothing mattered except that he ease the throbbing ache he was building inside her.

Boone Benoit might be an entitled jerk, but apparently she had a type too.

* * *

Tilly rolled to her back on the bed and stared at the ceiling. Her stomach rumbled. She wanted to ignore her hunger pangs and avoid any possible contact with Boone while she was still annoyed and anxious, and hadn't yet decided what to do about it. Knowing she ought to quit rather than risk everything for a paycheck, still, she was tempted by the man and everything that came with him.

She glanced down at the nightgown she'd donned after her bath—a sheer pink negligee. So lovely and delicate she was afraid a hangnail would snag it. It fit perfectly, was nearly transparent. She'd never worn anything this beautiful or sexy.

Her stomach rumbled again, and she sighed. There was no way she'd last until morning.

Although she'd promised herself she intended to keep a low profile until they boarded the helicopter to return to Bayou Vert, she couldn't resist the urge to primp a bit. For herself, because there were all those beautiful clothes hanging in the closet, and she'd missed the feel of fine fabric against her skin.

At least, that was her story, and she was going to stick to it. And if she happened to meet him in passing, well, Boone had seen her at her worst. Why not let him see her at her best? So she chose a soft silk wrap dress the color of watermelon. Soft pleating beneath her breasts emphasized her hourglass figure. The hook at the side was the only thing holding together the dress. Her hair tumbled past her shoulders in soft curls, and she applied makeup. Her skin looked radiant, slightly flushed from a little too much sun, but glowed with health. Three-inch silver leather sandals were overkill for a refrigerator raid, but she felt like a princess.

Holding her breath, she let herself out of her room and made a beeline for the kitchen, half hoping she wouldn't meet Boone along the way, but half hoping she would. Peeking inside, her shoulders fell when she found the room empty. All dressed up and no one to notice.

Which was just as well. Her disappointment at his absence was frighteningly strong. She knew she was vulnerable to his overtures because she found him so darned attractive, so powerfully beautiful. Her nerves still felt raw after their conversation in the pool—from everything they'd said as well as his sheer physical perfection. She walked to the fridge, reached for the handle, and pulled, pausing when footsteps padded toward her. She stiffened.

A hand reached beyond her and shut the fridge door.

Her heart pounded like a snare drum. She didn't know whether it was her natural fight-or-flight response, or simply her natural reaction to him.

Boone stood so close to her that his masculine scent—of male musk and that elusive hint of cinnamon—filled her senses. She turned her shoulders, intending to put space between them, but was unable to resist the pull to be even closer to him. Her breasts brushed against his chest. Clasping her hands behind her, she leaned back against the door.

"Going somewhere?" he murmured, his gaze sweeping downward.

Was the widening of his pupils due to his approval of her appearance? "Dinner, I hope. I'm starved."

His eyes narrowed. A cool smile eased up the corners of his mouth. "You're in luck. I have something for us on the patio." He grasped her hand and tugged her behind him.

She should have declined, just to place their relationship on solid footing. But the past two days had been a whirlwind of changes and spiraling emotions. Her interest was piqued—she couldn't deny that. If he was a jerk, she'd find out soon enough. The man couldn't be that good an actor. And then the lust she felt every time she saw him would wither and die.

Why not take a chance? See where this led?

Tilly shook her head. The "why not" was obvious. Her cousin had been murdered and he'd been implicated. Her friends and family would be appalled. But she had good reason to believe he wasn't to blame. Even though the accusation didn't appear to have harmed him, she couldn't walk away and be just one more person who abandoned him.

Way to put a damper on things. Still, she didn't drag her feet as he led her out into the courtyard. The space glowed with Christmas lights shining overhead and candles glinting on a patio table. She couldn't help but sigh at the lovely setting. His people had gone to quite a bit of effort to provide a romantic meal.

She glanced around, assuring herself they were alone. "A table for two?"

"Just us. Disappointed?" he asked, pulling out a chair to seat her.

She didn't answer his question. She couldn't. But that was as much of an admission she was happy with the arrangements as she was willing to give him. Covered dishes sat in the middle of the table. The aroma of cooked beef, peppers, and onions made her mouth water.

He poured red wine into glasses for them both, and then lifted the covers to reveal the dishes. "I hope you like fajitas."

"I do," she said, feeling a bit pampered.

Small dishes of freshly made guacamole and steamed corn tortillas were uncovered. He placed a tortilla on her plate then ladled meat, green peppers, and onions beside it. He unrolled her silverware and flicked the napkin before setting it in her lap.

A gesture that if it had happened in a restaurant wouldn't have set her nerve endings afire, but *his* fingers brushed her lap. Not until he'd served himself and taken a seat did she draw a deep breath. "Thanks, this is lovely."

She fashioned a taco and began to eat, glad to have her mouth filled so she wouldn't be expected to hold a conversation with the man whose gaze seemed to notice everything. His stare didn't waver.

She put down her taco and dabbed her mouth and chin. "Am I wearing my food?"

"Are you nervous, Tilly?"

The corners of her mouth tugged downward. "I shouldn't be. It's just dinner."

"A little bit of edginess is warranted."

Her muscles tensed and she blinked her surprise. "Because we're alone?"

"Because I'm thankful there's a table between us."

Her breath hitched, and she slowly shook her head. "Otherwise…?"

"I'd be tempted to release that jeweled clasp holding together your dress."

Heat filled her cheeks. She picked up the fajita taco and took a larger bite than she should have, suffering through his chuckles while she chewed and chewed. How dare he laugh when he was the one who'd made such an inappropriate comment? Anger flared, nearly choking her.

Although the food was tasty, her stomach was too knotted for her to enjoy it. She refused a second serving and instead sipped her wine, hoping the mellow liquid would soothe her ravaged nerves.

Boone helped himself to more food, then sat back in his chair, gliding his finger around the edge of his wineglass—still watching her with those sharp, icy-blue eyes.

Silence stretched between them. Not a comfortable one.

Tilly shifted in her chair and took another sip. "Perhaps you should tell me what my duties will be once we return to Bayou Vert. Because the job wasn't described in the hiring notice, I don't have any idea of what my day-to-day will be."

He nodded. "I'll want you to start working with Colby Jones. You've met him."

"The construction foreman?"

"Yes, he's been supervising the hiring of workers and overseeing the reconstruction. If you could help him by interfacing with the locals, getting word out a little more effectively, I'd appreciate it."

She let his little fib about doing all his own hiring slide, but only because she was flattered he'd used the ploy. "Tired of Mae rippin' down the notices?"

He grimaced. "The existence of a local newspaper would be helpful."

A mountain breeze lifted her hair, and she smoothed it back. She cleared her throat. "I can help spread word. I assume he'll still do the actual interviewin' since I won't know what questions to ask regardin' laborers' skills."

"Yes."

She glanced down at the wineglass she fingered. "You said I'd be a secretary."

"Only when I need office help while I'm at Maison Plaisir."

A twinge of disappointment dampened her mood. Of course he didn't need her; he had Beatrice's *professional* services.

Boone tapped the table with his finger, drawing her gaze again.

"When I travel, I'll want you with me. You can keep in touch with Jonesy, but I don't want you tied to the place twenty-four/ seven. You'll be responsible for hiring the hospitality staff to support our guests—clerks, cooking staff, housekeeping—but you'll also need to hire a manager who will report to you."

The thought of accompanying him on trips like this one was dizzying. "I'm sure you have people who could *liaise* for you."

"I do. But I find I've become insular." He steepled his fingers under his chin. "As you've seen, most of my staff is made up of former marines and navy buddies. They're intimidating to the locals. I'd like to make an effort to blend a bit more. The plantation will be my home, so the sooner I start making those relationships, the better. You can help me with that."

Tilly pursed her lips. "Folks in the Bayou can be standoffish."

"You mean they have long memories."

She sighed. "Yes, they do."

Boone waved a hand. "And yet you're here. And not afraid of me."

"Celeste was my cousin." Her thoughts flew to her relatives and friends. "Some will think of me as a traitor to my own family. I might not actually be of much help to you buildin' those relationships you want."

"You're a first step. I'll appreciate your ideas on how I can polish up my tarnished image."

A smile twitched the corners of her mouth, and she raised her head. "If you don't drive around in that Bentley like you're royalty, that might be helpful."

"Should I buy a pickup?"

"Wouldn't hurt." She smiled. "Might be nice to see you doin' some fishing or hiring an airboat for a swamp tour. Get to know the locals."

"Sure they won't try to toss me off the boat?"

She arched a brow and her gaze dropped to his muscled chest. "If you wore something besides dress shirts and suits, they might actually notice they'd have a hard time tossin' you anywhere."

His head tilted to the side "How about I put you in charge of my meet-the-locals campaign? And you'll shop for things I should be wearing to impress them a little less."

She grinned. "I promise I won't put you in a Bubba Gump Shrimp T-shirt."

His teeth flashed with his quick smile.

Darkness had deepened around them. Gone was her nervousness, although whether from the wine or the conversation, she wasn't sure. "I guess you really do need someone like me."

"Did you think I was hiring you just because you're beautiful?"

She blinked, her smile fading. "I thought maybe you were hiring me just because I was Celeste's cousin." Her mouth dried, but she forced out the words. "Because I look so similar to Celeste, folks are bound to be nervous, thinkin' you're bound to repeat the past. If I managed not to die, you'd have your proof you're not a murderer to wave in front of their faces."

Boone breathed deeply. "You must not have a very high opinion of me."

"I'm sorry if I'm bein' blunt, but I thought you might appreciate a little plain speakin'. I don't have any opinion of you at all. I don't know you. But I did my homework. I studied you. You led an impressive career while you were in the navy. And somehow, you parlayed what you learned and the connections you made along the way into this company that you've taken global in just a few years. So I know you're smart. That you've managed to inspire loyalty in the men who followed you from the navy. You hire the best. Have a stellar reputation." Tilly gave him a straight, unblinking stare. "A dangerous one as well."

Boone's glance remained steady, which encouraged her to continue. "I know what you've accomplished, but I don't know *you*. All I do know is that you've flirted with me, manipulated me into acceptin' an ambiguous position. You can have your choice of female companions. Yet you want me to become more than just your local liaison. Certainly not a secretary." A hand swept an arc in the air. "You're makin' this up on the fly."

His lips pursed and he leaned an arm on the table. "Tilly, I hired you as my personal assistant, my local liaison, because I think you're qualified. I decided that *on the fly* when I first met you."

Crossing her arms, she leaned back. "You should have hired me as your hospitality manager. You won't find anyone local who's better suited. I know the area, can work with the local suppliers, the staff…"

"You don't understand the nature of the guests I'll be opening my house to."

"You think I can't comport myself among wealthy guests. That's ridiculous." She leaned forward, jaw tight. "You know where I worked. Those hotels are the best in Houston."

Boone's eyes narrowed. "The wealthy clientele at Maison Plaisir are a discreet group with certain…proclivities and preferences. A place like Bayou Vert, with its isolation, will give them the freedom and the privacy to be themselves."

Unease crept along her skin and she shook her head. "Proclivities. Preferences. What are you talkin' about?" Her eyes widened. Good Lord, was he reopening the estate only to make it some sort of sex club for the wealthy?

Boone's gaze held steady, boring into hers. "I think the moment some of the more dominant men and women see you, they won't rest until they can claim you for their own."

Chapter Seven

Her meal settled like a lead weight in the middle of her belly. She couldn't have heard him correctly. "I don't understand."

"No, you don't," he said, his tone a little cold. "And that's a problem we'll need to rectify. I can show you. But you'll have to trust me. Follow my lead. *In everything.*"

A wash of heat flooded her face. "Are you...? Is this about...?"

He gave a sharp nod. "Domination and submission. BDSM."

Preparing to flee, she shook her head and laid her napkin on the table. "I...I think you've made a mistake. I'm not into that—"

"I know you've never walked in that world. But in the short time we've known each other, I've seen certain instinctual signs that you might be a natural."

She wasn't ignorant. But just the acronym, BDSM, filled her head with images of black leather and leashes, paddles and chains. Ridiculous images. And he thought she might have leanings toward that lifestyle? She wasn't depraved, wasn't looking to be used or displayed in such a demeaning way. "I'm sorry you've gone to all this bother," she said, her voice becoming hoarse. "But you're mistaken."

His expression softened. "Tell me, Tilly. What do you think BDSM is all about?"

"It doesn't matter what I think," she said faintly. No way would she describe the images in her mind.

"Blunt talk. You were ready for that from me. Give me the same courtesy."

Her fingers were clasped tightly in her lap. She drew a breath and let her gaze fall away. "I think it's for people who haven't learned to connect with others in a healthy way. Or who have something missing inside themselves."

He stayed silent for a moment, his expression shuttered. "Are you open to the possibility that entering that world can help a person find what's missing in their lives?"

She raised her gaze and gave him a frown. "Maybe that's what you choose to believe about me, but twisting my words doesn't make it true."

"What do you think might be missing inside me?"

She shook back her hair and lifted her chin. "Like I said. Connection. Being forced to leave everything and everyone you knew behind can't have been easy. You were the high school football star. On the honor roll. Everything was ripped out from under your feet."

"So, you think my lack of control over what happened made me seek the ultimate control over my body and someone else's?"

Her chest pinched, and she sucked in a deep breath before she gave him a nod.

His gaze studied her. "Does that thought disturb you? Surrendering control to someone else?"

"I can't imagine trusting anyone enough to allow them to tie me up and do whatever they want. It's dangerous."

"It can be," he said, nodding. "But creating fear in my submissive is never my goal. Inspiring trust. Giving pleasure. Helping her discover her own potential for pleasure and submission... Now, those acts are things that excite me."

A shiver worked its way down her spine, although whether from what he described or the silky tone of his voice, she didn't know. A knot lodged in her throat, and she swallowed hard. "What did I do to make you think I might be like...that?"

His grin was easy, startling, and at odds with the stern set of his jaw. "You gave me your foot." He leaned over the table, his eyes alight with humor. "You didn't want to, but you were curious. The action, lifting your foot, put you physically off-balance. You, Tilly Floret, gave yourself over to me."

Her breath hitched. The memory flashed in her mind and she remembered the jumble of sensations and emotions that simple action and his care had engendered in her. "All you did was slide a shoe on my foot. I wasn't acceptin' anything else from you."

"You let me touch you," he said softly.

She blinked. A subtle tell, she realized, because his crooked smile widened. His eyes narrowed as he studied her face. His expression was...expectant, his body unmoving. "Can I show you it's not all about whips and chains?"

The silkiness was still there in his tone, a teasing quality that tugged at her willpower.

"Will you allow me to show you that surrender can be subtle and beautiful? That the lifestyle isn't really about sexual perversion at all?"

Maybe the wine was to blame for her body's reactions. Her skin tingled, flushing hot. Her nipples tightened. She shifted on her seat, squeezing her thighs together, because the timbre of his voice, so deep and smooth, felt like a physical caress.

He leaned closer. "We're alone. Just you and me. Answer me."

She cleared her throat, shaking her head slightly, a halfhearted gesture because her body was already leaning toward his. "That's a lie. You have people all around us. For all I know, you have this courtyard filled with bugs and cameras. Observin' people is your business. The way you live."

"True, but only my most trusted are here. They won't intrude. Or ever speak about what they see or hear."

Tilly drew in a deep breath. "And that's supposed to reassure me?" Her eyes narrowed. "Are the bedrooms wired?"

This time *he* blinked, and her back stiffened. She'd paraded around nude after her shower, while she'd sifted through clothing to find the most flattering outfit.

His mouth tightened a fraction. "The cameras are for your protection, you know. You entered my world willingly. This is one of the prices."

She remembered the way he and Serge had watched her on the flight to Monterrey. Certainly his large, rugged next-in-command was one of those overseeing her "protection." Renewed irritation tensed her muscles. "You expect me to learn to be comfortable knowin' your men watch me?"

"I expect you to learn to take comfort from the fact that I'll keep you safe," he said, his words slightly clipped.

Tilly's shoulders drooped. Suddenly, she felt weary. "At what price?"

Boone leaned back and set his napkin beside his plate.

A door opened onto the patio and a servant walked to the table and took their dishes.

When the woman's dark-eyed gaze rose to Boone's and he gave her a nod, Tilly snorted. Not just for her protection or his. For his comfort and amusement as well. He didn't have to ring a bell to bring the staff. All he had to do was give a subtle signal, placing his napkin beside his plate, to bring someone running.

"You're entitled to your anger," Boone said, his voice once again soothing. "But please stay for dessert. Marta will be disappointed if you don't try it."

"I think I've had enough," she said quietly. Right this moment, the only thing she wanted was to run as far away from this man as she could.

"If staying would please me, would you? A taste is all I ask."

And he wasn't talking about the dessert. She was certain of that.

The door opened again. The woman, Marta, brought out a tray. She set down plates with molded flan and half a dozen raspberries beside the custards. Then she left again as quietly as she'd come.

The chair across from hers scraped.

Her pulse raced as Boone carried his chair and his plate toward her. But she didn't move. She couldn't. Her damnable curiosity kept her frozen in her chair because she was dying to know what he intended to do next. If he moved close enough to touch her, would she have the will to resist?

He sat the plate beside hers, his chair as well, and then leaned back. "The fact that a table separated us gave you courage," he murmured.

"Now you want to intimidate me?" The quaver in her voice matched the trembling in her body.

"No, I want to be close enough to you that I won't miss anything."

Close enough that he couldn't help but note how flushed her skin was or how her erect nipples pushed against the front of her thin bra. Pretending she didn't care, she lifted her chin defiantly.

Boone gave her a half smile and leaned toward her. "Indulge me?" he whispered. "I promise I won't do anything that will embarrass you."

She met his steady gaze, her fearless pose unraveling because he was so close she felt the heat from his thigh right beside hers.

"Tilly...close your eyes. I want to feed you."

She searched his expression, carefully neutral except for the slight curving of his mouth. He was teasing her. "This is silly. I feel silly."

"Indulge me. We'll both enjoy the experience."

Huffing a breath, she closed her eyes. Not trusting him for a moment, but she'd let him play his game. Fact was, she enjoyed the intimacy of sitting so close to him. She liked the way he smelled: like cinnamon and male. Liked the heat emanating from his body.

"Open your mouth."

She complied, opening like a baby bird waiting for a worm. At that thought, she wrinkled her nose. Then she tasted the metal bottom of a spoon on her tongue and an explosion of sweetness as she closed her mouth around the flan. She groaned in ecstasy.

"Open."

She opened again and received a second spoonful of the sinfully delicious dessert—creamy, smooth, sweet like caramel.

"Open."

This time, she didn't hesitate. But a spoon didn't enter her mouth. Instead, two fingers, tasting slightly salty, deposited a raspberry on her tongue. She shivered, fighting the urge to close her lips around his fingers as she had the spoonfuls of flan.

A fingertip dragged across her tongue as it left her mouth. She bit into the berry, tart, sweet, and salty exploding on her taste buds.

"If we were lovers," he said beside her ear. "I'd take advantage of the fact you can't anticipate my moves," he whispered. "Open."

Without a thought, she did, and his finger daubed flan on her tongue. The taste was even better than before without the metallic aftertaste of the silver spoon.

"I'd open that clasp and part your pretty dress. Open."

Again, his fingers entered her mouth, dropping another raspberry. Her breaths grew ragged. Her heart raced.

"I'd thumb open the clasp of your bra and expose your pretty breasts. Open. No talking."

She was just about to ask how he knew her breasts were pretty. How had he known? The thought of cameras entered her mind and for the first time, they didn't horrify her. They became part of his seduction.

Flan, again, was delivered by two fingers.

The urge was too strong. She latched her lips around them and sucked.

His breath gusted against her cheek.

Not as steady as before.

She almost smiled.

He withdrew his fingers. "Open."

She did. And this time, a hand cupped her cheek and tilted her head back. His lips touched hers, his tongue sweeping into her mouth. She could taste the flan on his tongue and she swallowed greedily, taking him even deeper inside her mouth. An arm settled on her shoulders, turning her slightly. The kiss deepened.

Flan, wine, raspberries—none tasted quite as wicked as Boone Benoit's mouth. His lips sealed hers. When he began to move, dragging her lips in slow circles, she was helpless to follow his lead, drugged by the sensual tug.

When he drew back, she licked her lips and slowly opened her eyes.

His blue eyes gleamed. "There's pleasure in submission, Tilly." He tapped her nose and drew in a deep breath. "You should go now."

She wanted to argue. But he'd made his point. Even the simple act of eating a tasty dessert could be filled with sensual pleasure. Her body's response proved that.

He dropped his arm and stood, helping her to her feet. Cupping her elbow, he led her back into the kitchen through the living room to the hallway. At the first door, he stopped. "I'm in here, should you need anything."

As she continued down the hallway, she couldn't help the sway of her hips, aware that he still watched her. Her steps were light, her body awakened as never before.

As she sought a nightgown from the clothing hanging in the closet, she closed the door for privacy, hoping his security concerns didn't extend to her dressing room or bathroom. The thought of him watching her as she slept was still disturbing, but not for the same reasons she'd had before they'd shared that kiss.

As if he'd sit in front of a monitor to watch her sleep. She really did need to keep this in perspective. Boone might find her a challenge, but for how long? Maybe he did think he needed her to help smooth his way in Bayou Vert, but time and money would do the same.

The town was dying. Losing its young people to the city. In another generation, the town might not exist at all. Sad, given its long history. Bayou Vert had survived storms and its own pirate past, but it couldn't fight progress. Small fishing operations were giving way to larger, better-equipped companies. Fishing and acting as guides for the odd hunting or fishing tourist were the only jobs left. If she didn't have a brother who needed familiar sur-roundings to feel safe, she wouldn't stay either.

As she turned off the bedside lamp, she admitted to herself that Boone was her only hope. Her resentment was for the fact she didn't have a choice. And yet she was excited in ways she'd never experienced before.

A handsome, wealthy man wanted her. She'd have to keep her head free of the clouds, remember their disturbingly linked past, and hold true to who she was. More dangerous than their past was the secret she kept. Every day she walked in his world, the urge to tell him what she'd found grew stronger, because she was getting to know him, and feeling more and more empathy for the man. The closer she drew, she had no doubts the guilt would weigh heavier and heavier. She had the means to cast doubt on the town's foregone conclusion that Boone was a murderer. If he ever found out what she withheld, how would he feel about her?

* * *

Moments after watching Tilly enter her bedroom, Boone entered the situation room, dragging off his tie.

Serge turned from the computer screen he'd been reading. "Boss, is your head in the game?"

Boone narrowed his eyes. "Are you talking about Ms. Floret?"

"Just wondering. You don't usually let your personal life inter-fere with work. Not sayin' that's not a good thing."

"Have we received another communication?" Boone rolled a chair beside Serge's.

"No, it's been quiet. Alejandro thinks we might have some-one on the inside. Makes sense. If they know we're putting more sticks in their spokes, they might be thinking of ways to punish us. If this is the first of a concerted campaign, and they know where Black Spear's assets are, they'll want to teach us a lesson."

Boone's stomach roiled. They'd been here before. Waiting for a deal that wasn't going to happen because the kidnappers wanted to make a big splash, reinforcing a brutal reputation for the lengths they would go to ensure the biggest payoffs.

And this cartel was particularly frightening. Composed of ex–Mexican Army commandoes, they had skills only his own men could rival.

Yes, he'd been here before. Images of headless bodies left in front of a mosque in Afghanistan made his body tight.

"It's not Kabul, Boone."

"These bastards are studying terrorists' playbooks. It could happen. You see what they do to their own people when they cross them. We need to find these guys. If there is someone on the inside helping them, it's our fault for not finding the link. I want more assets on this."

"How long are we staying here?"

Boone raked a hand through his hair. "Alejandro's perfectly capable of running this op."

Serge gave him a one-sided smile. "Hard being the big kahuna. But you have to be willing to let go of the details. Maybe now wasn't the best time to return to the ole hometown. It's—"

"Distracting. I know."

"So's she." Serge arched a dark brow. "Enjoy your dessert?"

"Didn't touch mine."

"Wasn't talking about the flan."

Boone grunted, annoyed his friend had witnessed so much.

"She's not into the scene. You sure you want to lead her there?"

Boone aimed a deadly glare at his friend. "I could just tell you to mind your own damn business."

"I have your back. Always will." Serge shook his head. "But she's not part of your revenge. You drag her through it, she might get hurt. You like to think you're always on target. That you don't feel. But she's getting to you."

The memory of Tilly, opening her mouth so obediently, flashed through his mind. Turning her reluctance to eager enjoyment had given him an erotic thrill he hadn't experienced in a long, long time. He could still feel the moist pressure of her lips closing around his fingers. "Maybe it's time I let someone get to me."

Serge glanced back at the monitor. "Thinking about settling down?"

Boone grunted again. "Fuck, I don't know. But when I look at her, I don't see Celeste. Her murder has haunted me for so long, you'd think that's all I'd be thinking about when I look at Tilly. Instead, I'm racking my brain for ways to seduce her. To please her."

Serge chuckled. "If you want, I'll butt out."

"No, I need you to be my conscience. Sometimes, when I want something, I don't know when to stop."

Serge's expression sharpened, and he held up his finger to alert Boone that he was receiving news. He tapped his Bluetooth. "No wire. A physical drop?"

His gaze went to Boone, who shook his head. Too many things could go wrong, but then again, they might find a way to tag the cash and follow it back to the enemy. Up to this point, the kidnappers had shown remarkable sophistication. They were due to make a mistake. "No more than a quarter of the total payout," he said.

Serge relayed their agreement to Alejandro, who was manning the burn phone from the Tex-Oil building. When he removed the phone from his ear, he raised a brow. "Don't guess anyone's getting any sleep tonight. The drop's happening at three a.m."

"Peterson Group has the cash?"

"Alejandro had them primed for the possibility. He figured since we changed the amount, the Omegas were obligated to make the delivery harder for us." Serge pushed up from the desk. "I'm heading over there. How 'bout you?"

Boone nodded. "I won't sleep anyway." Another kind of excitement stirred in his blood. Adrenaline. Something he'd gotten addicted to from his years in the service, something he desperately missed after he'd concentrated on the managerial aspects of his business. "Radio Bear to ready three cars."

They never left the compound without ensuring necessary firepower. But it was also designed to confuse anyone watching as to which vehicle he might be inside.

Serge slipped the phone over his ear and relayed the message, then called for a replacement to monitor the cameras at the house. Tilly and his staff would remain safe within these walls while they were gone. Then they left the house through the garage door.

Bear met them at the cars. Not only was he Boone's personal pilot, he was also his preferred driver, having undergone extensive training in defensive driving tactics. Bear had earned his nickname due to his burly, rugged appearance. Although Boone had offered him positions with more authority, even his own region to manage, Bear refused, preferring to "keep it personal."

Boone rewarded his loyalty with a generous salary and certain perks, including his own membership at The Platform.

Bear took the Glock from his holster and handed it to Boone.

Boone made a quick inspection of the half-dozen men who'd be accompanying them on their run to the Tex-Oil offices. All were dressed in black military cargo pants, long-sleeved uniform shirts, and Kevlar vests. Each man carried a military assault weapon—AK-47 or M4.

Boone lifted the back hatch of the Esplanade and reached inside for a vest, and then gave the signal to roll out. The men loaded into the vehicles, with Boone seated beside Bear in the front. When Boone became part of a mission, he no longer wanted to be the one protected. Like his brothers in action, he was just another soldier prepared to enter the fray to save a few of his own.

Chapter Eight

The next morning, Tilly bathed and dressed, making use of the cosmetics and toiletries that somehow reflected the exact items she used at home, down to her brand of perfume. The thought of some burly ex-military buddy of Boone's pawing through her bathroom to make a list of her needs was unsettling.

Remembering the fact her every move might be watched, she wrapped a towel around her body before heading to the closet. Her own blue sundress hung there, newly washed and pressed. Her fingers fanned the silky confections in a rainbow of colors beside it, but since she was suffering a major case of morning-after regrets, she firmly pushed them down the rack and donned her simple blue dress.

Tilly was determined to keep her feet firmly on the ground. No matter how hard Boone worked to turn her head, she'd resist. His way led to heartache, and she'd had enough sorrow in her life.

At least that's what she told herself as she followed her growl-ing stomach to the kitchen. The house was dead silent. She poked her head into the living room, but found no Boone or Beatrice lurking inside, so she skimmed through to the kitchen, grateful for a little alone time to settle her jumbled emotions and shore up her determination to keep Boone at a distance.

Fixing herself a breakfast of leftover tortillas, which she nuked in the microwave, and slices of avocado, lightly salted, she poured fresh orange juice and took her plate outside to the patio.

With sunlight only starting to creep over the edge of the walled patio, the heat was pleasant rather than oppressive, the air filled with the fragrance of roses. She gobbled up her simple tacos and rested on a chaise, enjoying the sight of the mountains. Especially without the distraction of Boone or any of his minions to interrupt.

She hadn't rested long when in the distance she heard the roar of engines. She closed her eyes, deciding to ignore the sounds. But tires bit gravel, engines revved. Curiosity got the better of her, and she swung her legs to the ground. Letting herself out the garden gate, she circled the house to the garage.

The doors were open. Three black vehicles, likely the same that had comprised the caravan from the airport, were parked inside. Large men dressed in black and bearing a frightening array of weaponry spilled from the doors.

She held back, hiding behind the corner of the building to watch, fascinated to find Boone among them. He was every bit as built as the soldiers around him, every bit as fierce. And apparently vulnerable, since he needed the extra protection. The thought of him facing dangers that required this much firepower and security made her a little weak at the knees. At the same time as she feared for him, arousal stirred. Odd, but the thought he could hold his own among men like these turned her on. As did his expression. His features were set in hard, determined lines. Velcro scratched as he opened his armored vest and dropped it into the back of the vehicle.

One of the men spun on his heel, raised his weapon, and pointed it in her direction. The rest reacted, crouching, rifles and handguns rising.

Her breath stilling, Tilly raised her hands and waved them as she stepped around the corner. "Sorry to alarm you."

Boone's expression didn't change.

Was he irritated to find her spying? She walked toward the group as weapons lowered. Where she found the courage to approach such a well-armed assembly of men, she didn't know. But she refused to betray the fact butterflies flitted in her belly and her pulse thudded hard in her ears.

"Looks like you've been busy," she said as she drew closer.

Eyes narrowing, Boone didn't crack a smile. His arms crossed his chest. "I should have laid down some more ground rules. Wandering outside alone isn't safe."

"There wasn't anyone around. I took advantage of it." She pressed her lips together and dropped her gaze to her toes, heat filling her cheeks.

Boone's breath eased out in slow exhale. "We were longer than I expected."

She peeked up from beneath her lashes. "I had no idea you were so hands-on with the operations."

One corner of his firm mouth twitched.

A flush at her word choice heated her cheeks. "It was the 'hands-on' part, right?" she whispered.

He didn't answer, instead sweeping her body with a hard gaze. "You're not happy with the clothing I provided?"

"Oh, I love it, but I haven't earned it," she said, frowning at her deplorable choice of words.

He grunted. "Seeing as you're ready, we'll leave now."

"Going home?" she asked, raising her head.

Ice-chip eyes narrowed. "Disappointed we're leaving so soon?"

Tilly tipped up her chin. "Not at all. I'm not used to lazing poolside. I'd just as soon get started at the new job."

Boone opened the door to the backseat of the Esplanade, indicating with a sweep of his hand that she should slide inside.

"My purse?"

Serge tapped his Bluetooth and asked Marta to retrieve her purse from her room.

She stared at Serge. "When do I get one of those?"

"Do you really want to be wired in," Boone murmured, shockingly close to her ear, "at my beck and call?"

Tilly wrinkled her nose. "Guess I can wait." She slid into the backseat, surprised when he slid in beside her.

He shut the door. "Serge will ride in the lead vehicle."

As the remaining doors slammed, she shook her head. "This must be like driving in a presidential motorcade."

"It's necessary," Boone said, patting her knee. "My profile was raised when my team rescued a diplomat's daughter last year. The cartel would love nothing better than to get their hands on me or one of my men, just to prove I'm not invulnerable."

Her stomach knotted. "So there's a good reason, other than being a control freak, why you didn't like me wandering around alone."

His gaze held steady. "I promised to keep you safe."

She studied his face, the deeper lines bracketing his mouth, the redness of his eyes. "Did you get any sleep at all last night?"

He shook his head.

"You push yourself as hard as your staff."

"I won't ask them to do anything I'm not willing to do." A shoulder lifted and dropped. "They respect me. For all that display you witnessed, the night was pretty boring—hovering near a cell phone while we waited for instructions on where to drop the first payment."

"Isn't that dangerous? This business of dealing with kidnappers and extortion drops?"

He shrugged like it was ordinary. "One man on a motorcycle dropped a satchel in a park. We had him covered, and then pulled back, as per instructions. Nothing exciting. No one hurt."

When she opened her mouth to ask another question, he pressed a finger over her mouth. "No, I won't tell you any more. Details are revealed on a need-to-know basis. You don't need to know."

Tilly sighed and sat back. "This is definitely more exciting than I'd anticipated," she muttered, jumping when his hand closed around hers.

She swung her head toward him, but his eyes were closed, his head resting against the seat. Definitely more exciting.

* * *

They set down on the lawn at Maison Plaisir in the late afternoon. Neither Serge nor Boone had rested, but their grimly set faces didn't betray their exhaustion.

On the other hand, Tilly was drooping.

Boone took her hand as they strode toward the gate, something she didn't think she'd ever get used to but didn't bother to fight. Any workers watching their arrival would know something had changed between them.

The thought made her a little uneasy, but she shoved it aside. She liked the feel of his hand around hers. Liked the fact he seemed to do it naturally. Her morning resolution to keep her feet firmly planted had evaporated the moment she'd spied him in Kevlar and toting a weapon.

Never would she have guessed that some super-alpha macho man would excite her, but she couldn't fight the warm glowy feeling that always overtook her in his presence. As they approached the house, she drew a deep breath and tugged her hand away. "I'll need a ride home."

"You are home."

Her step faltered. "Then they moved my things?" At his nod, she gave him a smile. "I'm not sure where the foreman's cottage is."

"About that…" His head bent toward hers. "I made some changes."

At the narrowing of his eyes, she knew he had changed the arrangement they'd made. She frowned, a show of defiance, and braced herself for what was coming.

"You'll be staying in the main house."

What? She drew a sharp breath. "No, I won't."

"We've reached an understanding."

"No, we haven't." She shook her head. "You've made pronouncements and bullied your way around me, but I'm not moving in with you."

"You'll have your own rooms."

"Where? Across the hall from yours?" At the arch of his brow, she fumed. "This is moving way too fast. You're taking for granted that I'm willing to fall in line. I'm not some soldier taking orders. The cottage was already too much, but I agreed, and you know why I did. But moving into your house, especially considering the type of entertaining you'll be doing—" She waved a finger in the air between them. "Not happening."

"Think of this arrangement as temporary."

Exactly as she'd thought. She jerked up her chin. "And that makes it better? This lasts for as long as you remain interested in me?"

As he leaned closer, his brows furrowed. "The arrangement lasts for as long as it takes to convince you to move into my rooms."

Her eyes widened, and she glanced around to see who else might have heard his bold pronouncement.

Serge was looking elsewhere, no doubt *pretending* he was speaking into his Bluetooth.

Tilly stepped close and dropped her voice to an angry whisper. "You don't have any respect for me or my reputation. Working for you is bad enough. Most of my friends won't understand that choice, but to live under the same roof?"

His back stiffened. "Because I'm a murderer?"

She huffed. "Don't be ridiculous—because you're a man and I'm not married to you."

His eyebrows shot up. "You'd rather we were married?"

"No!" Her eyes bugged and her hands jammed on her hips. "I'd rather you treated me like your employee, not your mistress," she hissed.

"That's an old-fashioned word."

She rolled her eyes. "Seems appropriate given the arrangements you've likely already made. When did you decide this?"

"After our dinner."

"Because I let you kiss me? You're unbelievably arrogant."

Boone's cheeks billowed around a gusting huff. "You'd really rather live in the cottage when you could have the cook prepare your meals, maids clean your rooms—"

She balled her fists, glaring upward. "I want some privacy," she said, enunciating every word. "Someplace you're *not* when I need to breathe."

"I smother you?" he said more quietly, his forehead wrinkled.

"Yes. No. You're just a little...overwhelming."

Boone stepped closer. His hands lifted to clasp her upper arms; his thumbs rubbed her bare skin. "The cottage is ready. Your things are there. If you'd agreed, I'd have had them moved during dinner."

"You didn't think I'd agree?" she asked, irritated he'd been toying with her.

"I'd have been a little disappointed if you'd fallen right in line." He crooked a finger and tucked it under her chin, lifting it. "I don't want a soldier taking orders," he said, his gaze boring into hers. "I want you choosing me. Trusting me enough to place your well-being in my hands."

His words took her breath away. He wanted her willing submission, and for the first time, she had an inkling what that might mean. She was helplessly intrigued. "This...thing you want me to learn to be...Will I have no choices beyond accepting your...dominion?"

"Baby, I don't want some Stepford wife in my life. Our relationship would be equal. We both have choices, both have things to learn about each other. Me learning how to please you, you learning what I need."

She bit her lip. "I won't say yes—no matter how much I want to. I won't move in with you."

"Will you let me try to convince you?"

As she studied his face, she narrowed her eyes and pursed her lips. "And if I do?"

He came closer, his head dipped, his breath brushed her ear. "From that moment, don't expect me to *ask* you for something ever again. It's not how it works. Just know, you do have choices even if they aren't spoken. You can tell me no. You can decide to take a step back."

Liking the sound of that more than she was willing to admit, she shivered. If she were asked to do every little sexy thing he might want, she'd feel obliged, for pride's sake, to object. This way, she imagined she could follow his lead without any embarrassing drama. Simply living in the moment. Inside, she felt a fluttering of happiness. A raw surge of quietly blossoming need. How had he known she needed that when she never would have imagined she'd respond this way? She dropped her head, not wanting to meet his gaze as he pulled away.

"What's your answer, Tilly?" he whispered. "Will you let me seduce you?"

The low rumbling tenor of his voice was like a caress. She moaned. "So not fair. You're standing too close. I can't breathe without taking you in." She licked her lips.

His mouth curved, and he bent deeper, taking a kiss, his mouth scooping at her lips.

She leaned into him, her breasts flattening against his hard chest. The finger under her chin moved to stroke her cheek. A hand fit into the arch of her back, giving the barest pressure, but she rubbed against his front, feeling the swell of his sex, her knees weakening. As she sagged, that hand pressed harder, holding her upright and mashing her against his front.

He ended the kiss with a crooked smile. "Can I take that as a yes?"

Because she didn't trust her voice, she nodded.

Boone's smile became harder. His eyes glinted with satisfaction.

Her throat tightened. Lord, what precisely had she agreed to?

"Serge will take you to the cottage. Rest. I'll see you in the morning."

When he released her and stepped back, she found herself swaying.

"Ms. Floret?" Serge said, giving her a little bow of his head, his dark eyes twinkling.

"Tilly, don't you think? Seeing as how I'm going to be here a while."

"Tilly, I'll show you to your quarters."

She glanced back at Boone, but he was already stepping through the front door of the mansion. She wanted to follow him. Beg him for another kiss. Could he be right about her? About what he suspected was her true nature?

Clearing her throat, she pasted on a bland smile and followed Serge, who led her along a shell-pink gravel pathway lined with bricks. To either side was more wildly overgrown garden.

"How soon does he intend to open the house to guests?" she called out to him.

Serge glanced back, his face set. "You'll need to direct your questions to Boone."

Another avenue of control. Irritation prickled her skin and she frowned at his back.

Circling the house, they followed a path that skirted a wide lawn and passed a gazebo with a collapsed roof, overtaken by wisteria. Behind it was a cottage—a charming house by anyone else's standards, one larger than Mrs. Nolan's home and garage apartment combined.

Beyond the cottage were small cabins. Old slave quarters, she knew from her study of the history of the place. The cabins were undergoing renovation as well, men working like ants, replacing roofs and shoring up sagging porches. The cabins formed a square. In the center, the ground had been dug up, dirt hills sitting in front of acres of sugarcane beyond the cabins, evidence that some sort of major landscaping project was under way. "Is he constructing another courtyard area?"

Her question met with silence. She frowned again. "You do know he expects us to work together," she called after him as he climbed the cottage's porch steps and unlocked the front door.

When he turned, his mouth was a straight line, but one brow was arched.

She brushed past him to walk through the door.

"You're just what he needs, Tilly Floret. Save your questions for him. He'll enjoy answering them." He tilted his head toward the interior of the cottage. "You should find everything you need. If there's anything the staff has forgotten, make a list and give it to Boone or Jonesy."

"My car?"

"In the garage."

"Will I need a key or a code to access the garage when I want to take out my car?"

"You'll need to speak to—"

Her hand rose in a halting motion. "Boone, I get it." She glared at him, then slammed the door in his face.

When she heard his heavy tread descending the steps, she leaned against the door and glanced around the open living area. Dark hardwood floors, white canvas-upholstered furniture. Nothing fussy. Clean lines, overstuffed cushions. Netting here and there to give the area the feel of living on a plantation. Rattan fan blades stirring the air from above.

She sighed, loving the buttercream walls. Curious now to see the rest of the place, she pushed away from the door and began to explore.

The kitchen opened to the living room and had white tiled counters, cherry cabinets, and the same pale yellow walls. The first room down the hallway off the living room was the bathroom, outfitted with a white claw-footed tub, a pedestal sink, and a deep white baker's rack filled with rolled towels in black and yellow.

Another door was a large closet filled with blankets and sheets. The last door was a bedroom. Here the walls were a light turquoise, the floor covered in a looped-pile white rug. The bed had a white iron frame and thick white duvet.

A phone, sitting on the bedside table, rang.

"Hello?" she asked, tucking the French white-and-gold receiver into the corner of her shoulder.

"Will you be comfortable?" came Boone's silky voice.

Of course, who else would call? "Your timin' is mighty suspicious."

There was a pause. "You know I'll keep you safe."

Her gaze slowly scanned the room. "Are there cameras in the bathroom?"

"No."

She didn't ask any more questions and he didn't offer up any further information. She supposed he had his reasons. A murder had happened on the grounds, years ago. Perhaps he was entitled to a little paranoia.

A long indrawn breath sounded in the receiver.

"You're yawnin'," she said, smiling. "Have I already bored you?"

"Your clothing is in the drawers. Your personal items are in boxes in the hall closet for you to sort through and decide where to place them."

As she realized what was among those personal items, her heart stopped. Her folder of news clippings and historical records regarding Boone, the house, and the murder had been lying on her coffee table. She pulled a strand of hair behind her ear and forced herself to be calm. He could see her after all. "I hope," she said carefully, "my privacy was respected."

"Their instructions were to simply pack up your things as they were. Your every secret is safe."

To hide her shock, she schooled her features. But a chill ran down her spine. She'd been so enamored of his attention, of the whirlwind pace of the changes he brought into her life, that she'd forgotten. Or had she deliberately shoved The Secret to the back of her mind?

"Get some sleep, Tilly. Your day will begin early."

"Where will I report?"

"Find Jonesy in the morning. He'll give you a rundown of everything we're doing."

A flash of disappointment shot through her body. Already he was pawning her off on another of his minions. No mention of where he'd be, or when she'd see him again. Perhaps the arrangement was just as well.

Chapter Nine

Darkness settled. Cloying, sultry. The odor of stagnant water drifting from the bayou battled with the sweetness of honeysuckle and roses. Despite the fact that he hadn't slept the night before, Boone couldn't fall asleep. He felt edgy, beyond exhaustion, restless.

If the time wasn't too soon to seek Tilly's company, he'd be at her door. As it was, he'd already roamed past her cottage and noted the lights turning off in the living room.

Earlier, after assuring himself she'd found her accommodations suitable, he'd forced himself to leave the security room, resisting the urge to watch as she readied herself for bed. Somehow, just seeing her soothed his raw edges, but he couldn't sit still. So he wandered around the estate, passing armed guards who nodded but didn't stop him to speak. Maybe that was just as well. They were wise to leave him to his thoughts.

He walked through overgrown brush toward the ramshackle cabins, which formed a square. Moonlight painted the structures—old slaves' quarters from the plantation's dark past. Missing roofing shingles allowed spears of white inside a few of the cabins. Scraggly weeds grew through floorboards.

Renovations had begun on several of the cabins farther down the square, but he couldn't have cared less. He hated this place. Hadn't stepped foot in the slaves' square in years. Not since that horrible night so long ago. He'd have been content to let them and the big house continue to rot—if he could have forgotten about them and what had happened here. They'd been ravaged by storms and disuse, but still stood. While he'd leased the fields to local sugarcane growers, he hadn't wanted anyone stepping foot inside Maison Plaisir or any of its outbuildings. As though he was punishing the place. Or the spirit of his father, who had loved it so well. He'd wanted it gone, but couldn't let it go.

Because of the one cabin he now drew near.

Heaviness settled on his shoulders. His stomach revolted, tightening as memories he usually kept too busy to dwell on flooded his mind.

Standing in the doorway, he stared into the dark, empty room, seeing the old iron bed with its missing mattress, which had been carried away to a forensics lab, where it had been "lost." Tattered remnants of crime-scene tape were caught on a splinter in the doorframe.

Boone remembered that last night. Heard echoes of laughter as Celeste opened her gift to find yards and yards of red silk ribbon, her pale arm waving as she held it up for him to tie her to the spokes of the white iron bed.

Closing his eyes, he tilted his head, catching a waft of roses and mint, her scent. Remembered her blonde hair, straight and wispy, sticking to her cheeks.

He'd tied her to the iron bed, facing her forward on her knees. To still her laughter, he'd gagged her with the ribbon, afraid her sounds would carry to the house where his father and mother were entertaining. Then he'd taken her in sure strokes, finding pleasure in her shuddering frame and her cries, muffled behind her gag. Together, they came in wet waves, the bed's springs squeaking.

Afterward, he'd walked her to her car, parked outside the gate, farther down the lane so no one would see. He'd kissed her, slow and deep. She'd clung tightly to his neck.

"Wait for me," he'd asked, his forehead resting against hers.

She'd promised she would, but he knew she was lying. Perhaps when she followed him to Tulane the next year, they'd hook up again. He'd like that. She was perfect. Liked his games.

But the next time he saw Celeste was early the next morning when the sheriff shoved him to his knees in the cabin's doorway. "See what you did? Boy, your daddy's not gonna fix this one."

Blood pounded in his temples and Boone sucked in a deep breath. He uncurled the hands fisted at his sides. The crunch of footsteps made him stiffen.

"Boss," Serge said from beside him. "You decide what you want done with this place?"

Boone's lips curled in a snarl. "Burn it."

* * *

Tilly awoke to the smell of burning wood and the sound of hushed voices outside her window. Her eyes smarted from the smoke. Fear clogged her throat.

She didn't dare turn on her lights until she knew what was happening. So she felt around for her thin bathrobe, knotted it around her waist, and then made her way through the cottage to the front windows. Holding open two slats of the blinds, she stared in horror at one of the cabins across the square ablaze, sparks flying high into the air like fireflies.

Men surrounded it, holding hoses they used to wet the nearby ground and the surrounding cabins, but they pointed no water toward the burning cabin.

Everything seemed under control until her gaze found Boone, standing frozen in front of the gaping cabin door, watching the flames consume the structure.

Then she understood. Celeste had been found lying in one of the cabins on a dingy, blood-soaked mattress. That was all the detail the newspapers had given. Enough to fill her mind with images of a vivacious young woman who'd laughed while Tilly jumped on her bed, forever stilled. Although they were cousins, too many years lay between them for them to be close, but Celeste's loss had changed everything.

Goose bumps raised on her skin. She wanted to sneak back to her bedroom and pretend she hadn't seen a thing. But the sight of Boone, standing so still, his body rigid, hands fisted at his sides, made her stomach knot.

Her guilty secret made her feel slightly ill. She could ease his pain—shift the shame from his shoulders. All she had to do was come forward with her brother's treasure box and the bracelet that hadn't been found at the crime scene.

Watching him standing so silently, with his grim-faced men giving him worried glances as they worked, her eyes burned more. She hurried back to her bedroom. Not wanting to think about what she was doing, she dressed in shorts and a tee, slid her feet into flip-flops, and hurried back to let herself out of the door. Flapping sounds echoed in the air as she passed Serge, whose lips tightened. She ignored the shake of his head, which told her to mind her own business. She passed Mr. Jones, who didn't give away his opinion by so much as a movement or change in his harsh face. Ignoring everyone but the man whose rigid body stood like a silent sentinel, she sidled up beside Boone and cupped his balled fist in her hand.

His hand tightened more, but didn't shake hers away. Desperate to keep hidden the tears forming in the corners of her eyes, she kept her gaze down and stood beside him as the roof groaned, then collapsed, sending sparks raining out the gaping door.

Only then did he act, his arm coming around her to urge her backward. Then he pulled her against his chest and cupped her head, his hand smoothing over her back.

Maybe he was only making sure none of the firefly-like embers hadn't landed on her, but he held her close, his heart thudding against her cheek.

Slowly, so that he wouldn't jerk away from her, she raised her arms, encircling his muscled torso. Providing comfort and finding some for herself. Her hands roamed his back as she snuggled closer to his chest and let her tears fall, wetting her cheeks and the front of his shirt.

At last, he inhaled deeply, the tension in his body draining away. A kiss landed on her hair, and she leaned back, wiping her tears away with her fingers then checking his expression and finding it haggard, ravaged. "I think your men can handle the rest," she said softly.

Boone shook his head. "I don't want them turning on the hoses until it's ashes."

The harshness of his voice nearly broke her heart. "I'm certain they understand."

Boone dropped his gaze to hers. "Why are you here, Tilly?"

The hollowness of his gaze made her mouth tremble. For all his strength and accomplishment, he was still a man haunted by his past. "I'm here because I know what this place is…" She took a deep breath. "And I know you didn't do it."

His lips twisted. "There's believing, and then there's knowing. Which is it, Tilly?" he asked, his gaze sharpening as he studied her face.

Tilly quivered beneath his hard gaze but tilted up her chin. "I know," she whispered, "but don't ask me how." Her gaze pleaded with his to leave her admission alone. She wouldn't tell him any more.

His jaw firmed, but he nodded, pulling away. "You should go back inside."

"There's too much smoke."

A dark brow rose. "Then you haven't any choice. You'll come with me to the Big House."

Pressed close to his body, she didn't miss the stirring of his sex against her belly. She dropped her head, staring at his throat, but gave him a nod.

He swallowed. "Serge…"

"Yes, boss," Serge said from a few feet away.

"See it to the end?"

"Of course. We don't need you here."

Boone slipped an arm around Tilly's waist, and turned, leading her away.

They followed the path, lit by moonlight.

Tilly had known this moment would come. From the first touch of his hand on her foot. She'd been drawn to him from the start. So tall and strong, so smart and accomplished, but inside, he was tormented, something she understood only too well. Pity and guilt didn't have a thing to do with her surrender. She needed Boone every bit as much as she sensed he needed her.

Her heart tripped inside her chest, knowing she'd accepted an invitation for more than a place to rest while the fire continued to burn. She was ready to explore this tantalizing attraction they shared. Already, her skin felt on fire. Her breasts tightened. Her hips swayed, bumping against his, because she couldn't contain the excitement curling in her belly.

She was going to his bed. She knew it. He knew it. What he'd do once he had her there… well, that was the mystery.

They climbed the back porch steps and entered through a door that opened to the servants' staircase. He dropped his arm and grabbed her hand, pulling her up the steep stairs.

She didn't bother giving even token resistance. She wanted this. Not to ease his pain or her guilt, but because she wanted to know what being with Boone was like.

Tonight, witnessing his raw emotions had humanized him. Boone might be hardened by the things that had happened to him, by war and his dangerous profession, but at his core, he was vulnerable to hurt and sorrow. For tonight, that was enough to know.

She'd revealed something, but he hadn't pressed her. No doubt tomorrow he'd think about it, and maybe redouble his effort to discover what she knew. But for now, he'd take what she offered instead. Comfort. Sexual release. She'd submit to him too, if it was what he needed.

She almost smiled, because he'd predicted this. He knew her in ways no other man had ever bothered trying.

He'd guessed the moment she'd balanced on one foot, curious to see what he would do.

They reached the upper floor and he headed left, unerringly finding his way in the darkness. At his bedroom door, he opened it, not bothering with the overhead light, but walking straight to the curtains and pulling them open. In the distance, over the roof of the foreman's cottage, they could see the glow of the fire, but not the burning cabin itself.

Once again, he stood rigid, his hands on the window ledge. "Why are you here, Tilly?" he asked again.

"Because I want to be."

His glance shot her way, taking note of her expression, which she masked, tilting up her chin.

His gaze went back to the lit sky. "Undress. Take everything off. Do it behind me if it helps knowing I can't see."

Shock quivered through her and held her still for a moment. His harsh whisper frightened her with its coarseness, but part of her was relieved he was doing exactly what he'd said he would—demanding her submission. This wouldn't be a romantic seduction. No sweet pauses to gauge whether he'd wooed her sufficiently to proceed. This was about raw need and desires about to be fulfilled. Somehow, her pride was salved by the fact she didn't have to voice her agreement. Her role was simply to obey. So she stepped out of her sandals and fumbled with her clothes until she stood nude in the shadows behind him.

"Go to my bed. Slip between the sheets and wait for me."

Nervous but also terribly excited, she couldn't force words past the lump growing in her throat. But what would she have said? She was panting, her breaths so short and rasping, he had to hear. She walked to his bed, noted the rumpled bedding, and slipped between cool cotton sheets. When she glanced back to the window, she saw he had turned and was watching her. But for how long?

He unbuttoned his shirt and shrugged out of it, letting it fall to the ground behind him. Then he toed off his shoes, unbuttoned his pants, and drew down the zipper.

At the moment he shoved down his pants, she realized she hadn't been breathing, and she gasped.

Not that she could see much of what he revealed. The fire glowing in the distance illuminated his shoulders, but shadow hid the front of his body.

He stepped away from his clothing, striding straight to the bed as he stared down at her figure. "Pull away the sheet, Tilly. It's dark in here. Your modesty will be preserved."

"I'm not afraid," she whispered, tossing back the sheet.

He reached down, and she held her breath, but he didn't touch her. His fingers grasped the coverlet and sheet and pulled them to the end of the bed. Then he knelt on the edge of the mattress beside her.

Even a shadow couldn't mask the desire in his eyes.

Her gaze snagged on his erection, which stood straight from his groin, rising nearly to the center of his belly. When she lifted her gaze, his teeth gleamed in a narrow, tight smile.

He bent over her, grasping her wrists and placing them beside her head. "Keep them here."

Swallowing hard, she nodded—then gasped again as he set his big hands on her thighs. His palms smoothed up and down, the rasp of light calluses causing goose bumps to lift in their wake. He gripped her, pushed apart her thighs, and climbed on his knees into the space he made.

Now she was open, as vulnerable as a woman could be. Tilly concentrated on her breaths, dragging them between her pursed lips, blowing them out in a slow, steady stream to calm her racing heart.

But he only looked at her, his gaze caressing her breasts, her belly, the apex of her thighs. His fingers raked through the hair on her woman's mound. "I'll be shaving this."

Her breath hitched at his touch, and then again at his words. When he tugged her short, curling hairs, she groaned because her sex tightened in reaction, and he could see.

A finger stroked the length of her slit, the moist sound seeming to please him, because again, his lips parted in a strained smile. He bent, landing his hands on either side of her shoulders, and then slowly lowered his body.

The first touch of his chest to hers, crisp curls rubbing against her sensitive nipples, made her shiver. When he lowered his hips and pressed his hot, hard cock against her belly, she closed her eyes, afraid she'd reveal too much of the pleasure washing through her.

"No hiding."

She opened her eyes, staring back at him. He was resting on his elbows, bracketing her shoulders, their bodies mashed together. And all she could think was how much more of him she wanted.

He cupped one side of her cheek and rubbed his finger across her bottom lip. She stuck out her tongue and licked it, eyes widening when she tasted herself.

His head lowered, bringing the shadows with him. "There's so much I want, sweetheart. So much I'll do. If anything makes you afraid, don't hesitate to ask me to stop. There's nothing I consider taboo. Nothing I don't want to touch or enter. With you, I'm finding it hard to hold back." He bent closer and kissed her mouth, licking her bottom lip, and then eased his tongue inside her.

His kiss was more than just a kiss. It was a promise. A sensual threat. He controlled it, using his hands to hold her head still, his lips to seduce her into wanting to follow. His tongue invaded, licking at her lips, stroking her tongue, thrusting in a way and a rhythm that made her hips curl.

With his mouth and tongue, he drew from her emotions she found foreign—wonder at his thoroughness, sublime lethargy that left her feeling boneless. Heat licked at her breasts and sex, although he concentrated all his efforts on exploring only her mouth.

When he drew back, she blinked slowly, her gaze going straight to his lips and then rising slowly to lock with his darkly hooded gaze.

"I think...I'll play with you later," he murmured. "For now, I'll keep this uncomplicated."

"Uncomplicated? For whom?" she grumbled.

His chest shook against her as he chuckled. Then he dipped down and kissed her chin.

She tilted back her head, begging him silently for more. He gave it, sliding his lips down her throat, his tongue touching the pulse hammering there. Then he scooted down, kissing the tops of her breasts.

More than anything, she wanted to sink her fingers in his hair and pull his mouth to the aching tips of her breasts.

Boone didn't make her wait, lips latching on one beaded tip and drawing on it, pulling it into his mouth, where he tortured it with flicks of his tongue.

Muscles tensing, her legs moved restlessly, widening beneath him. Moisture seeped from inside her, but he couldn't know, could he? He wasn't touching her there, where she needed him most.

He let go of her nipple and nibbled and sucked her skin, making his way across her chest to the other nipple.

When he bit the tip, she arched beneath him, groaning, aching for release.

He leaned on one elbow and cupped the breast he tortured,

molding it in his large hand. Then his hand glided down her ribs, and lower still, fingers sliding into the top of her folds.

Heart pounding, her breath hitched and held as he pulled her nipple between his teeth and nibbled. His fingers swirled atop her cloaked clitoris.

Letting go of her breast, he glanced into her eyes. "No rules. No inhibitions, Tilly. Give yourself to me." His fingers swirled and swirled, pausing now and then to gather the fluids seeping from inside her, then rubbing again, each slow circle tightening the desire coiling inside her.

She couldn't look away. Couldn't hide behind the sweep of her eyelashes. Locked in his gaze, held captive by his wicked fingers and the steady gleam of his darkened eyes, she began to writhe, thighs tightening and opening, her head turning side to side. Her breaths deepened, growing more ragged by the second.

When the moment arrived, she forgot to keep her hands at her head and reached desperately for his shoulders, fingernails digging into his skin while her back arched and her moans grew louder.

"That's it," he whispered. "Fly, sweetheart. Fly."

Released by his words and the pressure of his fingertips, pleasure exploded, radiating outward from deep in her core, quivering through her limbs, curling her toes. Tilly's cry cut off as she fell back, shattered, pleasure pulsing, rippling up and down her channel.

Fingers plunged inside her, twisting, finding a sensitive spot that wrested another wave of wicked pleasure. When she tumbled down, she lay sweating, the sheet wet beneath her bottom.

Boone kissed her belly, the top of her mound. When his tongue touched her clit, the caress soothed rather than taking her into that dark pleasure again. She sank her fingertips into his thick hair and rocked her hips, the motions slowing until she fell still.

He moved up the bed, turned her on her side, and spooned his body behind hers. His arms wrapped around her, a tight-muscled embrace. He pressed a kiss against her cheek and simply held her.

Tilly waited breathlessly, eager and yet dreading what came next. Her breaths were still settling. Leaving her no way to pretend she'd suddenly fallen asleep. But what did one say at a moment like this? She'd given herself to a man she barely knew, one she couldn't trust with her secrets.

And his cock was still rigid, poking against her bottom—no! Resting between her cheeks! Her breath hitched in her throat.

"It's all right to sleep," he drawled, his fingers rubbing along her arm.

Tilly sniffed. "I don't need your permission."

"But you need my cooperation."

She heard a smile in his voice. "But you didn't…"

"I had some satisfaction. I've learned a few things about you."

"Really? You got all that…just now?"

"Mmm-hmm." His head nodded against her hair. "You're not a screamer."

To hold back a laugh, she pressed her lips together.

"You mutter. And mumble. Whisper a lot of 'Oh Gods.'"

Surprise slackened her jaws. "Where was I? I didn't hear any of that."

"Because your eyes were closed. You were too busy with your orgasms to know what you were saying."

Her eyes widened. Had she blurted anything else? "You're teasing me."

"Yes, I am. And I thank you."

"For what? You still haven't…"

"Come, yes, I know," he said, his voice wry. "But I'm also not thinking about the cabin. Or what you said to me out there."

She held her breath, certain now that he had her naked and vulnerable, he'd press his advantage. But he wasn't pressing anything, which got her thinking about how she could distract him from what she'd said.

To stall, she dragged in a breath she didn't really need and snuggled deeper against his chest, and then gave a subtle wiggle of her butt.

His breath caught. Thick, muscled biceps tightened.

At his restraint, she bit her lip and gave an exaggerated sigh.

"Tilly," he rumbled, "I'm trying to be a gentleman."

"Why?"

"I can't remember now," he murmured against her ear, his breath hot against her neck. His cock nudged harder against her backside.

Tilly squeezed her eyes shut and called on her courage. Slowly, she stretched her leg down, then lifted it, sliding her calf atop his, opening herself to whatever he might want to do.

"Training you is going to be a bitch," he growled.

"Some things don't need a lot of thought," she whispered. "No plan. No campaign."

"Something you will learn is anticipation builds tension and that makes what happens next so much richer and deeper."

"I promise to take notes tomorrow," she sassed breathlessly.

"You won't be responsible for remembering anything. My task is to train you well enough that you act out of instinct. Without thought. Or campaigns."

She liked the rumbling tenor of his voice and the way his

hands stayed still on her hip and belly while she couldn't help pulsing softly against him. She was incredibly turned on, because she knew she was getting to him.

The things he said, promising her something she really didn't understand but was growing eager to embrace, made her hot. Not because of any image they brought to mind, but because she could tell how much he wanted her to submit to his care and tutelage.

And maybe that was the point.

From behind, his thigh moved, nudging between her legs.

She tilted her ass and let her pussy rub against his thigh, leaving a trail of moisture he couldn't miss.

"Tilly," he groaned, warning in his voice.

But she wasn't paying him any mind. Her breasts and the moist slit of her sex were growing hot and engorged. She ached and she didn't bother holding back a moan. "Do something, Boone. Please."

He grunted and shifted behind her.

The moment she felt the thick hot column touching her inner thigh, she tensed. Her pussy clasped, making a lush wet sound that made her cringe.

His hand smoothed down her belly and fingers slid between her labia, spreading them. The hand on her hip moved, reaching between her legs and beyond. And suddenly, his cock was snug against her entrance. Instinct tightened her thighs for a second and then she relaxed.

"Dammit," he bit out. A soft chuckle followed. "I never have these moments."

Frustrated, Tilly felt on the edge of some discovery. "You can't find it? You're right there."

His chest rocked against her back. "No condom," he said, licking her neck.

"Where do you keep them?"

"There should be a box in the nightstand."

In a flash, she shoved away his hands and scrambled for the side of the bed, his chuckles following her as she felt around for the drawer, slid it open, and reached inside. When she found the box, she dumped most of the contents on the floor, but didn't really care. Her eagerness was giving him a giggle fit.

In triumph, she raised a packet. "You have to put it on. I'm not learnin' now."

"You're a bossy little thing." He reached for her hand and took the packet.

Shadows hid most of what he did, but she heard plastic tear, and then the sounds of latex smoothing down.

When he was done, he leaned on one hand and patted the mattress with the other. "Come here, Tilly."

There were no more thoughts of stalling. Modesty was already out the door. Her knee landed on the mattress, and she crawled, coming to a halt beside him, but careful not to touch. At that moment, her courage fled, and she didn't want to show her ineptitude one more time by doing something clumsy, or something he didn't want.

Boone studied her, his gaze sweeping her body slowly. He reached out and tugged a nipple, letting it bounce back when he released the pinch. Then he trailed a finger down her belly, pausing to trace her belly button.

Her belly jerked. She'd never considered that part of her body an erogenous zone, but the feel of his callused fingertip on her soft skin made it one. Then his finger trailed down to her mound and into the top of her folds. It rasped her clit, and her thighs tensed. She wanted badly to open her stance and invite him to burrow deep inside her, but she held still. Waiting.

He didn't make her wait long.

Boone dropped his hand and lay back, putting both hands behind his head, stretching his body, and parting his legs. "Play, Tilly. For tonight, do anything you want. Touch me anywhere."

Chapter Ten

Boone held his breath as Tilly's greedy gaze raked over his body. She'd surprised him with her shy lust and humor. He'd surprised himself with his indulgence—and by the fact he was eager to see where her desire and curiosity led.

So he stretched his body, placing his hands behind his head and threading his fingers together to resist the urge to reach for her soft body. His belly sank, his thighs were tense and spread. His cock rose against his belly, demanding attention, but he didn't think she'd have the courage to go there first. So he waited.

With quick swipes, she licked her lips. "I feel at a disadvantage," she whispered.

Boone arched a brow. "How so? We're both nude."

"Your body." She waved a hand. "It's so perfect. Not an ounce of…laziness…anywhere."

A smile tugged at his mouth. "You haven't looked away from my cock. How do you know?"

Her gaze shot to his face. "Sorry. I thought you might be…large, but that…" She pointed at his groin. "I'm a little intimidated."

"It's not Mount Everest."

"It's the *mounting* that worries me." Her lips twitched.

His smile stretched wide. "You're funny. That's unexpected."

"Only when I'm nervous. Maybe. I don't know." She groaned and shook her head. "Maybe I'm just funny to you because you know I don't know where to start."

Boone watched her, loving the way her gaze darted over his body, looking for just the right spot, but lingering again on his cock. Taking pity on her, he cleared his throat. "Run your hands over me, sweetheart. Begin at my shoulders. Straddle me if you like. Nothing will happen unless you do the mounting."

She swallowed hard, the harsh sound impossible to miss. But then she lifted her chin and crawled closer. When she began to lift one thigh, she glanced away.

For a moment, he was tempted to follow her gaze. Then he realized she'd looked away because she'd hoped he'd do the same. She was clearly nervous about opening her legs and exposing herself.

"You know it's very dark in here. I can barely see anything," he murmured.

"*Liar.* But thanks." She finished the movement, gasping as she fit her pussy against the length of his shaft and settled down. Her breasts shook with her quick breaths.

At her touch, his thigh muscle tightened. "You're very wet, Ms. Floret," he teased.

"Quiet. I'm nervous enough."

Boone's cock pulsed, and he clasped his fingers tighter.

She gasped, then blew out a stream of air.

Good Lord, she better move, and soon. "You have me at your mercy," he said, in the way of encouragement.

"Why do I suddenly think I'm doing exactly what you wanted me to do?"

"Your slick pussy is pressed against me, but not embedded. Do you really think that's what I want?" His pulse pounded.

"I'm glad you can't see how red my cheeks are right now. It's not like I haven't had sex before, but…" She bit her lip.

He shifted his thighs, juggling her a bit.

With another gasp, she clamped her hands on his chest.

"You could pleasure yourself. Use me," he whispered, his voice like a caress.

"Maybe you could give me a few more hints."

"Do you really need them?"

"Not really, but maybe you're thinking of something other than what I am. I'm a little one-tracked right now." Warm liquid spilled from inside her and she moaned, followed by a breathless laugh.

Her one-track was exactly in line with his. Relenting, he gave her another hint. "I'd love to feel your breasts against me."

She gave a little nod, and then lowered her torso until hardened, beaded tips touched his chest. Her eyes slid closed, and she swayed slightly side to side, scraping them on his skin and tangling them in his chest hair.

"Do you know what I'd like to do with those pretty peaks?" he murmured, relieved she'd finally done something to get the action started.

"No," she said, biting her lip and swaying again.

"I'd like to attach alligator clamps to the tips and tighten them, just enough to make you gasp."

Her face was close enough, he saw her nose wrinkle. "Sounds painful."

"It's exquisite. Some women can come from just the pinch of the clamps tightening. Once they're attached, I'd flick the tips with my tongue."

Her breaths deepening, she swayed again. "My breasts might

not be that attuned. That sensitive," she said, dragging out the last word as she scraped them once more. She sighed and lowered again, mashing her firm globes against him. Her cheek slid alongside his, and her breaths rasped in his ear.

He undulated his hips, sliding his cock forward and back between her vaginal lips, rocking her gently.

"Maybe I could come just like this," she said, her tone hopeful.

At her words, he rolled his eyes. His body wasn't going to cooperate for very long. Her hot sex was spread, oozing honey he'd love to feel melting on his shaft. "If you lift up your hips, you could take me," he whispered.

Her head lifted above his, and her mouth hovered over his lips. "But then the sex would all be over. And somehow, I suspect this is a pleasure you won't be awarding me again, any time soon. This freedom."

He drew a deep breath. "Smart girl."

"Not a girl." She licked his bottom lip, dragging off it and groaning, and then pressed her mouth firmly against his.

Boone shuddered beneath her, his control ready to snap. He nearly laughed at that realization because he wasn't one to lose himself in sex. He prided himself on control, but there was something special about Tilly, something…innocently carnal about the way she approached making love with him. His restraint was fraying. Quickly. The moment her tongue entered his mouth, he pounced, sucking it inside, taking control of the kiss as he lifted his head and locked his mouth to hers.

He'd kissed a hundred girls. Probably more. He didn't know, didn't care. This kiss was hotter, purer. Her whimpers leaked into his mouth.

She drew back, her brows drawing together. "I didn't know a kiss could be like that."

"Like what?"

"Like sex."

"Kisses are sexy."

"But they're not…" She swallowed. "Dirty."

His cock twitched. He dropped his head and clenched his fingers tighter. "Continue, Ms. Floret."

Her thighs straightened, bracketing his, and she applied pressure, urging him to close them, which he did. Then she scooted down his body until her head was level with his chest.

Her hands molded his muscles. "They're like thick slabs. Curved, but not like mine. Flatter, but thicker." She dipped her head and touched one small nipple with the tip of her tongue, flicking it, and then she latched her lips around it and sucked, drawing off it then burrowing again, using both lips and teeth to pull it into a point.

Boone felt the sensual tug all the way to his groin.

She fingered the tip, glanced up to meet his gaze, and then moved to the other nipple, twisting the one she held as she sucked.

Her mouth pursed and drawing against his skin nearly broke his control again because he could easily imagine her mouth on his cock, pleasuring him with those strong pulls. "Tilly… sweetheart…"

"Mmmm?" She shook her head, dragging his nipple left then right.

The sting went straight to his balls, which were hard as stones and drawn up tight. His closed thighs felt like a vice clamping down on them. He growled a little.

She giggled, then moved lower, licking and nipping his ribs, her fingers trailing just behind, until she reached his belly button, which she rimmed lovingly over and over. The point of her tongue dove into the center and pressed.

His cock jerked against the center of her body. Boone gritted his teeth but remained silent, refrained from offering her suggestions because she was doing just fine without his guidance. His cock was so hard, so swollen with lust, he half feared he'd split the condom.

Again, she moved downward, raising her head and coming up on her arms as she stared at his cock. Her head was bent so he couldn't see her expression and her hair tickled his pelvis.

"My balls," he bit out, unable to endure another minute of pressure.

"Oh." She leaned one way then the other as he parted his legs and let out a sigh at the relief from constriction. "Do they hurt?"

"Uh-huh." Maybe she'd show a little mercy.

Her small hand slipped between his legs, and she cupped his balls. After a second, her head shot up. "Would you like me to lick them?"

He couldn't get a word past his throat without first clearing it. "I want you to suck them."

"Oh," she said again, and took a deep breath before bending, one hand pushing against his cock, the other cradling his stones.

The moment her mouth opened and she took him inside, he let out a ferocious groan.

Her tongue laved them inside her mouth as her lips sucked.

His cock swelled again, and he knew he wouldn't last a second longer if he didn't take back control. "Enough," he growled, holding his body rigid.

In an instant, her mouth disengaged, but she didn't look up.

He sat up, gripped her shoulders, and pushed her away, then got his knees under himself. Without pausing, he pushed again, shoving her to her back. Her knees remained folded. He pressed them farther apart and crawled over her, not stopping until he had her body under his, his cock snug against her opening. He dipped his head, his mouth an inch from hers.

"Did I do it wrong?" she whispered, her eyebrows doing a teasing dance.

With one shake of his head, he tightened his jaw because every instinct screamed at him to plunge deep. But she'd been worried about his size, and he didn't want this first time to be anything but pleasurable.

So he waited until he had his lust firmly under control, dragging in deep breaths. Only then did he reach down, spread her lips with his fingers and push his cock inside, just a couple inches, just far enough that her entrance swallowed his head. Her pussy tightened around him, clenching him, holding him there.

Her mouth was open, her breaths coming in jagged pants.

The excitement he heard heightened his lust. "I want to fuck you, Tilly."

"I want that too. God, I swear I do."

He dropped his head, resting his forehead against hers. He settled his elbows on either side of her shoulders and cupped her face between his hands. "If I go too fast for you…"

"I'll let you know," she said, then closed her eyes. "Please, Boone. Please."

With a gentle move, he flexed his hips and drove slowly inside, giving her shallow thrusts as he worked his way into her channel. She was hot and tight. So wet, he nearly groaned. Ripples were already massaging his shaft.

She was perfect. He was accustomed to noting the details, clicking off every sign of a woman's arousal, but he couldn't quite concentrate on her body's reactions. His own pleasure was eclipsing his mind. He rocked his hips, churning into her sweet, wet cunt.

Boone rose on his arms, needing larger motions, needing to thrust deeper and deeper, because he couldn't hold back a moment longer. He leaned on one hand and cupped her butt, bringing her closer, locking her against him as he powered into her.

Her legs straightened, toes curling. He wrapped his arm around one then the other, and shoved her thighs forward, pausing to kiss the inside of one knee, then powering harder into her.

Her head thrashed on the mattress, rocking side to side. Her mouth was open—breaths shortening and whimpers rising in tenor. She was close. He could feel the tension inside her body, the way her inner walls and succulent opening clamped around him.

Boone gasped and stroked harder, sweat rolling from his hair to drop on her chest and belly. He still wasn't deep enough, not close enough. With a groan, he pulled free and sat back on his haunches. He patted his thighs and waited until she opened her eyes.

Unhesitating, Tilly clambered up and straddled him.

He reached down, planted his cock at her entrance, and then gripped her hips and forced her down.

Her head lolled back, but her knees scooted closer to his body. She began to rise and fall, her belly undulating, her thighs quivering. Her moans came fast, one on top of the other, and her soft hands squeezed his shoulders.

When next she rose, he dove toward her chest, latched on to a nipple, and bit it.

She screamed, her body shuddering hard, stiffening.

A wash of liquid heat coated his cock, and he groaned again, cupping her ass and urging her to move faster.

"Boone, Boone," she chanted.

"Baby, come. Do it now," he growled.

If she didn't come quickly, he'd spend himself before she did. Not something he'd allow. He slipped a hand between them, slid a fingertip into the top of her folds, and toggled her clit.

She keened, the sound broken by wild downward thrusts of her body.

Waiting, waiting, he ground his jaws together. But she bit his shoulder and his balls exploded, cum shooting through his cock in hot spurts. His fingers dug into her voluptuous ass and he pushed her down as he jerked upward, impaling her in strong, centered thrusts—stroke after blinding stroke until he was wrung out, his chest heaving and her body quaking, falling limply against him.

He thrust his hands deep into her hair and brought her mouth to his. Their kiss was wet…ravenous. When their movements slowed, they drew back, breathing hard, staring into each other's shadowed faces.

His fingers tugged her hair, and he bent to press his forehead against hers. "I'll be in charge from here on out."

"I think that's best," she whispered.

But he saw the white of her teeth as she smiled. "Minx, sleep."

"You can manage single syllables. Can't have been that good."

His chest shook. Eight inches deep and he was laughing. Now, that was a first.

* * *

As he lifted her from his lap, Tilly felt as boneless as a rag doll. She was exhausted. Sated as she'd never been before. For now, she was content to let him take over and arrange her body.

He dragged her up the mattress, rolled her to her side, and spooned against her back, a thick arm resting in the curve of her waist. His hand slid under her head, and he placed his arm beneath her. His beefy bicep would be her pillow. Harder than she was accustomed to, but also reassuring. She sighed and snuggled against his heat.

"None of that," he growled.

"Don't worry. I have no further designs on your body." A yawn threatened, but she swallowed it. "Can't keep my eyes open anyway."

"Might be fun to see if you'd wake up for your next orgasm."

Liking the fact he felt comfortable enough to tease her, she smiled. "You're teasin', right?"

"Go to sleep, Tilly."

"Yes, Boone."

His hand smoothed over her hip then back up to her waist, over and over, lulling her into sleep. "Tilly?"

At his tone, her eyes blinked open, and her body stiffened. Was he going to ask? *Please, no. I don't want to lie to him.*

His hand smoothed again, and he sighed. "Just sleep."

She felt his disappointment. And the fact his breathing wasn't that of a man relaxing meant he was still thinking. Now she couldn't relax. "I guess I'm not used to sleepin' with a man." Not really a lie. A diversion, but true just the same.

"Glad to hear that," he said, stroking her hair.

"Are you?"

"Am I used to sleeping with men?" he asked, laughter in his voice. "No."

She sighed. "I wish you weren't quite so…"

"What?" he asked, pressing a lingering kiss against her shoulder. "Intimidating?"

"Nice."

"Tilly, I'm not nice."

"I think you are. You've been nice to me. I know I sound like an idiot. Like I'm twelve years old. I do know you have reasons for hirin' me, and I don't want to hear what they are. But you didn't have to be nice." She released a sigh. "I would have slept with you anyway."

"You'd have slept with someone you didn't think was nice?"

"I'd have slept with you because I've wanted you from the first moment I saw you."

He was silent, his hand slowing on her hip.

Well, that felt awkward. She didn't expect him to reciprocate. "Just thought you should know," she mumbled. "You don't have to keep bein' nice. I'm not some wiltin' Southern lily."

"I'll keep that under advisement."

Another kiss landed on her shoulder, and she relaxed. Boone didn't know it, but he was a nice man inside his hard-edged, calculating businessman exterior. He was a survivor and not likely to show anything he considered a weakness, especially toward someone he might consider an adversary.

And for all that she wished she weren't, she was keeping something from him, something so vital he might not forgive her if he ever found out. Releasing a tired sigh, she snuggled deeper into his embrace, taking pleasure from the heat of his body and the measure of security he gave so effortlessly.

I'll take care of you, Boone, if you let me. I'll build those bridges between your world and mine. It was the least she owed him.

Chapter Eleven

Early the next morning, a soft knock sounded on the door. Boone opened his eyes, surprised to find light flooding the bedroom. He'd overslept.

The reason lay draped across his chest, her knee dangerously close to his balls. Gently, he moved Tilly off his body, but needn't have worried about waking her.

Muttering softly, she rolled to her side and fell back to sleep.

Boone climbed off the bed and padded to the door, opening it a crack.

Serge stood in the hallway, his gaze lifting beyond Boone's shoulder to the bed. "I hate to disturb you, boss," he said, his troubled gaze boring into Boone's, "but you've got visitors—the sheriff and some pencil-neck who's all up in arms about the fire."

Boone stiffened. "Give me a minute. I'll be down."

His friend arched a brow. "No rush. Beatrice arrived. She's serving them coffee and crumpets."

The idea of Beatrice serving anything but a starchy stare was laughable. Boone's mouth twitched.

He shut the door and turned back to the bed.

Tilly was sitting, the comforter pulled under her chin to shield her body. "Leon's here?" She rolled her eyes. "Bet he's checkin' to see if I'm still all in one piece."

"Maybe you should put on my robe and join us," he drawled. "Just to put his mind at ease."

She shook her head, her lips pursing in a gentle rebuke. "That wouldn't be the best foot to put forward, Boone. No need to give him another reason to distrust you. The man's been after me forever."

"Exactly my point," he muttered under his breath as he strode toward her. But Tilly's blush reminded him his agenda wasn't necessarily hers. "I'll shower. You can take your time."

"I have to wear my Daisy Dukes." She wrinkled her nose. "I didn't exactly prepare for an overnight."

Boone reached down to take her hands and pulled her forward. The comforter fell, and he glanced down at her naked body, a growl rumbling in the back of his throat at the sight of her pink nipples. Damn, but he wished he had time to savor sucking the tender flesh into full, beady erection. "I think you'll find clothes in my closet."

"Wow." Her eyebrows rose for a second, and then they lowered. "You took a lot for granted. Or should I expect to have to squeeze into someone else's size two?"

He knew better than to let his gaze dip again, and met the militant gleam in her blue eyes. "I didn't expect anything, Tilly—I hoped."

She lowered her head, slowly tugging her hands from his. "Go get your shower, Boone. Leon doesn't like to wait. He can be ornery when he's pissed."

Boone left her, not liking the tension that remained between them, not after the night they'd shared. But then, maybe the distance was for the best. Tilly was a distraction. She tempted him to rethink his plans, and he'd worked too hard to arrive at the point where he actually had the power and influence to set things in motion. So why was his chest tight?

When he entered the parlor fifteen minutes later, he felt as though he'd entered enemy territory.

Leon Fournier stood with his hat in his hand, his uniform pressed with knife-edge creases and his badge shiny. The stare he leveled on Boone was hard and cold. The man who accompanied him was short, bald, and wearing a light, badly fitting suit. He held a large yellow envelope and wore a piggish, self-righteous expression. Neither was sitting or drinking the coffee set on a side table.

Beatrice offered him a thin smile, and then began the introductions. "You know the sheriff, Mr. Benoit. And this is Mr. Gentry from the state's division of historic preservation. Both gentlemen have some concerns regarding the fire last night," she said with a pointed glance.

Leon sniffed as though smelling something bad. "Was wonderin' why you didn't call in the fire, *Mr. Benoit*."

Boone smiled. "The blaze was small, contained. My employees were able to put it out."

"You do know that every buildin' on this property is listed on the national registry?" Mr. Gentry lifted his pointy chin. "If it was purposely set..."

Boone winced at the man's irritating whine. "It was an accident. Wood as old as that." He shrugged, staring the man down.

"Funny, no storms, no lightning strikes to explain it," Leon said. "And that particular cabin... You can see why we'd be suspicious."

Mr. Gentry's shoulders stiffened. "And there are the renovations goin' on now. I'll need to inspect. You didn't request any variances. I can find no record of a request coming through our office."

"I can assure you, sir. The house and grounds are being restored to their previous state. If my staff overlooked any documentation they should have forwarded you, I apologize. Beatrice can show you around. There have been a few upgrades to the electrical wiring and amenities in the kitchens and bathrooms, but nothing that should alarm you. I trust you can inspect quickly, because I have a crew eager to continue the work."

The little man's jaw jutted. "You should have applied for permits. In advance."

"This is my home. I didn't need permission."

"It's a public treasure."

Narrowing his eyes a fraction, Boone smiled. "If you'll check with Mr. Axiom at the office of cultural development," he said, naming Gentry's supervisor, "you'll find he has reviewed my plans. If they weren't properly filed, you'll need to take him to task."

Mr. Gentry swallowed, and then nodded. "I'll get in touch with his office. In the meantime, I accept your invitation to inspect."

Boone gave Beatrice a steady stare, telling her they would have a conversation later. She hadn't been called to the estate and should have been working at the New Orleans office, but he thought he knew why she was here. In the past few months, she'd become possessive of his time. Not something he'd encouraged. Worse, her presence now might prove awkward for Tilly, and he wanted no setbacks in his campaign to seduce Tilly Floret.

When Beatrice and Mr. Gentry left the room, he turned his gaze back to the sheriff.

"Hello, Leon," came a sultry voice from behind him.

Boone glanced back, satisfaction flooding him at the sight of Tilly entering the room. She wore a casual turquoise blouse with thick shoulder straps and a narrowed waist, white silk capris, and silver ballet flats. Her hair was wet and pulled back into a high, tight ponytail, the barest hint of makeup brightening her cheeks and eyelids. Her mouth was a little swollen, but maybe he was the only one who noticed, because he knew the cause.

"Tilly," Leon said, his narrowed eyes sweeping her body as she came to a halt beside Boone.

"I see you've come to check out all the excitement we had last night. Everything happened so fast," she said, her Southern drawl a tad exaggerated. "Boone and his workers were all over it, makin' sure the other cabins didn't catch a spark as well." She shivered delicately. "The smoke was awful. Chased me right out of my cottage."

Leon's stare lasted a second longer than it should have, but then he blinked.

Boone wondered if the sheriff was equally as fascinated by this Tilly—chicly dressed and smiling confidently.

Leon glanced at Boone, winced, and then returned to Tilly. He cleared his throat. "Mae's worried about you. Said you left without givin' her any notice."

Tilly's down-turned mouth reflected real regret. "I'm sorry I left her in such a rush, but there was an incident that Black Spear had to respond to. The timing was perfect for me to see the operation in action. It was all very excitin'. I got swept away."

Boone nearly snorted, but kept his expression neutral, letting Tilly do exactly what he'd hired her to do.

A flush creeping up his neck, Leon cleared his throat again. "Tilly, perhaps you could make time to stop by and speak with Mae. Ease her mind and assure her you're doin' well."

Tilly reached out and touched the hand clutching his uniform hat. "Tell her I'll be by soon." She gave him a pat and her hand dropped away.

Leon nodded, his fingers clenching hard around the brim. His gaze hardened the instant it landed on Boone again. "I'll be outside waitin' for Mr. Gentry to finish his tour. Tilly, Boone…"

When the sheriff was out of earshot, Boone turned to Tilly. "That was some performance."

Her gaze narrowed. "Thought you might need a little Southern honey to sweeten that sourpuss. Leon's not a bad man, Boone. He could be a valuable ally, but if he's got his back set to keep you under the microscope, he can be a real pain in the ass."

Bemused by her sudden change from smooth honey to vinegar, Boone's mouth twitched. "I'll keep that in mind." His gaze flickered downward. "I see you found something suitable to wear."

She leaned closer. "I shudder that someone on your staff knows my bra size," she whispered. "It's unnerving."

Boone quirked an eyebrow. "Join me for breakfast?"

"That might be awkward," she said, lifting her chin. "Don't you think if we're gonna keep this thing under wraps, that we ought to—"

He pressed a finger to her lips. "It's just breakfast. After the night we had, I'm starved. You must be as well."

Her lips pressed against his finger.

His skin warmed as he remembered her mouth on certain parts of his body. But he quickly leashed the feeling. What he wanted to do—sweep her up and lay her down on the nearest soft surface—and what he should do—protect her modesty—warred inside him. The last thing he wanted was to leave her embarrassed over the fact everyone would know she'd screwed the boss. His people would be discreet, but Leon was just outside…

Her eyes were wide, perfect windows into her pretty head. She was worried about how everyone would treat her today, knowing where she'd slept. But also worried about how *he* was going to treat her. She'd behaved fiercely proud in front of his company to save face.

Boone dropped his finger and picked up her hand, setting it on his arm. "Breakfast, and then I'll have you shadow Jonesy for the morning."

Her breath left in a sigh, rosy color flooding her cheeks. She lifted her head and gave him a sideways glance that was at once kittenish and bold. "Mornin', by the way."

Warmth spread through him at her husky greeting. "We have stools in the kitchen now."

She laughed. "I'm almost disappointed."

* * *

Tilly was relieved Colby Jones, or "Jonesy" as he'd insisted she call him, didn't seem to mind her company throughout the morning. But then again, he didn't show any pleasure either. In fact, he showed absolutely no emotion. She wondered if being impassive was a SEAL thing or just the fact they were accustomed to hiding their thoughts. She could only imagine the things they'd all seen.

Jonesy was another ruggedly built man, nearly as burly as Bear, and with a jaw the WWE wrestler John Cena would have envied. Hazel eyes, dark hair that glinted gold when the sunlight struck it—he wasn't handsome, but he was so masculine that she wondered how she would maintain a professional demeanor when all she wanted to do was simper. She wondered what he'd do if she raised the back of her hand to her forehead and faked a faint.

The thought of his dismay made her smile.

"We've been working from photos from the Historical Society, the library, and Boone's family album," he said, sweeping a hand across the long table set up in the library next to the French doors that opened onto the backyard patio.

"I remember how it was," Tilly said, nodding. "The Benoits used to open the estate for Fourth of July. There was a big picnic, then fireworks on the lawn where the helicopter lands now. It's the only cleared spot in Bayou Vert that's big enough. I remember the trees along the drive, and the fact that there were always flowers in bloom, but not much else about the festivities." She glanced down at the printed scan from a photo and then looked out at the garden behind the house.

Workers were busy clearing flower beds and pruning roses. The far side of the garden was a mess. Debris from the rising bayou during some great storm was tangled in bushes and the lower tree branches. Stones framing rose beds were being dug from the debris and stacked to one side.

She gave Jonesy a hard glance. "Looks as though he's planning to reconstruct the garden exactly as it was. Why's that?"

"You'll have to ask Boone," he said, reaching out to open the doors and then indicating she should exit first.

Ask Boone. She wrinkled her nose. She was getting very tired of that answer. *Ask Boone, my ass*, she mouthed because she didn't want Jonesy to hear her disparaging his employer and friend.

They strode toward the gazebo, or what was left of it. The roof was gone, panels of latticework missing as well. "You don't think it would be easier just to demolish it and start fresh?"

He arched a brow, but his mouth remained a firm line.

"I'll ask Boone why not," she muttered. They walked a path

recently cleared through the woods, dappled light peeking through the canopy of oaks and sycamores above. The ground grew spongier with a thick blanket of leaves.

The path they followed led to a small clearing beside a dredged canal, a finger of water too perfectly formed to be a natural eddy. Huge oak posts stood at the bank and ten feet into the water.

"This was a dock," Jonesy said with a wave of his hand. "We'll do a better job of clearing the path, then rebuild the dock. There used to be slips for a couple of airboats and a pirogue."

"I suppose guests might like a swamp tour," she said, shrugging.

Having been born on the bayou, she never quite understood tourists' fascination with the dank, dark waters and the frightening creatures that lived there. Men in town enjoyed hunting and fishing; they knew every twist and turn of the waterways that fed into the bay.

Before her father had left when she was very young, he had taken her brother and her into the water. She'd enjoyed the hum of the boat engine. But when he'd cut it off and used a pole to get closer to the banks, she'd grown frightened by every wake in the water, imagining alligators ready to leap and clamp their giant jaws around her arm. Her father had laughed at her apprehension and pulled her into his lap to give her hug. One of the few memories she had of her father. Warm, but confusing. How could he have seemed so loving, and yet leave them so abruptly? She remembered grieving when he'd left, more because her mother cried for so long than for her father. Her mother had always been the hub of the family, and Tilly had been comforted, knowing her mother's hugs would keep her warm and safe.

Listening to the sounds around them, she shivered, glad she

had someone like Jonesy near. Otherwise, she'd be jumping like a frightened rabbit at every watery splash or crackle in the underbrush.

"There's a gator's nest across the way," he said, pointing to the far side of the narrow canal where tall grass was flattened over a mound of dirt.

She sidled closer to Jonesy, who gave her a level stare that she returned without explanation.

"I'll keep you safe, Tilly," he said in his deep, gravelly voice.

Lord, she liked the way these men talked. "Can we go back?" she asked, rubbing her arms.

He nodded and waved a hand toward the trail they'd come down. "I'll follow."

Although the hour wasn't yet noon, the air was thick and muggy, hard to breathe. By the time they got back to the house, her hair was rumpled and frizzy.

"Why don't you cool off?" he said, eyeing her hair. "I'll be back after lunch to show you what we're doing with the house."

She thought about heading back to her cottage, but since she had time alone, and access to the house, curiosity drew her inside. Wandering through the downstairs rooms, her jaw dropped as she entered sumptuously appointed rooms—the formal Southern parlor she'd entered earlier with its warm yellow walls and pale green upholstered sofas; a library with teak shelving to the ceiling, a heavy desk, and a thick Persian carpet on the floor; a formal dining room with a table large enough to seat twenty; and a larger living room with antique, Victorian-style raised wallpaper and rich wine-colored fabrics covering ornately carved chaises and love seats. Braiding dripped from the curtains.

This would be the place Boone entertained his *special* guests.

She wondered if they'd make use of the long braided curtain pulls, and then hurried out of the room at the sensual images that flooded her imagination.

All the downstairs floors were deep, honey-colored oak. All the rooms had twelve-foot ceilings with ornate crown moldings and molded adornments surrounding each chandelier. Twin restrooms faced each other in the back landing where the private stairs led to the bedrooms above. A peek inside showed that one was appointed as a ladies' room, with pink-and-wine wallpaper, a gold-framed mirror, and gold fixtures. The men's room bore pin-striped wallpaper in navy and wine, and the fixtures were less grand, with a masculine brushed steel.

The stairs beckoned her. She'd only seen his room, but was curious about the rest. And where was his office? There must a room where his security team monitored the estate. Was it inside the house or somewhere else on the grounds?

She tilted her head, listening for any sounds of movement above. She'd hate to meet anyone while she snooped.

* * *

Serge poked his head around the door, wearing a smug smile. "Boss, you'll want to see this."

The cause could only be Tilly.

Boone powered down his workstation, set his phone on vibrate, and followed Serge through the connecting door into the security room to the row of monitors.

Behind him, Serge quietly closed the door, which was hidden behind wood paneling in his office wall. And none too soon.

In one monitor, he watched as his office door creaked open. A blonde head peered around it.

"Boone," he heard her whisper, but she looked anything but disappointed to find his office empty.

Boone took a seat in front of the monitor, glad of the panoramic camera that sat on his desk in the other room, which had a view toward the door. He watched Tilly walk inside, her gaze scanning the room. She stopped at the bookcase and touched a couple of books, a finger trailing the spines, but then she glanced back at his desk.

"If she's a spy, she's not very good at it," Serge whispered. "She hasn't spotted any of the cameras."

"That's because she's not a spy," Boone muttered.

Serge grunted, arms crossing his chest, as he stood beside Boone, who used the roller ball to turn the camera and keep her in the center of the screen.

Hands clasped behind her back, she moved around the walls, looking at pictures, every once in a while glancing over her shoulder at the desk.

He could almost see the wheels turning. She was curious. He wondered how long before she gave in to the temptation.

"She'll need punishment," Serge murmured.

This time Boone grunted. And his cock stirred. Punishment was something he was looking forward to introducing her to. She was lovely, young, wholesome. Just remembering how she'd snuggled into his groin throughout the night was enough to make him ache.

She finished her circle and walked to the window, standing to the side to lift the blinds and peek outside. She sucked her bottom lip between her teeth, then straightened her shoulders.

When she circled his desk and sat in his chair, he switched the feed to the camera attached to the bottom of his monitor. Her image appeared, ensconced in the executive chair.

But she didn't seem interested with what might be on his computer, not that she'd be able to access a thing. Nor did she seem interested in anything that might be hidden in the drawers of his desk.

She sat in his chair, placing her hands on the arms, wrapping her fingers around them, then smoothing them up and down the leather. Turning her head, she drew in a breath that lifted her chest.

"Is she smelling the leather?" Serge whispered.

No, Boone would have bet anything she was sniffing his cologne. He smiled. "Come with me. Be quiet."

He pushed up from his seat and hurried to the door leading to the hallway, then quietly padded to his office door. He turned the handle and pushed the door open an inch. Pitching his voice loudly, he said, "Serge, I think I left the plans on my desk. This will just take a moment."

Serge's eyes wrinkled with laughter, but he cleared his expression.

Boone pushed open the door, hearing a gasp and a scrape. When he opened the door, there was no sight of Tilly.

Only one place she could have hidden.

"They're on my desk," he said, again overloud.

He and Serge entered, their gazes going to the desk with its enclosed well beneath.

From the front, she was completely hidden.

He winked at Serge and walked around the desk, standing behind it and shuffling pages. "Ah, here," he said, picking up a newspaper and sliding it across the surface before taking his seat.

Being careful to give her time to scramble backward, he spread his thighs and rolled his chair closer, trapping her.

He could imagine her expression, cheeks reddened with

mortification, nibbling her bottom lip as she tried to figure out how to gracefully get out of her predicament. A smile tugged at the corners of his mouth. When had anyone amused him so much?

Fierce satisfaction burned through him. She'd provided him the perfect opportunity for him to teach his first lesson in obedience.

While Serge picked up the paper and began a nonsensical monologue, Boone thrust his hand between his legs, palm up, and waited.

Her fingers stroked his palm, and he captured her hand. "If you'll take the plans and speak with Jonesy, I have some business to take care of here."

Serge's grin stretched across his face, and he pointed to the security room door, indicating Boone wasn't going to have the privacy he wanted, and knowing Boone wasn't going to give up the game to tell him otherwise.

Boone gave him a deadly glare, waited for the door to close, and then let go of Tilly's hand, placing both of his on the surface of his desk before speaking. "Should I even ask?" he said, adding a dangerous edge to his voice.

"How'd you know I was here?" she hissed.

"I'm the only one who'll be asking questions."

A dragged-out sigh was followed by a mumbled "I'm sorry."

"Sorry isn't going to cut it."

Fingers played with the crease of his trousers. "Are you gonna fire me?"

Boone glared into the monitor, knowing Serge was likely chuckling away. "No, dear, but there ought to be a punishment, don't you think?"

She snorted. "What are you gonna do? Spank me?"

"Funny you should mention that…"

Her breath caught.

He waited, wanting to see if she'd begin to backpedal nervously. But she remained silent, likely thinking hard about what he meant.

Boone schooled his face into a neutral mask and rolled back his chair. "Crawl out of there, sweetheart."

On her hands and knees, she came forward, her eyes the first thing he saw because they were wide. And curious.

He almost relented but was hard as a post and far too eager to test her. He hadn't left her enough space to straighten, not without touching him.

Tilly swallowed, placed her hands on his thighs, and slowly rose to stand in front of him, trapped between his spread legs and the desk. Her face was pale except for wild color balled in the centers of her cheeks. Her eyes were round. Her lips parted, the bottom one swollen as though she'd bitten it.

Boone eased back in his seat, setting his chin in the L formed by his forefinger and thumb, his middle finger riding the seam of his mouth as he studied her.

He noted the curls framing her face and escaping her messy ponytail, the healthy glow of her tanned shoulders. The lace of her bra didn't hide the constriction of her nipples, pressed against the turquoise top.

"Turn around, Tilly," he said, keeping his voice even.

Her chest rose around a deep inhalation, but she inched around in the small space.

"Open your pants and drop them. You may keep your panties on if you wish."

Her gasp was light but audible. "What about the door?"

"No one will interrupt us. I promise," he said, aiming another glare at the camera beneath his monitor. So Serge would see more than he might wish. This was too important an opportunity to let pass.

With her breaths shortening, she raised both hands in front of her. Her clothing rustled, and then her capris eased over her lush bottom and pooled at her feet. She'd left the pale lacy band of her panties in place.

"Bend over my desk."

She placed her hands on the mahogany top and leaned over it.

"Your chest against the wood. Place your hands behind you and clasp them together."

She gave a nervous laugh. "This feels awkward, Boone."

"Sir. Call me sir."

Her bottom tightened. The thin silk hugging her fleshy globes provided next to no protection from his hungry gaze. Already, he noted dampness at the crotch of her panties.

He'd said she could keep the panties, but he was eager to see how far she'd let him go before her modesty interfered. Serge could see the sleek, pale sides of her hips, but not the interesting bits behind. Knowing his friend watched was no impediment to Boone's pleasure. In fact, knowing he was watching added to his enjoyment. Serge would quickly come to understand his fascination with this woman.

With a gentle move, he plucked at the elastic band at the top of her panties and slowly slid them past the crease of her thighs.

Her pussy was wet and beginning to turn pink. He rested a hand on one round globe. "Have you ever been spanked, Tilly?"

A noisy exhalation sounded. "Not since I was a child, and then only a scootch on the butt from my mom."

"What do you think about receiving a spanking from a man?"

"I think...it's humiliatin'," she said, her voice getting smaller.

"Is that all?"

Her pussy tightened. More fluid oozed from inside her. "I think...that since I did something so grievous, that I deserve it...sir."

When she added that one little word at the end, Boone was lost. He'd thought her perfection before. She'd just sealed her fate.

Chapter Twelve

Tilly thought she might faint. With her chest plastered against the desk and her hands clutched behind her back, she couldn't draw in a deep breath.

She was bent over Boone Benoit's desk with her panties down, and if she was very, very lucky, he was about to give her lesson number one in submission.

She'd been surprised he hadn't fired her on the spot for sneaking into this office, but thought, maybe, he'd been looking for just the right reason to begin her training. Or at least, she hoped that was what he was about to do.

Because if she was right, it meant he might just keep her around a while longer. He couldn't be very angry with her snooping if his first impulse was to get her naked. Or at least the important parts bared.

She tried not to think about what he must be seeing. And hoped like hell there weren't any cameras aimed right at her backside. While she'd been looking around, she'd forgotten about that possibility—that he or one of his men might be monitoring her activity. What must they be thinking?

But humiliation was the furthest thing from her mind right this minute. She'd suffer for it later, trying to figure out who might have seen, and ducking her head every time she passed one of Boone's men.

No, she shoved that thought to the back of her mind, because right now, Boone was touching her bare ass, a finger sliding between her cheeks.

When the callused pad touched her tiny forbidden hole, she jerked up, her ass cheeks tightening. "You aren't spankin' that," she muttered.

His chuckle was low and dirty. "A few ground rules, Tilly. You aren't to speak unless I ask you something or give you leave. Do you understand?"

She almost blurted a sassy response, but instead bit her lip and nodded.

"And when we're like this, me giving you intimate attention—whether we're clothed or not, alone or not—you will call me sir."

Already wet and tense, she swallowed, thinking about the clothed part and about being seen by others when he was instructing her. Lord, why had her thrill-meter just jerked to the red? Was she really that depraved? Excitement caused her heart to thud hard against her chest, but curiosity kept her still.

His broad palms landed on both cheeks, gripping her fleshy globes and massaging them, moving them in circular motions that parted and closed her bottom. Was he looking there? Could he see how wet her pussy was?

Tilly waited, expecting the first slap to land, and bracing for it, but his hands dropped away. Then his feet padded on the wood floor, circling the desk, coming around the front. She lifted her head, but in this position could only raise high enough to glimpse his hard belly.

His hand gripped one shoulder and raised her, just enough so that he could reach beneath her and open the buttons of her blouse, spreading apart the material. Then he unlatched her bra, palming a breast and pinching the tip until it hardened, then doing the same to the other breast before lowering her chest to meet the cool wood.

She gasped and readjusted her stance, widening it and trying to control the shaking of her legs.

Her whole body quivered now. Blood pooled in her sex, causing it to throb in time to her galloping heart. Liquid trickled down the inside of one thigh. When he padded back around the desk to stand behind her, she shut her eyes, hoping he'd touch her, and that she wouldn't make a fool of herself, because she was hot and scared and so aroused she thought she might climb out of her skin.

* * *

Again, Boone glanced to the monitor and narrowed his eyes, hoping Serge would avert his gaze and allow him some privacy. He'd changed his mind about wanting him to watch. Knowing his friend like he did, Serge was likely chortling at the current situation.

Tilly needed this attention. He needed to administer it. The fact they were both intensely aroused proved a delicious complication. He'd love nothing better than to lower his pants and take her right there, but he wouldn't do that, not with an audience. And she'd find out sooner or later that every room was rigged for surveillance. He didn't think she was ready for that kind of exposure.

So he cupped his fingers, mounding them together so that his first clap would be thuddy as opposed to sharp, and raised his hand.

Her breathing had shortened to ragged pants. Her sex gleamed with moisture. Her bottom shivered. He swung his arm and clapped her bottom, not as hard as he wanted, but certainly enough to get her attention.

Her breath left in a whoosh, and he heard a soft whimper. He hadn't hurt her, but her tension made her hypersensitive to his touch.

He clapped the other side of her bottom and watched as she flung back her head, the motion curving her slender back and raising her butt another inch.

His breath hitched as he enjoyed the sight of her tightening posture. Again, he thought how perfect, how suited she was for training. And how lovely her body was. He stood to the side of her and delivered more claps, to different spots, watching her skin turn pink and her pussy release another gush of fluid while his own body warmed.

Pausing, he smoothed his hand over her hot skin. "Tilly, can you take more?"

She panted, swallowed hard, and then glanced slightly to the side. "Sir, I entered your office and sat in your chair." Her words were spoken in a throaty whisper. "If you hadn't come when you did, I might have looked inside your drawers."

He knew his amusement was stamped on his face, and hoped Serge wasn't enjoying the moment too much. "A simple yes or no, girl."

"Yes, sir," she whispered, then held her breath.

He flattened his fingers, raised his hand again, and gave her a sharp slap that caused her ass to quiver.

Her gust of surprise sent heat straight to his cock, a sensation he didn't bother fighting to control. He raised his hand again and swatted the other cheek, the backs of her thighs, the tops of her hips.

Her whimpers stretched to moans. Her thighs shook. His next slap landed the tips of his fingers on her swelling pussy, and she gave a garbled scream.

Boone trailed a finger down one flushed lip, following it downward then dipping into the top of her folds to skim her clit. The nub was hardening, and the next swirl had her rising on her tiptoes to lift herself higher, inviting his attention there.

"I have cameras in this room, Tilly," he said, dropping his voice while he continued to swirl on her clit. "I watched you sneak in here. Watched you sit in my chair and close your eyes while you sniffed the leather. I wanted to bend you over my knee right that very minute."

Her entire body shuddered, but she held still.

Liking the fact she hadn't spoken, that she was keeping to his rules, he pressed a fingertip on her clit.

Her back bowed, lifting her chest from the desk. When he removed his finger from her folds, she drooped again with a soft sob.

"Jonesy didn't take you into the cabins. Do you know why?" he asked, smoothing a hand over her warmed rump again.

She cleared her throat. "I assumed they hadn't been renovated yet, sir."

"I told him to keep you away, because I didn't want you shocked by what you might see. Each is uniquely equipped." He traced the other swollen lip, his own breaths deepening, his arousal tightening his belly. "There's one dedicated to spanking. I might take you there. I have floggers I'd love to use to stripe your ass. A padded bench I'd love to bend you over."

A whoosh of air released through her mouth. She groaned and bent her forehead to touch the wood.

Smiling softly, he tapped her clit. "I have one light flogger in my desk. I'm going to test it on your pretty ass."

After she jerked, he pressed on one buttock, holding her down, and bent to slide open a drawer. A deerskin flogger lay inside. He gripped the handle and laid the flanges on her shoulders, rubbing them across then trailing down her spine.

Because she wasn't fighting him, he dropped his hand from her buttock. Stepping behind her, he trailed the suede strands up the backs of her thighs and over her flushed pussy.

Boone stepped farther back, giving himself room, hoping too that the distance and the fact he wasn't touching her smooth creamy backside, would give him back a little control. His cock was thick and heavy, poking at his pant leg. More than anything, he wanted to free it, wanted to sink inside her slick, hot cunt. Instead, he raised his arm to the side and swung across her buttocks, striking the right side.

She didn't jolt, didn't cry out. The deerskin was the softest flogger he had, and a perfect place to begin building her tolerance and hunger for more. As he stroked her bottom in steady, side-to-side motions, he welcomed the constant motion and the calming affect it had on his sharp edges. Tilly's passivity, the evidence of her growing arousal, were everything he'd hoped for.

* * *

Each stroke of the lashed implement he wielded warmed and soothed Tilly's fiery bottom and mind. Awash in sweet sensation, her pleasure built to a slow crescendo. She lay acquiescent, her mind drifting to last night's pleasures.

Boone filled her thoughts. His large, hard frame, his thick molten cock churning relentlessly inside her. She couldn't help the groan that leaked between her lips, or the shudder that racked her torso.

Again and again, he stuck her bottom, her thighs; occasionally he gave gentler strokes that padded against her pussy. She was wet and swollen, her body readying to be taken. If only he would.

When suddenly the strokes stopped, she held her breath, hoping he wasn't finished with her, because she needed release. Her body ached for it.

She heard his body settling into the soft leather chair, the whir of the wheels as he rolled closer to her spread legs. Hands cupped her buttocks, thick digits slid into her soaked slit, fingering the edges of her inner labia. Then one pushed inside her entrance.

She gasped. "The cameras," she whispered, then bit her lip because he'd said she couldn't speak. "Sir," she added, but she knew she'd made a mistake and hoped he'd overlook it because she couldn't bear for him to stop touching her.

"Serge is no doubt watching us now, but he can only see your side. He can't see what I see," he said, stroking over her slit. "Are you sore, Tilly? I was rough with you last night."

She wanted to lie, because she didn't want him to stop doing more. "A little, sir," she said softly.

Fingers parted her folds. Breath gusted against her wet open flesh. His pointed tongue entered her.

Good Lord, she'd never had a man do that before, and the action was excruciating in its intimacy. What was he feeling? Did he like the way she tasted? Tempted to close her legs out of embarrassment, she suffered through several moments while her thighs quaked.

He withdrew and then pushed inside again.

This time her pussy clenched, trying to capture his tongue. She wanted to tell him to use his fingers, to fuck her with his cock, to hell with what Serge might see, but held still. She sensed he was testing her, seeing whether she could control her emotions and her responses. Wishing she knew for sure what he wanted, she kept silent.

"I'm going to make you come. Will that please you?"

"Yes, sir," she said, her voice tightening with rising excitement, hoping he'd fuck her, ready to beg, but she bit back the extra encouragement.

A drawer slid open and closed. Then something cold pushed inside her. Something considerably smaller than his thick fingers. Something that felt heavy. Something metallic? A hum sounded and then vibrated inside her. She sucked in a deep breath and held it.

His fingers pinched her clit. "Listen to me, Tilly. Can you do that? Can you concentrate for a second?"

She nodded vigorously. "Y-yes, sir," she said, her throat closing, the tension in her body expanding, curling in her womb.

He pinched her again, hard. And her bottom jerked.

"You can't come until I say so. That's a rule as well. Try very hard to please me."

"Yes, sir," she said, her voice rising. Her head felt light. She clamped her jaws shut, because she didn't know if she could do this, not with the delicious vibrations hitting just the right spot inside her.

His breath blew against her moist folds. His tongue stroked through them, then back down. He tapped her clit with his tongue, used a rough finger to draw back the hood. Just the air hitting the hot little bundle of nerves nearly made her come unglued. Her thighs quivered.

"This will be tough," he murmured. "But do what you have to do. Make some noise. Bite that pretty mouth. Just don't you come until I say so."

She expelled a hard gust of air. Released from silence, she moaned. "Jesus, sweet God, Boone, please." Tilly moaned again, then rubbed her chest on the desk, soothing her nipples with the smooth wood. Her thighs went rigid, her pussy convulsed. She was getting close, so close.

Then his mouth latched around her clit, drawing on it, his tongue lashing the top of the knot with his tongue inside his mouth.

The sensation was exquisite agony. The small metal egg inside her began to pulse, felt as though it was rolling inside her, striking the spot again and again. His mouth pulled on her clit, forcing it erect. The suctioning so strong, he pulled it into his mouth, his lips sliding around the small base.

She screamed. At the edge of torment, Tilly couldn't ignore the sensual pressure building in her core. She had to come. It had to be now.

He released her clit and she sank, gasping for air.

"When I squeeze your knee, you can come, baby. Wait for it."

And then he was sucking her clit again, pulling it hard, his teeth nicking it, causing her to jerk. The little rounded knot was thick, hard, so sensitive that each draw sent electrical pulses straight to her womb. Her channel rippled, her cunt pulsed in time with her heartbeat.

She couldn't stand it, couldn't resist. Sliding her hands beneath her, she cupped her breasts, needing the comfort and then pinching her nipples to try to hold back.

A hand slid around her knee and squeezed.

Tilly arched off the desk and shouted as her orgasm exploded outward from her clit, rippling through her vagina, shivering over her buttocks and thighs. Shock held her erect for a long dizzying moment, and then she collapsed, her heated body pressed against the cool wood desk.

The vibrations slowed, lulling her. His lips relaxed, his tongue stroking her bared knot in wet, soothing laps, until, at last, she lay limply, her hands still hugging her breasts.

She closed her eyes and let out one last reedy moan.

Kisses landed on her pussy and covered her inner thighs, her bottom. Hands gripped her waist and pulled her up. Boone turned her, sliding her over his lap, her capris and undies dangling from one lolling foot.

With a strong arm, he held her against his chest and stroked her belly, between her legs, providing a brand of intimate comfort she'd never experienced from a man. Then fingers entered her and tugged on the small egg. He placed it on his desk, and she pushed her face into the corner of his neck, because the whitish fluid that coated it embarrassed her. After everything that he'd done, that she'd accepted, she knew the reaction was silly, but she hid.

"No showering." Boone pressed a kiss against her ear. "No changing your clothes. Not until tonight. I want your panties wet and sticky."

She groaned. "I'll smell."

"No one but you will notice. But I'll know you're uncomfortable. When you see me, you'll blush. When you're thinking about that lovely orgasm, I want you to lower your gaze."

"Will your men know? Is this something you always do?"

"No, it's a new rule. Just for you." The corner of his eyes crinkled. "Lower your gaze. Wait for me to come to you. I'll touch you. Not anything that will cause anyone else to know what we've been up to, but you and I will know."

She'd said he used this kind of play to create a connection. Now she understood how right she'd been. Every time she lowered her eyes, she'd be thinking of her hot bottom and the pleasure he'd given her with his mouth.

With a slow move, she bent back her head to look at his lips.

"Do you want a kiss?"

Her gaze flitted up to his eyes.

His blue gaze was glinting.

"Yes, sir." She wrinkled her nose. "You ask me questions just because you like hearing me say that, don't you?"

A smile curved his mouth, and blue eyes reflected a smoky heat. "I do. You please me, Tilly Floret."

"But you didn't take your own pleasure."

He sighed and tightened his embrace, pressing her down on his erection. "That's my penance for my lack of control."

Drawing her eyebrows together, she frowned.

She thought he'd shown a great deal of control, taking care with her body to the exclusion of his own orgasm. But before she could ask what he meant, he tapped her nose.

"I'm sending someone around to your brother's group house to do an assessment. We'll want to know how best to integrate him here."

Tilly sighed. If the moment wasn't already perfect enough... "I'm sorry if this is getting complicated—my problems shouldn't become yours."

Boone shook his head. "I wouldn't be taking them on if I didn't want to. I'm not a selfless man, Tilly. Don't go thinking there's more to me than what you know."

His warning didn't convince her. Boone had a softer center than he let the world see. His care with her proved it. She closed her eyes and rested her head against his shoulder. "I don't know how this will work is all. I want you. But I don't know how Denny will fit. How I'll manage to keep him out of trouble."

"Leave it to me, Tilly. I'm not without resources. When there's something I want as much as I want you, I'll move mountains."

She grunted, fingers toying with the buttons on his shirt. "There are no mountains in the bayou, Boone," she muttered.

His chuckle shook her, and she smiled, happy to let him ease her worries, if only for a while.

Chapter Thirteen

The moment Tilly let herself out of his office, Boone went to the hidden door and entered the room where Serge sat, his feet propped on the desk.

Serge glanced his way and smirked. "Don't worry, boss. I turned off the feed the second you pulled down her panties." He cleared his throat, still not looking Boone's way. "Didn't see a thing."

Boone gave him a glare, but couldn't manage to muster a reproach. He was still too hard to think straight. He shook his head to clear the memories of what he'd just done. "Anything from Alejandro?"

Serge grunted. "Said the tracking device took them to Cancun then headed west into the jungle. Must have either found it or changed bags, because the signal stopped a few miles in. He has a team scrambling to pick up the signal from their last location and see if any of the locals can be bribed into committing suicide by ratting out the Omegas." He shook his head in disgust. "Rotten business, that. Families will be lucky to get their bodies back for a proper funeral."

Boone's body tightened. Serge tended to see the bleak side of things, but Boone's business was to create miracles. "We still have leverage. That final payment. They'll keep them alive at least that long. In the meantime, we'll grease some palms and see what might shake loose in Mexico City. Someone knows something. I don't like trusting they'll hold to the deal. They're a ruthless bunch." He ran his hands through his hair in frustration. "The handoff, if we can get them to agree on something public, will be tricky."

Serge nodded, and then gave him a sly sideways look. "You really like that girl."

Boone didn't respond. Fact was, he did like Tilly. Liked her sense of humor, her wide-eyed curiosity, and especially how she'd responded to him just now.

When Boone answered, Serge gave a soft whistle. "Never thought I'd see the day. Was sure you'd marry some stuck-up cover model who'd bore you to tears and maybe agree to a kid or two so long as you paid for the plastic surgery to make her perfect again. I like Tilly."

Boone settled into the chair beside Serge and sighed. "I hear a 'but.'"

"Maybe it's not the right time, boss. And maybe there's more to Tilly than we know."

Boone gave him a questioning look.

"That folder Jonesy found. I know he mailed photos to your phone. She's been keeping it for years. It's a little strange. Something that terrible happened to her cousin, you'd think she'd want to forget, but she's obsessed with you and the murder." His brows drew together. "You don't find that disturbing?"

"If I'd known that before I'd met her, maybe. I know she's keeping secrets, but she's not very good at it. She doesn't have a

secretive nature. Whatever she's withholding is eating her up."
His gaze locked with Serge's. "My hope is that once she trusts
me, she'll confide."

Serge's mouth puckered, then drew into a straight line. "Like I
said, I like her. And you know I don't like many people. Just keep
a little emotional distance. At least until you find out what she's
keeping from you."

Giving him a vague nod, Boone settled into the seat beside
Serge and dialed Alejandro in Monterrey. Anything but think
about the fact Tilly might be lying. His stomach roiled at the
thought. Whatever she was hiding, whatever she might be
involved in, he hoped he'd be able to protect her. Her safety came
first. But when all this was over, he hoped his faith in her would
still be intact.

* * *

Tilly didn't seek out Jonesy right away. She stopped by her cottage for her phone. Boone's mention of Denny brought a jolt-
ing reminder that she hadn't spoken to him for a couple of days,
so she checked her messages. Nothing from him. And only one
missed call. From Mae.

She stared at the number, feeling guilty over the way she'd left
the woman high and dry. The only way to make it right was head
to town and stop in at the restaurant. She dreaded seeing the
older woman face-to-face and could already picture the condemnation in her dark eyes.

Mae had been good to her. Good to Denny. When Denny had
still been living in Bayou Vert, she'd hired him as a busboy and
dishwasher. Simple tasks he could perform, although Mae had to
stand over him to see he did things right.

Denny had been pumped about having a job and a paycheck. He hadn't understood that the wages didn't go far enough to pay their bills and save their home. He'd thought he was rich because he had a check to bring home every week.

Thankfully, the garage door opened without requiring a secret decoder ring. Climbing into her car, she smiled, thinking about Denny's pride over his pitiful paycheck, and missing her fuzzy bear. His hugs were uncomplicated, filled with unconditional love. Tilly hated that her relationship with Denny, at least from her side, was tarnished by the discovery of the bracelet. It ate her up inside that she couldn't ask about where he'd found it. First, because she didn't want to know whether he was the one responsible for Celeste's death, although she couldn't picture it. Sure, Denny did throw tantrums. And with his size and strength, but without the ability to hold back, she recognized full well the possibility existed that he could have lashed out at Celeste, who'd always goaded and teased him mercilessly. But where had he gotten the knife? It wasn't something he'd have carried around with him. And if he'd slashed her, he wouldn't have thought to hide it. He'd have panicked and said something…to someone. Wouldn't he?

Second, she couldn't ask him because whatever Denny got into his head, he repeated over and over. He'd never mentioned the bracelet, and might well have forgotten how he'd come to have it. Yes, he asked about his treasure box, but she didn't think any one of his treasures meant more than the other. If she asked him pointedly about the one bracelet, he'd never shut up about it, and might mention it to someone who would recognize its significance, just as she had the moment she'd picked it up and held it to the light.

A delicate charm bracelet with golden bells attached and tiny hoppers that tinkled against the insides of the bells as the brace-let moved. Celeste had worn it in her prom photo. Worn it when she'd posed with the homecoming court, wearing her queen's crown and looking radiant in a royal blue gown as she stood beside a tall and lanky Boone.

Tears welled, but it wasn't really for sorrow over her cousin. She'd lived years with her death, even resenting the way it hovered in everyone's minds and tainted her town.

She felt weepy for the fact she no longer trusted her brother, not when she couldn't be certain he hadn't been the one who'd killed Celeste. Maybe the bracelet didn't mean a thing. Maybe Denny hadn't killed her, but he'd certainly been there that night. He might know who else had been there.

It was odd, the fact she didn't trust her own brother, but knew with all her heart that Boone hadn't killed her. All because he'd shown her brother kindness all those years ago, her belief in him only cementing the more time she spent with him.

But what to do about Denny? She always felt like a lodestone of guilt weighed her down. He shouldn't be a burden.

The restaurant loomed. Another worry to replace the one that would never go away. She pulled into a parking space and let herself out of the car.

A chirp of a siren sounded behind her, and she glanced over her shoulder.

Leon double-parked his sedan beside hers and exited his car. "Boone finally let you off your leash?"

Tilly planted a hand on her hip and glared. "Am I wearin' a collar?" Good Lord, her cheeks blushed, because she wasn't so sure that wasn't where their activities were heading. But Leon couldn't know that, could he? "Don't be a jackass," she muttered as he strolled toward her.

Leon came close, staring down at her, his gaze raking her slightly rumpled clothes.

She sincerely hoped he didn't have an acute sense of smell. Not that she was ashamed to be taking up with Boone, but Leon had a thing against him and she didn't want the added aggravation of his constant taunts.

"You look good, Tilly. Although I do miss the Daisy Dukes."

Her lips twitched into a smile. "I was a little tired of my ass cheeks gettin' sunburned."

Leon laughed and pushed back his hat. "Heard you moved out there."

She heard the question in his voice, knew he had his suspicions, but she wasn't about to confirm them. What she was doing with Boone was none of his business. Strangely, she wasn't embarrassed. A day ago, she might have blushed at this conversation. "I have the foreman's cottage."

"Seem a little weird, him puttin' you up out there?"

Pretending a nonchalance she didn't feel, she shrugged. "Most of his staff lives in the mansion for now. Not the local workers—they commute back and forth—but I don't think it's strange at all he wants me there."

Leon gave her a pointed look. "Is he botherin' you?"

Tilly shook her head, keeping her smile set and her eyes wide. "Boone doesn't bother me, Leon. And fact is, I wouldn't mind the attention."

His expression quickly shuttered. "You be careful, hear?" he said, his voice deepening with his doubt.

"I always am. Don't you worry about me."

He lifted his chin toward the restaurant. "Can I buy you lunch?"

Relieved he'd dropped the interrogation and because she

wanted to make nice, she smiled and nodded. "I'd like that, although I did come to talk to Mae. I left without giving notice. She might spit in our food," she teased.

"She wouldn't dare do that to an officer of the law," he said, giving her a wink, and then he held open the door, waiting for her to enter.

Tilly took a deep breath and walked inside the cozy restaurant. Mae wasn't anywhere in sight. Had likely spotted her through the window and gone to the kitchen to sulk. LeRoy Duhon, the bait shop owner, was the only customer inside, and he gave her a narrow-eyed stare. Tilly knew her moving to Maison Plaisir had made her the talk of the town. And not in a good way.

She glanced at the corkboard. A handwritten note was posted there: WAITRESS NEEDED. Mae had pinned it right over the latest of Jonesy's notices. Notices she hadn't bothered tearing down.

Tilly shook her head. She'd never understand the gruff woman. "Find us a couple of seats, Leon. I'll go talk to Mae." She straightened her spine and pushed through the swinging door, entering the kitchen.

"Only folks who work here are welcome in the kitchen," Mae said, her voice surly, her gaze on the onions she chopped on the cutting board, her knife slicing with practiced ease.

"Mae, I'm sorry I didn't give you notice," she said quietly, hovering by the door. "I left you in a lurch. You have every right to be angry."

Mae huffed a breath through her nose. "My baby's dead 'cause o' dat man, and you're off gallivantin'—flyin' to Mexico and havin' a gran' ole time—an' she's dead an' in her grave."

Tilly knew there was no use defending Boone. Not when Mae had been cultivating her hatred for him for all those years. "It's a good job. One that'll allow me to bring Denny home."

Mae raised her head, but looked out the window to the restaurant rather than look at Tilly. "Don' guess there's anythin' left to say. Don' ever say I didn' warn ya."

Knowing she'd lost a friend, Tilly sighed. She had too few, and although Mae wasn't a warm woman, she'd seen her through some tough times. Guilt settled in her tummy. "The sheriff invited me to lunch. If you want, I can serve up today's special and take it out there."

Mae's shoulders straightened. "It's my kitchen. Don' need your help."

Tilly backed away and pushed through the door. Regret ached inside her chest, but there was also relief. Mae had never been easy to be around. She held her anger and grief at the world too close. Both tainted her view of the world around her.

Leon raised his eyebrows as she settled in her chair. "She must have taken it well," he drawled. "Didn't sound like World War Three was breakin' out."

She wrinkled her nose. "I would've preferred if she'd thrown a hissy fit. I don't think she'll ever speak to me again." Her eyes teared up, but she blinked away the moisture and pasted on a smile.

"She's been lookin' after you ever since you came back to town. I can't see her stayin' mad that long."

Leon was trying to comfort her, which she found sweet, but she knew she'd burned a bridge with Mae. "She's different than she was back then," she said, unwilling to say her cousin's name. "Harder. Even worse ever since Boone came back to town. Mutterin' and morose."

Leon's expression grew pensive. "Has to be hard for her. She was Celeste's nanny. That girl was her whole world."

Her body went still. "Her death wasn't easy on any of us, Leon. If I can get past it, why can't the rest of y'all?"

Leon's gaze drilled into her. "Because the rest of us aren't walkin' around with blinders, Tilly. The man who's responsible for her bein' dead is walkin' around like he owns the place."

Anger flushed her cheeks. She lifted her chin. She almost blurted that Leon had had more motive to kill Celeste than Boone had—he'd wanted Celeste too—but believing him a murderer was just as unfathomable. "It's been fifteen years. Don't you think if he had killed her, coming back here would be the last thing he'd do?"

Leon leaned forward and tapped the table. "He was a damn SEAL. He thinks he owns the place. And don't think he hasn't killed since—it's just all legal-like now." At her expression, he sank back in his seat, his gaze turning away. "I'm not sayin' a man can't change. I'm just sayin' folks can't forgive the fact no one ever paid for her death."

A plate slid in front of Tilly, filled with dirty rice and beans, fried shrimp, and corn bread.

Spicy aromas swirled upward and tickled her nose. Tilly's belly felt queasy, but she offered a smile as she tilted her face upward.

Mae's stony expression didn't relent. She slid a plate in front of Leon. "Anythin' else you be needin', Sheriff?"

"No, Mae. Smells good." He smiled at her and reached for his fork.

Mae grunted and turned away, her feet clomping hard all the way back to the kitchen.

Leon whistled. "I see what you mean. Might wanna give her some space."

Tilly's shoulders slumped. "She's not ever gonna forgive me."

"Probably not." Leon reached across the table and gave her hand a squeeze. "Not all of us are angry with you, Tilly. Just concerned. You be careful."

She dug into her meal, hoping she could make a dent and not give Mae another reason to hate her. Still, she wasn't sorry she'd come. Mae deserved the courtesy of a personal apology. Hoping to change the subject, she raised her gaze. "So, did that historical guy have anything to say about the renovations?"

"Other than complainin' about the loss of the cabin, he wasn't critical of the rest. Said that Boone was holdin' true to the historical details while making some necessary upgrades. Shouldn't have any trouble over them."

Her lips twitched at his grumpy tone. "You don't sound happy about that fact."

His eyes narrowed. "I know he's your boss, but I'd love to catch him speedin' through town, just once."

"What would you do?"

"Give him a ticket. I'm not out for blood, Tilly. I'm a lawman; I'll let justice find its own way."

They ate in silence, Tilly's mood spilling toward the floor. After the exhilarating night and morning she'd had, she supposed she was due to come down off her high. She forced down a final bite, feeling suddenly weary.

"Any chance you've changed your mind about goin' on a date with me?"

Tilly blinked and raised her head. She didn't have a snappy comeback. And she knew the moment she didn't, that he knew why. Regret lanced through her at his tightening expression.

Leon's mouth firmed into a straight line. He cleared his throat. "Don't guess I can compete with a billionaire," he said, his voice deepening.

She didn't bother reminding him she hadn't been interested before Boone came to town, but what was the use? She laid down her fork and pushed away her plate. "I'm done. Sorry to eat and run, but I have a lot to do today. Really appreciate it, Leon."

"Sure," he said, giving her a stolid stare.

She scooted off the seat and walked out of the restaurant, heading to her car.

The sound of an engine starting drew her glance. A dark car with tinted windows was parked across the street.

Tilly gave the driver she couldn't see a glare and opened her car door. No doubt Boone knew the moment she'd left the estate. He also knew who she'd joined for lunch. She wondered if he'd consider that a punishable offense.

Her mood kicked up a notch. A girl could only hope.

Chapter Fourteen

Tilly didn't see Boone for the rest of the day. She was on tenter-hooks all afternoon, wondering what he would say or do about the fact she'd met with Leon. Jonesy hadn't resumed his tour, but he'd let her dog his steps as he'd checked with the army of work-ers busy around the estate.

She couldn't imagine the amount of money Boone was pour-ing into the restoration, but just in the last two days, there was notable progress. The garden in front of the house had been cleared, dead plantings removed, bushes pruned, fresh dirt and manure and a layer of mulch put down. A delivery truck was parked in the front lawn, workers unloading trees, bushes, flow-ers in pots ready to be planted. The red-tiled roof looked good as new. Painters were building scaffolding to begin the work on the exterior of the house.

She had to admit, his money could perform miracles. The sparkle was starting to return to the grand old house.

Tired, she could do little more than drag her feet back to her cottage. She wasn't sure if she'd be welcome to join Boone for dinner, didn't know for sure how that worked, so she decided to shower and rummage through her well-stocked kitchen for something to eat.

Maybe she needed time alone to sort out her feelings. The many highs, followed by the thudding lows, had sucked out her energy.

When she entered her bath and spied that great big tub, she changed her mind about the shower. Instead, she poured rose-scented bath salts into the bottom of the tub and filled it high with water. Resting her head against the back, she closed her eyes. Maybe she'd have a little nap.

"I guess I should have been a little more specific. I did only say no showering."

She peeked between her lashes at Boone who strode inside and tipped down the toilet lid to take a seat. Her heart tripped, and then beat at a faster, heavier rate. "Thought I locked the front door."

"You should have turned the dead bolt if you didn't want me using my key," he said, his narrow gaze resting on her face.

"I'll remember that." She closed her eyes again and resisted the urge to smile. She liked the deep, rumbling quality of his voice. Warmth that didn't have a thing to do with the rose-scented water sent a flush through her skin.

"I came by to invite you to dinner—that is, if you don't already have plans."

Okay, so his edgy anger was a turn-on, but she didn't really want him having the wrong impression. What they had, whatever it was, was too new to tarnish with any misplaced jealousy. Better not to pussyfoot around what was actually on his mind. "I didn't go to town to meet Leon. I went to apologize to Mae. Leon just showed up. He invited me to lunch. It wasn't a date, Boone."

"You know damn well Leon's man at the gate radioed him the moment you left the estate."

She opened her eyes. "You monitor the police band too?"

He shrugged.

She sat sideways in the tub and rested her arm on the rim. "I noticed you had me followed," she said, giving him back the same narrowed glare. "Some women might be creeped out by that fact."

A dark brow arched. "Are you?"

"No." She shook her head, and then grinned. "You're a control freak, Boone."

Boone shook his head, a smile tugging at the sides of his mouth. "Since you're already wet…" He reached beneath into the bottom of the baker's rack and pulled out a black pouch.

She angled her head to give him a coy glance. "What's that?"

"How about you get out of the water and sit on the edge of the tub, and I'll show you."

As always, her curiosity won out. She pushed up and stood, then sat gingerly on the rolled lip of the tub. Her nudity made her blush, but she wasn't about to comment on it.

"Part your legs."

She almost blurted, "What? No 'please'?" But he was giving her one of those looks, the ones that said it was playtime. Excitement thrummed through her. She dropped her gaze and slowly spread her thighs, hoping the pressure of her muscles against the rim wasn't making her thighs appear massive.

He came to her, sliding an arm around her back.

"You'll get wet," she gasped.

He shook his head. "Lean back and grip the far rim."

She did just that, leaning on her arms and realizing how the awkward position left her open and vulnerable.

Boone unzipped the pouch and drew out an electric razor.

Her eyes widened as she realized he intended to keep his earlier promise. "I can manage that on my own."

He tsked. "What are the only words I want to hear right now?"

She sucked her bottom lip between her teeth, then let it go. "Yes, sir?"

Boone knelt between her legs and used a towel to wipe away the excess moisture.

She tried to resume breathing, hated that her face was getting hotter. All this attention to her private parts was a bit unnerving. And embarrassing. Did he think her terribly ungroomed? She'd always shaved her bikini line, but doing anything more seemed decadent.

"Did Leon get close enough to notice?" he asked softly, not bothering to glance up.

Holding a conversation with a man who couldn't bother to look away from her pussy was awkward to say the least. Having him ask whether another man noticed she's smelled like sex only made this whole scene surreal. "No, sir. Or if he did, he was too polite to tell me I smelled."

He pressed a button and the razor buzzed, reminding her of the hum of the vibrator he'd used earlier. Her pussy clenched.

With a finger, he tapped her mound. "None of that, now." Then, starting from the bottom of her pussy, he ran the razor up the right side of her folds.

The sensation was foreign—and delightful. She gripped the rim harder and leaned her head back, trusting he knew what he was doing and deciding she'd just enjoy this new experience.

He ran up the left side, then rubbed his fingers over her lips before parting them and repeating the process, but this time following the edges of her labia.

The razor ceased its humming and she opened her eyes, her gaze shooting down to inspect her bare mound.

He held a can of shaving cream and shook it, before pointing it on the opposite palm and pushing the nozzle to fill it with foam. Then he painted the foam on her mound, her labia, and the supersensitive area between her pussy and her anus.

Dying to speak, she sucked in a deep breath. If she could, she'd tell him this was way beyond embarrassing. Painfully intimate. When he dipped a manual razor into the tub water and then pulled her labia this way and that to glide the blades over her flesh, she was glad she wasn't speaking, because she certainly didn't want him distracted. But she needn't have worried.

Boone was ruthlessly efficient, shaving her bare in minutes, and then wiping her with the towel. When he'd put away his tools, he fondled her flesh, admiring his work. "Pretty and pink." He rose and slid an arm around her again, pulling her upright. "Rinse off in the bath. I'll be waiting for you in your bedroom."

Her heart racing, she lowered into the water, her cheeks so hot she wished she could curl up and die. Holding a breath, she sank beneath the water, hiding there until her head felt ready to explode. When she came up, she heard chuckling from the other room.

"Stop stalling."

Lathering up a loofah, she washed quickly, shampooed her hair, and then ran fresh water from the tap to rinse. She stepped out of the tub, making a face at the pubic hairs littering the floor and being careful to step around them. Men didn't think about their messes.

Wrapping her towel around herself, she walked into the room, her footsteps slowing.

Boone sat in an armchair, which he'd placed beside the bed.

"I'll just get dressed," she said, although she knew he had some nasty plan up his sleeve.

"Dinner will wait for us." The stare he gave her as he turned his head was at once hard and hot.

For a long moment, she held still, hoping he'd give her a hint of what he wanted next, but decided maybe what he wanted was for her to trust her instincts. She dropped the towel and stood with her gaze downcast.

Not because she felt in any way subservient, but because she sensed he'd be turned on by her willingness to play. Then she slowly glided forward, trying to keep her movements graceful. She was a little too self-conscious of her nudity and her flesh's tendency to jiggle, but she forced herself to put it out of her mind. When she drew near, she knelt between his legs, keeping her head lowered but watching him from beneath the fringe of her lashes.

His breath left him in a slow, steady hiss.

Because his legs were spread, she could see the promising bulge pressing against his slacks between his legs.

A satisfied smile tugged at the corners of her mouth, but she firmed her lips, sensing he wouldn't approve of her humor. This was "lesson time."

"When you kneel," he said softly, "place your hands on your thighs or behind your back. I'll let you choose what feels comfortable."

Placing her hands over her breasts or between her legs would be more comfortable. Since the point was proving her willingness to let him see her, she clasped her hands behind her back, aware her breasts jutted and the nipples tilted upward.

He reached down and gently plucked a nipple, rolling it between his thumb and forefinger.

She breathed deeply, heat stirring in her core.

He tipped up her chin. "I want you to lie on the bed sideways, place a pillow under your head. Then spread your legs, knees bent."

Her throat dried and she swallowed. "Yes, sir." With his hand helping her up, she moved to the bed, grabbing a pillow, then climbing onto the mattress, aware her ass and pussy were pointing at his face. She rolled and lay back, sliding up her feet to bend her knees. She slowly let them fall to the sides.

"Nice," he said, bringing his chair closer to the side of the bed. "Now, I want you to touch your freshly shaved cunt and pleasure yourself. Show me how you masturbate."

Her eyes widened. She began to shake her head, but saw him narrow his eyes. She blew out a breath, drew a deep one in, and then reached between her legs with both hands.

If she'd thought letting him pleasure her with his mouth was intimate, this would be agonizingly so. He'd know exactly how she touched herself when she played alone. An intimate act she'd never shared with another. And yet, the moment her fingers glided on her smooth pussy, she was fascinated by the texture of her freshly denuded skin. Soft as a baby's butt.

Softer, velvety almost. She skimmed a finger over her mound, then up and down her outer labia. He'd scraped her clean. Not a hint of stubble. She liked the sensation.

But he wanted more. He wanted her to show him how she got herself off.

Tilly steeled herself against the humiliation and dipped two fingers into her opening, swirling around her entrance, and then plunging deeper, encouraging the natural lubricant to ooze from inside her. When she'd coaxed sufficient moisture, and her fingers were coated, she pulled them free and traced the edges of her thin inner labia, up and down, touching them lightly, then tracing the edges upward to where they intersected. Her hood was swelling, protecting her clitoris, which was not yet engorged, so she rubbed the top of it, circling her wet fingers, and then diving back inside herself for more moisture.

Her pulse stuttered. She didn't dare look at Boone. If she did, she might come unraveled, might beg him to end this, to take over. The longer she smoothed her wet fingers over her flesh, the more she craved penetration. Her inner thighs tightened, and she eased them up.

Boone cleared his throat.

Casting him a glance, she paused. His face gave away nothing of what he might be thinking. She took his hint and let her thighs fall open again, but shifted her feet higher up and tilted her hips toward herself. So he'd see everything. Even her anus. Her arousal was building, fluid leaking past her perineum. Soon the bed would be wet beneath her.

His throat worked around an audible swallow, and Tilly took heart from that telltale action. He wasn't as unmoved watching her as he'd like her to believe. Tilly breathed deeply, pulsed her hips once, gave a little groan, and peeked beneath her lashes to watch his avid attention to her motion. Emboldened by his fixated stare, she scooped fluid with her fingertips and continued to rub, concentrating on the changes occurring there between her legs. She noted her labia were swelling and hot, her hood swelling more. Her clitoris was extending, growing harder, the glans protruding slightly. Gingerly, because it was engorging and more sensitive, she circled atop the growing knot, over and over, until her breasts tightened too. In her belly, deep, curling need swirled. Glancing down her body, she watched as the tips of her nipples became distended. She wanted to touch them, pinch them to add to the searing pleasure tightening her core. More than that, she wanted Boone with his wicked mouth to lash and suck her clit as he had the night before.

Again, she rubbed her clit, and knew she was getting close, but couldn't manage an orgasm without doing something even more embarrassing.

"Make yourself come for me, Tilly. Let me see how you do it. Don't torture yourself."

She held back, wondering how many women he'd watched doing this very same thing and whether they'd felt as awkward and exposed as she did now. She didn't want to do something that wasn't sensual or pretty. But he'd commanded her. She would obey.

Forking her fingers at the top of her folds, she pulled up, fully exposing her reddened, bulbous clit. She licked spit onto the tips of two fingers, then gave Boone a look she was sure showed every bit of her trepidation, but he gave her no encouragement.

Although he did seem to be holding his breath...

She reached downward, pressed her fingers against her clit, and rubbed it in quick, back and forth motions, heating it with friction, exciting it with pressure. She strained. Her head tilted back, her teeth gritting, and her fingers toggled faster and faster.

When the lubricant she'd applied was nearly gone, she felt the pulse deep inside, the unwinding of the fierce tension that curled so deep and hard. She moaned, thighs moving restlessly, her bottom lifting, and fingers toggled harder until, at last, she peaked.

Immediately, she eased the rhythm because her clit couldn't take the rougher motions. She dipped down and gathered liquid, then soothed it over the exposed knot, circling until the ripples moving up and down her channel slowed.

With one last ragged breath, she relaxed, closing her legs, and turning her head to the side so that she couldn't look at him.

The chair scraped on the floor, and then the bed dipped beside her. A hand rested against her cheek, a thumb pushing to turn her head.

Boone bent and pressed a kiss against her mouth, and then groaned and licked her lips. "I taste you," he whispered.

Tilly swallowed, unable to meet his gaze. What she'd done went beyond anything she'd ever shared with another person. Her body quivered in the aftermath. Mortification spread a deep flush of heat across her cheeks. She held silent, although she wanted to ask how her performance compared to all those other women he'd watched.

Again, he kissed her, and then drew back, settling beside her on one elbow. He ran a hand over her breasts, molding them gently, and then smoothed his hand over her abdomen and down to her mound. He cupped her sex, not penetrating with his fingers.

"I feel the after tremors," he said, and his lips curved into a smile. "I pride myself on self-control, but I'm hard as a post right now. I'd like nothing better than to fuck you, but you need to recover." His glance flicked to her face. "Now, was that so terrible a punishment?"

"Was that what it was?" she asked, her voice husky.

His teeth flashed. "I don't want everything to be a lesson, but rather to bring you along naturally. This was a punishment, but the lesson was that there can be pleasure in it. Punishments can be physical, which this certainly was. But more importantly, there was an element of initial humiliation. You didn't like baring your practices for me to see."

Her heartbeat still thundered in her ears. She pursed her lips, pouting them. "I don't think I've ever felt so exposed." As close to a complaint as she could manage, but he didn't seem to mind.

He patted her pussy, a hint of challenge entering his tight expression. "Be a good girl and get dressed. And...no washing. Also, no underwear. Wear something short."

Chapter Fifteen

Boone smothered a laugh at the look of shock on Tilly's face when they entered the dining room. He'd invited all his closest friends, men who shared his particular interests, to join them, having given them a heads-up that Tilly's punishment would require a little extra attention. His men stood to one end of the dining room table, dressed casually in blue jeans or cargo pants. They straightened as he and Tilly entered.

"You've met Serge, Jonesy, and Bear," he said, beginning the introductions and ignoring her beet-red cheeks.

No doubt she was horrified because he'd approved a very short black skirt and white halter top. More skin was exposed than she might want, especially since her nipples were still tight little beads, poking at her thin blouse. If she bent even a couple of inches, her ass cheeks would be exposed.

Boone didn't mind the fact his closest friends might get an eyeful of Tilly's sweet attractions, but he'd warned them against touching her, or making any sexual innuendos that might embarrass her. He'd reserved those pleasures for himself.

"You might remember Eric Thorson," he said, gesturing

toward the tall Swede, "from the first day you came here. Max..."
he said, pointing to the little pug who lay quietly in a dog bed in
the corner of the room, "is his. And then there's Lincoln. You
can call him Linc."

Linc's eyes twinkled in his dark face as he waved a hand
toward Tilly. "Nice to meet you, ma'am."

Tilly leaned closer to Boone, but offered the men a smile.
"Nice to meet you and Eric." Her hand sought Boone's and
squeezed hard.

He bent to her ear. "Punishment hasn't ended."

Her head dropped and her mouth firmed into a straight line.
More important, her arms remained at her sides rather than
moving forward in an attempt to hide her aroused nipples.

Boone smoothed a hand over the swell of her hips, all the
approval he'd give her, but she seemed to take strength from it.
Her mouth tipped up at the corner, and she gave him a sideways
glance from under her lashes. Cornflower-blue eyes held his gaze
for a moment.

Boone let the moment stretch, letting her know she was the
center of his attention. Then he waved toward the table. "Let's all
be seated," he said to his men. "I asked for grilled steaks tonight."

Serge rubbed his belly. "With Cajun seasoning?"

Boone nodded. "What else?"

The men circled the table and stood behind their chairs.

Boone ushered Tilly forward with a hand pressed against the
small of her back.

Her sandaled feet dragged, a hint of defiance, perhaps a reminder
that he shouldn't take her obedience for granted, but she let him
guide her to the chair beside the head of the table. When he pulled
it out to seat her, he bent to her ear. "As soon as they sit down, I
want your skirt hiked up and your bare bottom on the upholstery."

Her head turned slowly toward him, tilting up. Her eyes were round. "Seriously?" she whispered.

Amusement at her shock filled him. If only she knew what else he had in store... He tapped her nose. "That's 'Yes, sir.'" He paused, waiting for her response.

Her head dropped. "Yes, sir," she said, but there was grit in her voice.

Boone grinned as he straightened, then flashed a warning around the table before taking his seat.

The men scraped back their chairs and sat.

Boone gave Tilly a pointed stare before turning to Serge. "Any news from down south?"

Tilly's mouth tightened, and she shifted slowly in her chair.

He wished he was close enough he could run his hand up her thigh to make sure she was following his instructions. But the heightening color of her cheeks proved an excellent barometer of her discomfort. Tonight's lesson would feature a gentle humiliation. If she balked, he wouldn't press, but he was curious to see how she'd react. So far, she'd reacted as he'd predicted. Unsettled but acquiescent. For now.

"It's been quiet," Serge said, shooting a curious glance Tilly's way before meeting Boone's gaze. "Uh, Alejandro says the longer it takes for them to respond with the rest of their plan the worse it looks for those men."

Boone nodded and swept a hand toward the table. "Tilly, all of these men are involved with the security services division of my company, but they've volunteered to step away and help with getting me moved in."

She stopped wriggling in her chair, and raised her face. "It must be nice to have such loyal men surroundin' you."

"We're all vested in the success of the company."

Serge nodded. "We've grown wealthy together. Boone cut us in from the start. He was the man with the connections." He lifted an arm and flexed his biceps. "We provided the brute strength and training."

Around the table chuckles followed.

Tilly offered a little smile but was too wary to simply enjoy the conversation.

Boone moved his chair nearer to her and casually leaned an elbow on one chair arm while slouching in his chair. Now he was within reaching distance. Beneath the tablecloth, he reached for her knee and gave it a caress.

Her chest rose, and she sat up a little straighter. "So, I assume you all met in the navy?"

Linc flashed a smile, his eyebrows waggling. "We did. Not all of us came up as BUD/S at the same time. I met Boone and Serge when Boone was first assigned to Iraq. The others," he said, waving a hand around the table, "filled in…vacancies in our team. You get tight with men when you're having to watch each other's backs."

"When Boone decided to resign his commission," Serge said, pausing to sip at his glass of water, "he shared his plans. Said we'd keep doing what we did best, but get paid better. As we all became eligible to leave, we stepped into jobs with Boone's company, doing the security work ourselves. Now we train and supervise our own teams. Life's good."

Boone began sliding his palm higher, his fingers trailing up the inside of her thigh.

Her breath hitched. "And now you're in the back of beyond in a swamp," she said, her words coming in a rush.

"We'll go wherever Boone needs us."

Boone was glad they weren't going where he was as he moved

higher up her leg. Tilly's thighs were clamped shut. When he was a couple of inches from her mound, her hand reached down and pushed at his.

He'd expected her reaction but wasn't going to bend. Not now. Tilly had an important lesson to learn. Boone glanced her way, then bent the arm perched on the chair arm and crooked a finger.

Her glare could have roasted marshmallows, but she bent toward him.

"Since you've defied me," he whispered, "I want you to raise your skirt in back."

Her eyebrows lowered in a fierce frown that made him smile inside. She looked like a fierce kitten, complete with claws, which were digging into the back of his hand.

"They'll see my ass," she hissed.

"Only Bear, since he's sitting next to you, and he won't say a word."

Just then the door from the kitchen opened. His server was another member of his team, but Boone didn't introduce Manny Chavez. He'd let her sweat. "Now, baby. Do it. Do it because it will please me."

Her eyes rounded. "Is this the punishment?"

"You aren't playing by the rules. And you know there will be repercussions for every second you delay. But remember what I said—there's pleasure in the punishment." He gave her small smile to reassure her. "Your ass is lovely, by the way."

"Boone..." she groaned.

For a moment, he wondered if he'd pushed her too far, if she'd refuse. Schooling his expression, Boone shook his head. "You want to walk in my world, Tilly. Act like you're ready for it."

Dropping her gaze again, she sat still, her mouth trembling. Color rose high in her cheeks.

Boone nearly relented at that hint of her inner turmoil. Maybe she wasn't ready. Maybe she was too shy to ever be. He could adjust. The point wasn't that he wanted her complete submission, but rather that he wanted her to push through her own boundaries.

But Tilly surprised him. With her fingernails still gouging the back of his hand, she began to wriggle again. Fabric rustled. From the corner of his eye, he saw the black fabric of her skirt bunch around her waist. She'd bared her bottom and a little more than he'd asked for. Slowly, she parted her thighs and let go of his hand.

For the moment, the pleasure was all his. Warmth filled his chest at her courage. He rewarded her, slipping up to dip his fingertips into the top of her folds, giving her a caress.

Her breath hitched, and then evened out.

His men didn't miss their play. They shared glances, smiles tugging at the corners of their mouths. To the accompaniment of plates landing gently on the tabletop, the wet sounds he made, swirling on her sex, added tension to the air.

A plate slid in front of her. Then him. He glanced at Manny, dressed in dark trousers and a white dress shirt.

Manny gave him a nod. "I'll break out the wine."

Boone straightened, withdrawing his hand and reached into his pocket, taking out a small oval vibrator and setting it on the table between his place setting and Tilly's. He picked up his fork. "Tilly," he said, in a soothing tone loud enough for everyone at the table to hear, "put this inside you, then eat your meal."

As she reached for the vibrator, her hand shook. Her head remained lowered, but she did exactly as he asked, leaning back in her chair and slipping the vibrator between her legs. When her hand came up, she wiped her fingers on her napkin then laid it on her thighs.

Through the fabric of his pants, Boone pressed the remote, and a humming sounded.

Her eyes closed, her mouth rounding. "I'm going to kill you, sir."

Laughter rang out from his men. But Manny had already begun filling glasses.

Serge raised a glass, giving Tilly an approving glance. "Here's to Clotille Floret, the belle of Bayou Vert. Welcome to Maison Plaisir, sugar."

* * *

For Tilly, the toast and the praise she read in the rugged faces ringing the table filled her with a strange sense of accomplishment. For the first time since she'd entered the dining room, she relaxed. Pleasure at Serge's gesture flushed her cheeks. "Y'all certainly know how to entertain a girl," she drawled.

Boone flashed her a smile and lifted his own glass. "To your courage. My men appreciate that in a woman, even if she's not theirs to enjoy."

Warmth flooded her body. She wished she'd had enough courage to ask if she was truly his. The thought of belonging to him caused a deep yearning to tighten her chest. "I'd be flattered, but I wonder how many times this scene has played out."

"Funny you should use that word," Serge murmured, raising his eyebrows.

She didn't understand his meaning, but the amusement the men shared was a palpable thing. Just as their tension radiated from their thick chests and arms. *Lord, a woman could drown in the testosterone floatin' in this room.*

She didn't realize she'd said her thought aloud until Bear

choked beside her. Reaching behind him, she patted his shoulder. "Are you okay?"

He cleared his throat and threw her a scowl. "I'm fine, ma'am."

"Since I'm callin' you all by your first names, and you've been starin' at my ass, don't you think you should just call me Tilly?"

"Boone, you unleashed a monster," Linc said, his voice thick with laughter.

Tilly shook her head and picked up her knife, cutting a slice off the succulent steak in front of her. "Just tryin' to get into the swing of things. This is a very strange meal."

When the humming grew louder and the vibrations more insistent, she was given a hint of just how strange it was to become. She put down her knife and fork and curled her fingers against the tablecloth. "Boone?"

"Rules, sweetheart. It's time to play by them."

"Sir?"

"The moment you start to come, the meal ends. Let the men finish their steaks."

She shook her head, her gaze slashing around the table. Everyone's head was bent as they ate, but they were certainly taking their time. She didn't know how she was going to hold on. Her pussy was juicy and hot. Still a little raw from Boone's lovemaking of the previous night and her own manipulations not an hour earlier. And she was past caring that her expression had to be showing every bit of her dismay and arousal.

While they talked amongst themselves and shoveled food into their mouths, she tried to hold still, tried to think of something else other than the metal egg pulsing inside her, but the shiny gadget was striking just the right spot and shivering so hard she felt it vibrate through her belly and pussy. She closed her thighs, trying to trap the sound as well as stem the pulses beginning up and down her channel. With her breaths coming faster, she was sure someone was going to have to clean the wet spot growing beneath her on the chair.

Then the vibrations ratcheted up a little more. Her inner walls clenched around it, making it feel as though it was getting bigger, but it was only the swelling of her tender tissues as her arousal built. Her thighs slithered together, opening and closing. She let her head fall against the back of the chair and couldn't resist turning it side to side—the sensation was so delicious, and cutting through the last of her inhibitions. She closed her eyes.

"Very nearly done," Serge said, his voice demonically smooth.

"Thank you," she muttered.

He chuckled. "You're lovely when you come undone."

Boone cleared his throat with a rough rasp.

"Right, boss. We're not supposed to make any sexual comments."

"I don't know how you can refrain," she bit out, gasping against the tightness centering in her vagina.

"Might be easier if you didn't make those little moans," he said.

"I'm not…" But she was. She let another claw its way from her throat. And then she couldn't hold still another moment. She began rocking in her chair, forward and back, the motions soothing because her vaginal lips rubbed on the fabric. "Oh God, I'll never be able to look you all in the eyes again."

A large hand lifted her hair and cupped the back of her neck, massaging it. By the direction of the fingers, not Boone's. Her eyes shot open and she turned to Boone, who watched her, his expression blank.

Bear's fingers deepened their caress.

Another hand, Boone's this time, slipped into the top of her blouse and cupped her bare breast. He tweaked her nipple.

With an indrawn breath, she glanced up from her chest to meet his steady gaze.

"We're done eating," he said, giving her a little nod.

Tilly kicked off her sandals under the table and curled her toes into the Persian carpet. Locked with Boone's gaze, watching his eyelids lower and his nostrils flare, she leaned into Bear's caress, widened her thighs and ground down into the chair, pressing her pussy hard, causing the quickening vibrations to rumble through her pussy to her bottom. She cried out, chest jerking forward, her pleasure spiraling inside her. She forgot to breathe. Dropping her hands to the chair's arms, she rocked and rocked until at last she exploded.

When she opened her eyes, Bear withdrew his hand from her neck.

Boone pushed back his chair and came close, kneeling beside her. He cupped her head and pressed her face against his shoulder. "You'll understand if I ask you all to leave now."

Chairs scraped. Dishes rattled. Footsteps padded away.

Boone kissed her hair and scooted back her chair. Then he lifted her and laid her on the table, notably free of dinnerware.

With her legs dangling over the edge, her skirt around her waist, she didn't glance around, not caring whether Manny was still there, dutifully cleaning the table. She watched, fixed on the sight of Boone's ruddy cheeks. His hands tended to unbuttoning his trousers and sliding down his zipper, then lowering his garment past his hips.

Now, her attention was fixed on his thick, straight cock.

He lifted her knees into the crooks of his elbows and nudged her sex.

"Remove the vibrator then guide me into you, sweetness."

She wondered if the men had fled to the room where the

security monitors were. Whether they were watching. But she didn't really care. If she were more truthful with herself, she hoped they watched. Because Boone, standing as he was, with his cock poised to plunge inside her, was the epitome of masculine strength and determination.

And, at least for this moment, he was hers.

She reached down with both hands, spread her lips and delved inside for the vibrator, which she tossed away. Then she lovingly gripped his thick, hot shaft. Without breaking his gaze, she placed him at her entrance, rubbing the tip of his penis in her wet folds to moisten it, and then fed him slowly inside her as he pushed forward. "I love the way you feel," she breathed. "I didn't think I could take you, you're so large. But when you thrust inside me, I feel powerful too."

Boone hefted her thighs higher, pulling her bottom off the table and straightening his back. "Punishment's over."

She gave him a coy smile. "Am I free to play?"

Gaze sparkling with heat, he nodded.

Reaching behind her neck, she released the fastening of her blouse, then pulled down the front to expose her breasts. "Are they watching?"

"Probably," he muttered, pulsing inside her in shallow, circular movements.

She affected a shocked expression with gaping mouth and widened eyes. "What, you didn't give *them* detailed instructions?"

"No time. I was winging it." His hips delivered a delicious swirl. "When I went to your cottage, I had already asked them to dinner, but wasn't sure how far I'd take this." He circled again.

Her breath hitched. "I get it now."

"What?"

"Why they call this screwing."

Boone pushed all the way inside her, then paused. "Shall I demonstrate banging?"

She giggled. "Only if it pleases you, sir."

He growled and juggled her thighs, snuggling his groin against hers. "Okay, sweet sub, show me again how you play with your clit."

The door whooshed closed.

"Did your server just leave?"

"Uh-huh. Quit stalling."

"But they'll see," she said with a little playful whine.

"You'll get used to that."

The thought that he might want them to continue their relationship thrilled her. She pouted her lips. "I suppose you'll have me parading nude around them before too long."

"Only if it brings you pleasure."

"I think I like pleasing you."

"Then I'll command you to strip. Maybe I'll eat you out on the table while they actually finish a meal."

His suggestion sounded so decadent, but not beyond her imagination. At least not now that he'd begun powering inside her. She'd do anything to make him this wild.

She sighed. "I like this system of punishment and reward."

"You still haven't given me what I asked, Tilly."

"Oh." She gave him an impish smile and licked two fingers, then reached down and pulled up the top of her folds, liking how stretched they felt with his cock filling her hungry passage. She toggled her clit, working slowly at first while he glided in and out, his movements steady and controlled, until she began to wriggle, because her clit was already hard, already distended, and her fingertips were flicking faster. "Sir?"

"Not until I say," he gritted out.

She liked the surly undertones, and liked the tension he displayed, his face darkening, his jaw and cheeks looking like carved granite.

Dropping her eyelids halfway, she continued to watch him as his gaze fell to her pussy and her quickening movements. Her clit was molten hot with friction, her vagina soaking wet and making moist sounds that would have made her cringe before she'd learned he liked her sopping wet—for him.

Boone's motions grew shorter, sharper, his arms extended at his sides, widening her thighs. His gaze was on his cock sliding in and out of her body, and she wished she could see it through his eyes, know what they looked like, coming together. But she felt every inch invading her. Felt her body stretching wide, his groin crashing against her, his deep, targeted thrusts cramming his thick cock inside as he pushed and pulled.

And she could think those raw anatomical names without cringing either, because he made this something more than sex. Becoming his plaything wasn't just about this glorious culmination. Wasn't something she could feel ashamed about coming to crave. It was about surrender—of herself, of her inhibitions.

Boone pounded harder, sweat dripping from his hair and streaking down his cheeks. His lips were pulling back from his teeth. "Now, Tilly."

"Jesus," she groaned, and pinched her clit, twisting it slightly and arching her back off the table. She let loose a shout, knowing his men could hear whether they had their ears pressed against the door or were watching through their monitors. The issue wasn't about her not caring. She was proud of this moment, of the overwhelming release, of her capitulation. In this moment, she didn't belong to herself, but to Boone, just as they did.

Boone gave a muffled shout, and the sound made her smile.

While he continued to pump inside her, spurts of hot cum filling her, she hugged her breasts and thrashed her head, panting so hard she felt light-headed.

When he slowed, she felt a moment's disappointment the moment was ending. Then Boone dropped her knees and bent over her, sliding his hands beneath her back and lifting her.

Bodies still connected, her thighs wrapping around his hips, he walked her to the door.

Wearily, she smiled, glad they weren't finished. Hoping they never would be.

Chapter Sixteen

Tilly awakened, disturbed by a sound she didn't recognize. Turning, she glanced behind her, but Boone wasn't in the bed at her side. She searched the dark room, then saw the curtain beside the French door flutter. The balcony door was open.

She slid from the bed, searched the shadows for something to wear, and grabbed the first thing she found. Boone's white dress shirt. She shrugged it on, breathing in his musk and spicy cologne, rolled up the sleeves to her wrists, and fastened a few buttons for modesty's sake before padding to the opened door.

Boone stood with his back to her, his hands clutching the porch rail. Moonlight shone on his bare shoulders.

A slight breeze ruffled her shirt, and she pulled it tighter around her as she stepped nearer. "Can't you sleep?" she asked, leaning her hips against the rail to look up into his face.

His features were drawn and hard, his jaw tense enough that a muscle rippled along the edge. "You should go back to bed."

He'd looked like this before. When he'd stood in front of the burning cabin. Tilly's chest fell as she let go of a sigh. "What's wrong, Boone?" she asked softly, although she was pretty certain about what haunted him, what haunted them both—although Boone wanted closure, to know for a certainty who had killed Celeste, and Tilly was fearful of that truth.

Another balcony door opened farther down, and Serge stepped outside. "Boss, you hearing bells again?"

Boone's head turned toward the sound of Serge's voice, but not far enough to meet his gaze. "Yeah, you go back to bed. It's nothing."

The way he said it, *it's nothing*, his voice so harsh the sound made her shiver, said something was sure bothering him.

Serge knew it too, giving her a worried glance but stepping back inside.

"Tell me about it, Boone," she whispered, although now she wished she'd stayed in bed. Anything to avoid this.

He didn't look at her, his eyes focused on the dark treetops across the way. "I hear bells, Tilly. I know they're not real. But I hear the tinkling of Celie's gold bracelet."

Tilly didn't breathe. She knew the sound as well. Thought about it now and then, when chimes tinkled in the distance.

"The sound comes and goes, like when she walked, her arms swinging at her side. It's barely there, but…" His gaze dropped to hers, dark eyes accusing. "I don't believe in ghosts, but she's fucking haunting me."

Tilly closed her eyes and dropped her head. She'd known the moment would come when he'd ask her what she knew. What she hadn't prepared for, what she'd never considered, was that she wanted to tell him. Her secret was eating her up inside. And he didn't deserve this.

As far as the law was concerned, Boone might be untouchable, but he'd never let it go, never rest. Celeste's death was a burden he'd never relinquish, not until he'd found the truth.

Her throat tightened and she drew a ragged breath, and then slowly raised her head, afraid to meet his gaze. But she knew she couldn't cower away from this. "I've been tryin' to figure this out for years. I have a folder of every newspaper clippin', of every family photo of her I could find. I remember her, Boone, clear as if it were yesterday. When my mother went to visit, I'd hang out in her room. We'd listen to music, talk about boys. She talked about you all the time." Tilly's eyes filled, but she blinked away her tears. "She said she was gonna marry you. That you just didn't know it yet."

Boone grunted and nodded his head. "Seemed preordained. She was the prettiest girl in these parts—"

"And you were the senator's son. Only, she had another boyfriend." Her gaze fell away. "She snuck around on you, at least once." He held so still, she wasn't sure if he'd known. "I saw her leave with Leon Fournier. He didn't park in front of her house, and I was out walkin' with Denny, my brother. Denny shook his head and said she was headin' to hell."

She closed her eyes, remembering the smarmy spring heat that had made her shirt stick to her skin, and Denny's hand sliding inside her grasp. "Mama was always sayin' Celeste was too pretty and too fast. Said it ruined her. That she'd earn herself a ticket straight to he—" She bit her lip, because judging Celeste didn't seem fair when she wasn't there to defend herself. "Denny liked Celeste. He sure didn't like you, but he knew enough to be polite. But he *really* didn't like Leon."

Tilly turned to stare over the balcony beneath her, anything not to have to meet Boone's hard gaze. "That day, when I saw them drive off together, Denny told me he'd seen them together before. That he'd followed them to where they went and took off their clothes." She laughed, but the sound was anything but funny. "He didn't know why they'd want to do that when mosquitoes were out. That's how I knew there was at least one more person who might want her dead."

Blood pounded in her ears. She glanced sideways at Boone, whose body stood taller and whose features had grown rigid. It made her nervous to continue, but she'd already said so much. "Made sense to me that the evidence went missin'. Couldn't have that mattress or the semen samples showin' the sheriff's son might somehow be involved."

"And you never said anything," he said, his voice dead calm.

"Who would I tell? Leon's daddy? Leon himself, once he took his daddy's place?" She shook her head. "It's Bayou Vert. You know better than anyone someone placed like that can get away with murder."

Boone's hands were fisted so tight, his biceps bulged. "Dammit, he might not have been tried, but I'd have known. Everyone would have known."

"But I didn't know. Not for sure." Her glance fell away again. "And then I found something…" Her stomach churned sickeningly, and she paused.

Boone gripped her arm and turned her to face him. "What did you find?" he asked in a scary calm voice.

"I have to show you." She shrugged, her lips trembling. "I want to explain. You don't know him…" Standing in his grip, she waited, hoping he wouldn't press her for more. Not yet.

His hand dropped. "Go get dressed, Tilly."

Her head shot up, eyes widening. "It's the middle of the night."

"This thing you're going to show me, do you have it in the cottage?"

She shook her head. "I buried it. We'd have to head into town."

"I'll wake Serge."

Tilly shivered. The thought of heading to the secluded spot in the dark, all of his men simmering with judgment, left her breathless. Again, she shook her head. "If we head into town in the dead of night with your security team, folks there will think you're launchin' some sort of invasion."

His jaw clenched, a ripple working along the edge. "I've waited fifteen years for something to shake loose," he said, his tone harsh and biting. His stare turned cold and hard. "I can't believe you kept this to yourself."

He considered her secret a betrayal, what she'd feared most. Tears welled again. "I had my reasons."

His head tilted, eyes narrowing as he stared. "Someone close to you, then. Someone you care about." His face turned to stone. "Your brother."

Panic clutched her chest and she shook her head. "It can't be," she said, then gasped, the sound more of a sob.

Boone ignored her distress, walked down to Serge's door, and rapped on the glass.

Serge opened a moment later. "I heard. Already have Bear bringing the car around front."

Boone stomped back and stepped past her, entering the bedroom.

Tilly eyed Serge, who shook his head, warning her to keep silent. She followed Boone inside, doing her best to stop the tears welling in her eyes from escaping.

He switched on the light and began picking up her clothes and throwing them onto the bed. "Get dressed," he ground out. "We go now."

Her steps leaden, she went to the bed and stripped off his shirt to dress in her rumpled clothing. Her hands shook as she pulled her skirt close. "I don't have any underwear."

"Check the wardrobe in the closet."

She found a small pile of lingerie, all her size, and pulled on a pair beneath her short skirt. Last night, she'd been nervous about exposing her body. Now she'd revealed something even more shameful. She'd been dead wrong. Cruel, perhaps. And he and everyone around him would know she'd let him down.

By his tone and his hard glares, she knew what she'd revealed had likely killed whatever had been growing between them. Her chest felt thick and sore. Nausea roiled in her belly. And her brother, Denny, was about to be pulled into the middle of this mess. She'd promised to protect him. And she'd failed. Her words had condemned her own brother.

"Tilly."

Before she glanced his way, she closed the drawer and straightened her shoulders. She lifted her chin and forced her expression into something she hoped didn't show her fear. Her eyes were dry, and they'd stay that way.

They left the room, Serge falling in behind them. Linc's door opened and another behind her, but she didn't glance back to see who'd joined them. His friends were gathering. They'd watch his back.

No mercy would be shown her. No matter how pleasant and easy they'd made last night's experience. Their blood bond with Boone kept them loyal.

Lights came on as they moved through the house. Although who was flipping switches, she couldn't tell. Not anyone with them, because their footsteps never paused. The air was eerily quiet, other than the heavy tread of their boots and her own jagged breaths.

Once in the garage, Boone turned to her. "We'll need a shovel?"

She nodded, her hands clasped into fists at her sides.

He lifted his chin to Jonesy, who slipped out a door, then returned moments later holding a short military entrenching tool. Where he'd had it stashed and why, she wasn't even sure, but the question floated through her mind. Maybe because she was in shock, her mind and body separating.

The Bentley's door opened, and Serge guided her into the back, taking a seat beside her. Boone sat in front beside Bear.

As far away from her as he could get.

She closed her eyes.

"Where are we going, Ms. Floret?" Bear asked, his tone no different than any other day. Deadly. Emotionless.

"Belle Tierre Road, just off of Main," she said, her voice a little hoarse because her throat was tight with tension.

The car reversed, another's engine started. Two cars left the property, heading to Bayou Vert.

Just four days. That's all the time that had elapsed since the moment she'd met Boone, all the time it had taken for everything to unravel. In the cold silence, she had time to think.

From the start, he'd played her. Recognized her weaknesses—her need for financial security to bring her brother home, her sexual inexperience. He'd used his considerable talent and expertise to seduce her.

Likely he'd done it for the very reasons he'd given her at the start. He needed her to smooth his entrance into this end of the parish. Romancing her assured her enthusiastic cooperation. The fact she'd held a vital key to his investigation was a bonus—one he'd ruthlessly exploit. Not like they'd actually been falling in love.

Only maybe she had been. Tilly stared out at the darkness and wondered where she'd be when the dust settled. Out of a job? Back to square one, but without a fallback, because Mae would never hire her back.

Could she have screwed things up any worse? Was she making him a villain in her mind so that she could bear the pain of the break? Get angry enough not to cry? She dared a glance at Boone. His profile limned in dashboard light looked unfamiliar. Harsh lines, thin lips. This was the man who negotiated with terrorists and drug cartels. She'd been playing with his doppelgänger.

Until they entered town, the silence remained unbroken. She scooted forward on her seat to direct Bear, resigned to helping rather than hindering at this point. The sooner this was over, the sooner she could hide herself away from everyone's condemnation.

"This is the turn," she said as Belle Tierre came into view.

Bear turned the car onto the narrow street, passing small square clapboard houses.

"It's on the right," she said, then indicated with her finger. "But park by the trees up ahead."

The car pulled quietly to the side of the narrow, pitted track. No shoulder on this road. Trees and thick brush crowded the edge of the pavement.

They exited the car, the three men holding flashlights. Boone handed one to her, not speaking. They waited until she got the hint that she should lead the way.

She followed the road to a culvert, then stepped off to the side, trying not to think about the night creatures around them, and watching the ground for snakes and gators. About fifteen feet off the road, she halted at the base of a tall oak, moss draping its branches. She shone the light upward, noted the carvings she and Denny had made when they were younger. Their initials, and their dog's.

Then she walked around the base to the far side and knelt to push away leaves and fallen dried moss to get to the snug corner in the exposed roots. "Dig here," she said, then pushed herself up and stepped away.

Jonesy dug into the soft dirt with his short shovel. He'd only turned two shovelfuls of ground when a metal clunk sounded. Tossing aside the tool, he went down on his knees and cleared the rest with his hands.

When he pulled the small tin from the hole, Tilly felt a little dizzy, swaying on her feet.

Lights shone on the tin. Jonesy pushed at the lid, opening it.

Denny's little bits glittered inside.

"Jesus. Fuck."

The voice was Boone's. He shouldered closer and knelt beside Jonesy, his hand shaking as he reached into the box and plucked the bracelet by its clasp to hold it up in the light. The little bells tinkled, not a clear, musical sound as in the past because they were encrusted with dirt and no longer shiny.

"There's dried blood on it," Boone said, staring across at her, his gaze hard and accusing.

Tilly's eyes filled, and she whimpered, swaying. Her knees crumpled, and she went down. Crouched in front of him, she had no defense.

"What is this box, Tilly?" Boone asked, his voice hoarse.

"You know," she rasped. "Denny's treasures. Bits he found and kept. His p-pirate's hoard."

"There's blood on it. She was wearing it when she was murdered."

She shook her head, then raised it, her eyes pleading. "Maybe he found it somewhere else."

Boone gave a curt shake of his own. "Well, you don't know that, do you? Didn't you ask him about it?"

"I couldn't." She knelt back and pushed a hand through her hair. "He tends to go on and on about things when they're on his mind. I couldn't ask and have him say anything to anyone else. He's my brother," she whispered over a clogged throat.

Boone dropped the chain into the pocket of his shirt, then handed her the tin box.

Pressing it against her chest, she dropped her head as tears streamed down her cheeks.

* * *

Boone stayed silent the whole way back to the estate. Excitement held his body rigid. The possibility that not all the blood would be Celeste's made his stomach knot. The moment they got back, he'd have Bear take it to a lab for testing. It didn't matter that even if they did find someone else's DNA on the bracelet after all this time, they still couldn't bring the killer to justice. But he'd know. And he'd make sure *everyone* fucking knew.

The blight on his reputation, on his soul, would be erased.

A soft sob coming from behind him interrupted his thoughts, and he glanced into the rearview mirror at Tilly.

He could understand why she'd never mentioned her brother's involvement. She loved him, but why not Leon? Had she been afraid that once she'd dredged up the past, new light would shine on all those surrounding Celeste?

Her face was white, her eyes large. She was afraid, and up until this moment, he'd been glad. His thirst for vengeance demanded someone pay, but looking at her tortured expression made his chest hurt.

They pulled in front of the Big House's porch steps. He and his men exited the car, but Tilly still sat frozen in the back. The fury that had fueled his actions bled away, replaced by a sharp ache in the center of his chest. Blowing out a breath, he opened her door and extended his hand.

She glanced at it but scooted across the seat without taking it. When she stood on the cobblestones, she turned and walked toward the path leading around the house. Toward the cottage. Motion-detecting lights he'd had installed the day before lit her way.

He strode after her. "No, you don't," he said, catching her arm and drawing her around.

She twisted her arm, trying to break his hold. "I'm tired."

"I don't want you anywhere near a phone," he said, refusing to let her go.

Eyes narrowed to slits, her head tilted high. "Am I your prisoner now?"

He tightened his grip. "Tilly, it doesn't have to be this way."

"What way is it, Boone?" she said, her voice shredding with tears. "You have what you wanted from me. If it doesn't give you all your answers, you'll move on to someone else who might." Mouth pressed into a tight line, she shrugged her arm again. "Let me go."

For a moment, Boone was confused by her anger. He knew he'd treated her harshly, but did she really think he'd only been using her to flush out the killer? Boone sighed. "I can't let you go."

She stopped struggling but kept her head down. A slight tremble shook her frame. "Look, I'm tired. Dirty. I need to be alone."

Boone took a deep breath, wanting more than anything to bring her close for a hug. He sensed she wouldn't accept it, that she was holding on to her composure by a thread. "I'm sorry," he said softly, "but you're staying with me."

Her head came up, a smile twisting her mouth. "Maybe you should just go and call Leon. Let him hold me in a cell while you two figure out who killed y'all's old girlfriend."

Boone's lips pressed together. He was at a loss for what to say. Wasn't even sure what the next steps should be. His mind was still reeling. "Tilly…" He tugged her closer.

Her steps were wooden, her face turning, her gaze not meeting his. Her expression was shattered. Vacant.

And he didn't like how that made him feel. Didn't like how he'd treated her since she'd dropped her little bomb. But from the moment she'd confessed her secret, his mind and body had been seized, his laser focus locked on his target. Her.

He wasn't proud of how he'd reacted, and maybe she'd never forgive him for what he was about to do with the knowledge she'd given him. But he never fought his instincts.

The impulse was there, despite what his head was telling him, what his thirst for payback demanded. He pulled her closer, not stopping until her chest met his.

Only when their bodies touched did he know what he needed. Tilly under him. As plain and simple as that: there'd be no easing the tension riding his body until he was deep inside her.

"Boone, don't," she said, tears thickening her voice.

"Look at me."

Keeping her face averted, she shook her head.

Boone crooked his finger and tipped her chin toward him until the lights shining from the porch gleamed on the tears still trailing down her cheeks.

The weight in his chest grew heavier. Boone stood for a moment, a chill of realization washing over his skin. There was something he wanted more than revenge. Something he didn't think he could live without. He wasn't going to put a name to the emotion welling up inside him. So again, he followed his gut. "I need you, Tilly. Don't give up on me just yet."

Chapter Seventeen

Tilly didn't know exactly how Boone had done it, but she was grateful just the same. When he'd asked her to trust him, something inside her had given. Tears had dried. She'd nodded, relieved he wasn't that stranger anymore: the one who'd frightened her before.

In his eyes, she saw the same confusion she felt deep inside. They should be enemies, standing on opposite sides, but both yearned to find a way to make this relationship work. For now, she'd trust he would find a way to make this right for both of them.

As natural as breathing, she'd let him lead her inside to his bedroom and strip her, raising her arms when he asked, stepping out of her clothing when the rest of it fell.

Clasping her hand, he'd led her to the bed and had her sit on the edge and watch as he undressed. She'd grown painfully aroused watching, admiring the body exercise and discipline had honed.

Then he'd bent and reached to her side, snagging a pillow and dropping it in front of where he stood.

Inside, she melted. Gratitude and some poignant, fragile emotion crept into her heart. Perhaps it was odd, but what he wanted didn't feel like a selfish act on his part. He was making himself vulnerable to her, offering her another "lesson," proving to her he wasn't ready to toss her to the curb. He needed her. With her gaze lowered, she slipped to the floor, knelt in the center of the pillow, and leaned toward his cock.

As she rubbed her cheek on him and breathed in his tangy scent, she acknowledged she'd needed this reminder of how different they were—in physical form, anyway. All his strength and power were reflected in this bold, thrusting part of his male body. Satin skin cloaking a hard-as-steel rod.

There was comfort to be found in that masculine strength. Comfort he gave effortlessly, or perhaps in spite of himself. He'd given her so many gifts of delight and fantasy, he'd taught her a little about herself that she hadn't been aware existed.

He'd asked for her trust. And she knew, deep inside, he wouldn't have offered it if he didn't already trust her. What to do with that trust—well, that was the big question. For now, she could return a little of what he'd given her. She'd give him submission...and pleasure.

She warmed her hands between her thighs while she nuzzled his sex, giving his cock occasional kisses as she rubbed against him like a kitten. When she was sure the chill that had kept her hands shaking earlier was gone, she slid her hands up his taut thighs, inching her fingers slowly toward his balls. Her heartbeat thudded in her chest, the anticipation driving her wild.

His feet scooted farther apart, and she smiled to herself. She cupped him in her palm and hefted, liking their weight and firmness inside his bare, velvety sac. When she leaned toward him, she heard the soft whoosh of an inhalation.

Boone might like to think he was in control, but right now he was open and vulnerable to her touch. It was a heady thought, but one that didn't last long. She opened her mouth and sucked first one, then both hard orbs inside.

She lovingly caressed them with her tongue, following their curves then gripping them both as she gently tugged. Following her instincts to explore, she learned what pleased him by the slight tremble of his thighs or the raspy catch of his breaths.

While his arousal steadily escalated, so did hers, causing her belly to tighten, her chest to rise and fall a little faster.

Fingers dug into her scalp and pulled, and she reluctantly released him, slicking her tongue upward, tracing the veins carved on the sides of his shaft, and then lapping widely down to begin the ascent again.

A chuckle rocked him, and she opened her eyes, gave him a wink, and then gripped his shaft in her hands and eased it downward so that she could capture the soft cushiony cap in her mouth. Although the head was wider than her tongue, she found it oddly pleasurable to swirl and swirl around it. Still exploring, she teethed the cap gently and chewed, not deep enough to hurt and only on the spongy surface. With a gentle pressure of her thumbs, she widened his eyelet hole and slid the tip of her tongue inside, rocking her head shallowly forward and back as she stabbed inside. Every action felt natural, easy. As she gave him pleasure, her own increased, spiraling inside her, warming her, drugging her. Only the slight pressure of his fingers guided her, and she learned another important lesson. As his hips pumped slowly forward and back, heat pulsed through her body, centering deep in her belly.

But he was tired of play, and gripped the back of her head, pulling up to force her higher and aiming her mouth at his cock.

Opening, she let him guide her, accepted the smooth glide of his sex as it stroked over her tongue. Lord, the taste of his skin and the milky drop of precum had her groaning, because the way he fucked her mouth was the way she wanted him to move inside her pussy. She groaned and opened wider. His grip loosened and she bobbed forward of her own accord, taking him deeper and deeper, suctioning around him, lavishly stroking the sides of his shaft with her tongue, her own growing desperation fueling her sensual movements.

His hands surrounded hers, still holding his shaft, and he squeezed around them, showing her how tightly he wanted her to hold him, and then guided her hands to move in a slightly twisting fashion up and down his shaft.

When she bobbed forward far enough the tip bumped the back of her throat, he cupped her head and gently pressed her deeper. "Swallow around me, Tilly. Give my cock a sexy kiss."

Although doubtful she could, she tried it. Her throat convulsed, closing and opening, and she understood what he'd meant when he'd called it a kiss.

"Loosen your jaw, let me stroke deeper, breathe through your nose."

Her heartbeat quickened, but she did as he asked, widening her jaw and accepting his slow, gentle thrust, letting him come deeper than she'd thought possible. She gagged a little but breathed deeply, forcing herself to relax as he thrust again and again.

But at last he pulled away. Harsh breaths lifted his chest. He tilted his head to the side. "How is it you've never learned to give a blow job?"

Heat filled her cheeks. "Was I that horrible?"

"You were perfect, but, sweetheart, other than soft fondling, you weren't familiar with much else. How can that be?"

She shrugged. "Sex before you was really pretty quick and rarely repeated." Because she'd been left feeling used, but she wasn't about to admit that. College boys were selfish.

"How many partners have you had?"

Her jaw dropped and her gaze skittered to the side. "That's not any of your business."

"Of course it is. How am I to know where you need instruction if I can't know what you've learned, or haven't, along the way?"

Irritation tightened her body. She frowned, crossing her arms over her chest. "Four. Sort of. One who liked to finger me, because he didn't consider it fucking and so he wouldn't go to hell. The other three came inside me. One actually seemed to care whether I came or not, although he only accomplished it once."

His head shook slowly side to side. "Just vaginal penetration?"

"What other kind is there?" she quipped, although she wasn't really that naïve.

Boone pressed his lips together. "Get onto the bed, sweetheart," he said, a little gravel coloring his tone.

She pushed off the pillow and crawled onto the mattress. When she would have rolled to her back, he held her hips still.

Her heart fluttered in her chest. So he'd take her from behind.

"Move forward."

At his command, she crawled to the center of the bed and glanced over her shoulder, watching as he walked on his knees until he was right behind her. At the sight of the stern set of his jaw, she felt a moment's misgiving that she was here, ready to surrender everything again. Boone was a large man, hard-bodied, capable of horrible violence. Once a SEAL, now he was her lover. And he'd already proven himself capable of giving a woman unbelievable, dazzling pleasure. He'd been gentle with her, even when he'd pushed her past her inhibitions. If she was nervous now, it was because she feared feeling too much for Boone Benoit.

His hands landed on her bottom, smoothed down to her thighs, then up again. His thumbs spread her vaginal lips.

Quickly, she faced forward, taking short breaths through pursed lips as he thrust fingers inside her, drawing down silky moisture. The waiting as he continued to stroke her moist flesh made her tremble.

Then his cock nudged into her opening.

Arousal hit and her pussy throbbed. Tilly gripped the sheets in her fists and went to her elbows, lifting her bottom higher, readying herself for his thrust.

But he didn't move. Her pussy clasped his cap, making a sound like a lush wet kiss, but still he didn't move. Instead, he bent and wrapped his arms around her middle and then leaned back, lifting her up.

Feeling awkward, she didn't know where to put her hands or how to move. She clutched her thighs, wishing he'd signal what he expected. "I'm sure this would be easier if you let me back down," she said, lifting her hands to caress his tensed forearms. Offering encouragement, when she wished she could think of how to tempt him to go a little faster.

"Easier?" His breath gusted warmly in her ear. His tongue slid around the outer curve, following it down to the lobe, where he nipped it.

Her skin heated and she tilted her head to the side. "Yes, easier. You could…push into me."

"Why not push you down onto me?"

Why was he talking? She needed him to move. "Wouldn't that be awkward? And why waste your strength, because you know you'd have to help me move."

"Not if you spread your thighs and straddled mine. You'd have leverage and I won't exhaust myself."

His breath was warm on her cheek, and there was a smile in his voice. Her mouth curved. As if sex would exhaust him—the man with a body honed for action.

"Trust me. I'll show you how this works."

She didn't appreciate the delay, not when he'd been right there anyway. But she clumsily moved, with his help, until she was positioned with her thighs wide, straddling him. His cock pulsed beneath her, the shaft riding her slit.

"Now see? Everything I want to touch is open to me." He demonstrated, molding her breasts, and then smoothing a hand down her stomach to cup her pussy. "Plus, I can see over your shoulder." He gripped a breast. "I like your pretty nipples, Tilly."

Tingles ran along her skin. She certainly liked the way he molded her with his palm. The pinch he delivered with his thumb and forefinger made her gasp. Below, she was stretched, her entrance open. Cool air wafted between her legs, teasing her hot flesh.

Again, Boone nipped her lobe. "Reach between your legs, baby. Guide me into you."

A slight tremor in her hands, she reached down, gripped his cock, and put the head at her opening.

Boone's sweet breath drifted past her cheek. He shifted beneath her and pushed inside her.

She realized quickly there was a problem with this position. "But…" She bit her lip.

"But what?"

"You can't…I need you deeper."

A chuckle rocked his chest against her back. "We have time, Tilly. The rest of the night."

"But…" She wanted to whine, but his fingers pinched her nipple and she took that as a sign he wouldn't appreciate any more complaints. Boone wanted what he wanted, and he'd make her wait, just because he liked to drive her crazy with desire.

Two fingers curved over her bottom lip, and he stuck them in her mouth. "Lick them."

She swiped them with her tongue, while she wriggled her hips a bit, trying to ease down an inch or so more.

His fingers dropped between her legs and smoothed over her clit. Nice. Her body melted against him. Her back rubbing against his chest. Maybe he didn't intend to get her off by fucking. His clever fingers could easily coax her into orgasm. She settled her shoulders against his chest and leaned as far into him as she could while he swirled on her clit. Each slow circle tightened her womb, tensed her thighs and belly.

One of his hands disappeared. When it returned, he held two clips on his open palm.

Once again, her pleasure was arrested. She stared at the devices. "What are those for?"

"For your nipples. Open the clamps and attach them to the tips."

A frown dug a line between her brows, and now she was glad he couldn't see her expression. She swiped one off his palm, aware he peered over her shoulder, and opened the clamp, slowly letting it close around a nipple. The rubber-cloaked pinchers weren't exactly comfortable, but they didn't sting either. She let out the breath she'd been holding. She could handle this.

"See the screw on the side?" he said, his voice deepening. "I want you to tighten it."

With her fingers, she held the clamp still and tightened the screw turn by turn. Blood pulsed in her breasts. When the device felt plenty snug to her, she reached for the other, but his hand shut. "Two more turns, Tilly."

"But it's already tight. Any tighter and it'll hurt."

"You can take it. Two turns."

How strange it felt for them both to watch so intently, their heads side by side, both staring down at the cinched nipple. Her fingers shook as she gave the screw two more turns. When she'd finished, her breasts were tight and hot, the one tip filling and distending. The sting was harsh, but oddly erotic.

She glanced sideways and bumped her cheek against his. "Good enough?" she whispered.

Without speaking, he opened his palm, and she took the other, attached it to her nipple, then turned the screw until the stinging pain matched the first nipple's.

Before she had a chance to draw a deep breath to recover her poise, Boone's hands cupped the undersides of her breasts, lifting them. "Do you like that?"

"I'm not sure," she murmured.

He touched the tips of her nipples, just a soft side-to-side toggle, and she hissed between her teeth. Now engorged, her nipples were growing more sensitive.

"Just something else to think about while I'm not fucking you the way you want."

The more he toggled, the more she liked the sting. However, she caught the edge of his not-so-subtle criticism in his wry tone. She snorted. "I wasn't complainin', honest."

"But you wanted to. That's okay." Hands clamped the notches of her hips, lifting her.

Her hands went to his forearms to balance herself. Her heart leapt, because she hoped now he'd give her the release she craved.

His beard rasping against her shoulder, Boone let her fall, and at the same time he pushed upward.

His cock was deeper, spreading her folds. Not as deep as she craved, but pleasant.

"Spread wider, Tilly."

"I'm not a gymnast," she muttered, but she leaned a little forward and forced her thighs wider.

With nothing to hold on to now, she relied on his strong grip balancing her, controlling her movements up and down. She sank blissfully deeper than before, her pussy growing juicier, coating Boone's dick, and making lush, wet sounds. Greedy now, she wanted more—more of his thick, long cock, a bite of pleasure to push her over the edge. She toggled her nipples, slid a finger into the tops of her folds. He might be enjoying it, but he was moving so slowly she knew he wasn't going to allow her to peak any time soon.

He dropped her one last time, then wound his arms around her belly. "Am I boring you?"

Because there was a hint of laughter in his voice, she didn't worry about any hurt feelings. She eased her fingers from her clit. "I'm not bored," she said, unable to mask the petulance in her voice, "but I am frustrated."

"Are you questioning my prowess?"

She turned slightly, eyeing his expression. Secretly thrilled he was teasing her—even if she was teetering on the edge and annoyed he'd stopped her cold once more. "Am I allowed to question?"

His face tautened, his brows lowered. "If your master doesn't please you, you have every right to let him know."

Master. A word that in any other context would have had her back stiffening in rejection, but here…with him…she could imagine bowing at his feet or leaping to serve or service him. A crook of his finger, when she was this tightly wound, could make her crawl. And her body tightened even more. She nibbled her lip. "Is this some sort of punishment, Boone?"

The edges of his jaw and cheeks hardened. "Do you deserve punishment, Tilly?"

With a slow movement, she nodded, knowing she'd reminded him of everything she'd wanted him to forget while they were together like this. More than anything, she wanted the world and all their worries to recede, for at least as long as it might take for them to find pleasure in each other's arms.

"Well, this isn't punishment," he said, his voice even. "I actually intend to pleasure you. Because we both need it. And after what you told me about your previous lovers—"

Her body tensed. "I wouldn't exactly call them that. They were hookups. I know that makes me sound really cheap, but until I bought my first vibrator, I thought I needed them."

A finger pressed against her lips. "I wanted you aroused, but also frustrated."

With her mouth, she pushed his finger away. "And that's not punishment?"

Two fingers pinched her lips together.

Relief that he could let go of that little flare of anger again to tease her, and so quickly, kept her still.

"Shush. I wanted you pliable."

She couldn't help it; she bristled at the word. Wasn't she already? Hadn't she done everything he'd ever asked of her? She waited until he released her, then couldn't resist asking, "Why's that?"

His chest tightened against her back. Hands glided over her belly to the undersides of her breasts. "Because I'm going to introduce you to another form of penetration."

At that one word, a picture flashed into her mind. Tilly swallowed, shock widening her eyes, but liquid oozed from inside her. A slick of heat that quickened as her pussy clenched around him. She cupped the backs of his hands and gave them a squeeze. "Oh," she said in a small voice. "If what I'm thinking is what you're going to do, can I say I think it's really, really nasty?"

His cheek rubbed the side of hers, the bristles of his beard chafing deliciously. "Do we need to institute the rules again?"

"Only if you want to," she muttered.

"Do you *need* them, sweetheart?"

With her pussy clamping hard, and her nipples tingling, she couldn't suppress the quiver that shook her body at the sexy rumble of his voice. "I think I might," she whispered.

"Then no more speaking—unless I ask you a question. Do you understand?"

"Yes, sir."

He leaned away from her, removing his delicious heat. She heard the silky slide of fabric and then he straightened.

A purple scarf entered her vision. "Close your eyes."

He was blindfolding her. Intrigued, she complied, waiting patiently while he tied it around her head.

"Can you see anything?"

"No, sir," she said, her breaths shortening as she grew more excited. Without sight, his voice and hands would be her only anchor. She felt as though she'd relinquished power, placed her trust more fully in his hands, which was silly because she knew all she had to do was reach up and shift the scarf to take a peek. Something her curiosity wouldn't allow, not now. What was he up to?

"Good. Now, I want you on your hands and knees again, your ass raised for me. Do it now."

Although she cringed inside, at the evenness of his voice and for her modesty's sake, she leaned forward, bending at the waist. She caught her fall with her hands and crawled off his cock and lap. She halted in what she hoped was the middle of the bed and held still.

The mattress dipped and rose. His footsteps padded away, not far. To the bedside table. A drawer slid open. Something rattled, and then he was back, his weight once again shifting the mattress. A warm hand landed on her bottom. Fingers spread her cheeks. Although she tightened her ass in rejection, her pussy moistened. Good Lord, she hoped he'd be quick about whatever he was going to do, because once again, he'd embarrassed her.

Something cold touched her back entrance and she sucked in a breath.

"Just lubricant, sweetheart. And this is only an introduction, so don't worry I'll go farther than you're comfortable with."

Only because she was following rules did she resist a nervous quip. There wasn't any part of this forbidden act that was *comfortable.*

A firm finger rubbed the gel around and around her sensitive orifice. Oddly sensual, given she'd never understood the appeal. But something inside her told her Boone did. And she trusted he knew better after scores and scores of size twos. So she held silent and still, allowing herself to relax enough to enjoy the soft circling motions.

Fingers prodded her pussy. Two slid inside, twisting as they sank.

Her breath left in a whoosh. As his fingers penetrated deeper and deeper, she relaxed, her inhalations slowing, her chest expanding. Ripples of pleasure teased along her inner channel.

Until a fingertip pressed against her anus, and she couldn't help that her muscles contracted, trying to prevent his entry.

"You have to keep breathing, Tilly. Take a couple deep ones. Relax."

Breathe? Relax? Was he fucking kidding? But all she said was, "Yes, sir." Dragging deeper breaths through her pursed lips, she willed the tiny muscles to ease.

The thick digit entered her. Not very far, but the intrusion caused her body to shudder and her pussy to clamp tightly around his plunging fingers. Pleasure and unease blended, shredding her breaths, and soon, she didn't care which feeling eclipsed, because her stinging breasts swayed beneath her as her body moved forward and back, distracting her, and soon she was pushing backward, silently begging to be filled. She dropped her chest to the comforter and rubbed the exposed tips against the cool cotton for relief.

The finger in her ass pulled out, then sank again, twisting inside, this time deeper, causing her tissues to burn, but not in an unpleasant way. Startling. Perhaps even delicious, if she weren't so embarrassed.

His finger plunged and held. The ones curled into her pussy withdrew. Then the fat head of his cock pressed against her entrance and slowly slid inside.

Tilly gave a desperate groan. Everything clamped down— the mouth of her vagina, her tiny asshole. She pressed her face against the bedding, loving everything he was doing, but so shy she didn't know how she'd ever look him in the eyes again.

"Up on your arms, baby."

Her body stilled and she shook her head.

Finger and cock withdrew.

And she knew, her refusal had consequences because they

were still playing. Something she'd forgotten while she'd been so engrossed in the turmoil swirling inside her.

Disappointed in herself, she lowered her bottom and curled on her side to face him. When the weight on the mattress shifted, lightening, she worried that she'd displeased him even more than she realized. And why had she refused him? Something so simple. The fact her arms were shaking was hardly excuse enough. But she'd wanted to resist something, anything after she'd allowed him the dirtiest of intimacies, just to demonstrate a little free will and hold on to her pride.

Blindfolded and lying nude in the center of a sumptuous bed, waiting for a billionaire player wasn't something she'd ever prepared for. The fact she'd done her best to remain unimpressed with the trappings Boone brought had been a major feat, although she really hadn't had to try that hard. Since the beginning, he'd purposefully kept her on shaky ground. Too off-kilter to regroup.

Which was exactly where she was now, only the feeling was amplified by the fact she couldn't see him.

She followed sounds as he moved around the bedroom. The opening of a door, but not his bedroom door. The bathroom perhaps? Drawers slid open then closed.

"I'm a patient man," Boone said.

His voice was close and she jerked because she hadn't realized he'd returned. Had he come on tiptoe deliberately? The thought almost made her smile. Almost, but then she thought about what he'd said.

Was he out of patience? What might the consequences be? He'd been firm about the fact he wasn't letting her go, but would he care less? Would his desire for her diminish if she didn't give him exactly what he wanted?

Part of her hated how much that thought disturbed her, because it meant she really was falling hard for this man, and she couldn't protect herself from the hurt that would surely come when their affair ended. Already, the thought pressed against her chest, making it hard to breathe.

A hand smoothed over her shoulder and down her arm. A finger gently rubbed a swollen nipple. Small caresses, but enough—her thoughts stopped whirling.

"I think," Boone said softly, "and you're free to disagree, that you defy me for the express purpose of earning punishment."

Good Lord, was she that transparent? She shook her head, defiance once again swelling inside her. "That wasn't what I was thinking at all."

"Really? Then what did go through your mind?"

She sniffed. "That my arms were shaking."

"And that's all?"

Tilly didn't want to go *there*, but she sensed Boone wouldn't let her shy away from the truth. She turned her head, pressing her cheek into the mattress, wishing he didn't have a full view of her expression. "After what you did...what I'd allowed you to do, I wanted..."

"To take back a little control?"

Lord, she hated the fact he knew her better than she did. "Yes," she said in a small voice.

His hand glided up, stopping to cup her cheek. "Tilly, I don't want you to act against your nature or your instincts, ever. But will you agree, that sometimes, you don't act in your own best interests? That you make things harder on yourself?"

Was he thinking about the box or her refusal? She didn't know how to answer. Inside, she felt as shaky as her arms had. "I think...right now, I'm deserving of punishment."

He chuckled. "But you didn't answer my question."

"I don't know how, sir."

"I'll show you the answer you're seeking, sweet little sub. Trust me a little longer?"

She nodded. But only because he was using the voice again. The way he'd said *sweet little sub* in his dark, rumbling voice felt like a caress. Impossible to resist.

"Since your arms are so weakened," he said, his tone wry, "I want you draped over the edge of the mattress, feet on the floor, your ass pointed toward me."

Did he have a thing for asses? What about her pussy? The part of her that was swollen and wet and aching to be filled? But she didn't dare hesitate for more than a second, because she was done with introspection and needful of what she knew he would give her in the end. She just had to be strong enough to let him mold her however he wanted, and he'd reward her. So she slid backward toward the edge of the mattress, and then lay facedown, her hips bent over the edge, her ass pointing toward him, her toes touching the floor.

"Since you're so feeble, I'm using something to hold your legs spread. I don't want you exerting yourself."

"My legs are fine," she blurted, suddenly breathless because the humor in his voice held a bite. He was planning something, preparing to surprise her—no doubt, to push her further than he already had. She drew a deep breath and waited.

"This isn't for you, Tilly. It's something I want. Will you tell me no?"

She bit her lip, but then shook her head. She'd do whatever he asked, and not just for the reward at the end, but to prove to him she was no wilting lily. "No, sir."

"That's better." Then he was behind her. A hand patted her

rump, then smoothed down her inner thigh. Something was wrapped around her thigh, just above her knee. A band? She heard the metallic clink of a buckle as it tightened. He moved to her other thigh and fastened another band. Pushing apart her legs, he attached something else. Only when he moved away and she tried to close her legs did she understand its purpose. Her legs were held spread apart. Impossible for her to close. Now she lay, clutching the sheets, her feet completely off the ground and her most intimate bits vulnerable.

This time, there was no embarrassment warming her cheeks. Excitement heightened the tension in her body.

"Can't have you sliding off the bed when those weak hands let go of the sheets."

She heard him circle. Heard two somethings drop on the mattress beside her shoulders. Tempted to reach out a hand and touch, she didn't have to bother. He gripped her wrist and wrapped it, closing it with a scratchy Velcro fastening. He repeated the action, leaving both hands bound. Not until he pulled and she was gently forced to stretch out her arms did she figure out he'd somehow tied her to the bed.

Her chest tightened. Tilly wasn't sure she liked this. He could do anything he pleased. Or nothing at all. Her helplessness caused her a moment's panic, but then she reminded herself, this was Boone. He'd promised he wouldn't ask more of her than she could give. She took deep, calming breaths and relaxed into the restraints.

He came around the bed and patted her bottom again. "Very nice. Just one thing missing." He climbed onto the bed, straddling her waist but not dropping down his weight, and slid his hands around her face. "Open your mouth. I'm going to slip something inside. It's called a ball gag. And at first, it's not very comfortable. Don't fight it. Relax your jaws, Tilly. Don't hold them wide. Let the ball do the work."

Alarm shot through her. "Why do I need a gag?"

"Tilly, I know you, sweetheart. You'll try to protest what I do next. You'll beg me for release. Maybe even curse and rail, but only for your pride's sake. Let me set you free."

Heart pounding, she tensed her arms and tried to shake loose the bonds on her wrist. "Boone, this is a little—"

"Scary?" His hands massaged her bottom, thumbs digging into the small of her back. "Baby, this is just the beginning. I'll admit, I'm chafing at the bit to push you along. I shouldn't be this eager. I could slow down…"

The soothing motions relaxed her, and she slumped on the bed. The way he talked, he intended this to be a long exploration. Like maybe he wanted her around for a while. When his hands slid beneath her and massaged her breasts, she knew she wanted to experience everything with him. She gave a little moan and tightened her breasts, all the movement she could manage to show him how much she loved the way his hands gently cradled her. She hadn't thought about the future. But now that he'd put the idea in her mind, she wanted to be along for that long ride.

Tilly turned her head. "This all so new, Boone," she whispered, ready at last to accept his lead. "I'm not sure what's expected."

He leaned over her, kissing her cheek. "You don't have to think. I'll do that for you."

"That sounds a little arrogant." She wrinkled her nose. "Like I'm clay for you to mold. Like I shouldn't have my own expectations."

He bit her earlobe. "Try me, sweetheart. Let me guide you. After we play, we'll review."

"Now you sound like a coach for a football team."

"I *am* a coach." He leaned away and his hand caressed her lower back. "But I'm also your lover. And I'm the one with experience."

Tilly released a deep breath. "This is pleasurable for you? Teaching a newbie, know-nothing?"

"More than you can understand."

She girded herself to ask the question she hoped wouldn't make her sound too insecure. But he was so much more experienced than her. "And if I disappoint you?" She held her breath.

A kiss landed on top of her spine. "You can't. The fact you've let me take you this far in so little time... It's what tells me you're ready for more."

She released the breath, somehow reassured by his confidence in her. "What are you going to do?"

"You don't want to be surprised?" he asked, that smile back in his voice.

"I'd rather be prepared," she muttered softly.

Boone chuckled and then smoothed his large hard palm over her ass. His hand stopped and squeezed. "Baby, I'm going to flog you."

Chapter Eighteen

She went rigid, but not from dismay. She remembered how he'd gently stroked her with a flogger when she'd been bent over his desk. How the lashes had warmed her bottom, providing a surprisingly sensual pleasure.

"Tilly, nothing painful, I swear, but a little harder than what I gave you before," he said softly. "The first slaps of leather will surprise you. Once you're past that, relax. Enjoy."

"And after that?" she asked, hoping he'd at last take her. She didn't want to seem impatient, but her body was already wildly aroused.

"I might use my hand to spank your pussy," he said, his voice deepening into a gravelly rumble.

She let out a surprised laugh. "Seriously?"

"You'll be hot and moist. Your folds engorged. The slaps will feel sexy. Push you higher."

"But I'm already hot and...wet." She squirmed, her thighs tensing.

"See? Just talking about it excites you."

She shook her head, but then said, "All right," letting her

reluctance bleed into her voice, a subtle resistance he would note. "We'll do this. But, Boone…"

"Yes, sweetheart?"

"If I don't like it…?"

"Don't you mean if you get scared?"

He moved off her to the side, and immediately, she missed his weight.

His teeth nipped her ass. "You won't. But you also won't be able to tell me. I'll be watching you for signs. If you're too tense, I'll know to stop. While I'm stroking you, sweetheart, be thinking of a safe word for those times you can speak. Something not in your usual vocabulary, so I'll know you didn't accidentally use it."

A safe word. Funny, she didn't think she'd need one. She couldn't imagine him ever doing something so extreme she'd need one. He might embarrass the hell out of her, but she did trust him to know how much she could take. For such a strong, dangerous man, he was gentle with her. Controlled. Questions answered to her satisfaction, she opened her mouth.

Boone slid a hard knobby ball inside, pushing it against her tongue. A strap was fastened around the back of her head.

For a moment, she panicked, unable to breathe.

"Through your nostrils. Take a deep breath."

Quivering, she did as he instructed and instantly calmed.

"Good girl. Another." And then he left the bed.

A few moments later, something soft glided along her back and her buttocks, strands of something. The flogger. He was introducing the implement to her. Letting her know he was about to begin, giving her a feel for the material so she'd know that what he'd promised, that this would be another gentle introduction, was true. The strands were soft and pliable, although not as velvety as the last, sliding over her, a caress that made her skin retract in goose bumps. The moment the strands lifted, she held her breath.

The first stroke felt like the brush of a palm frond. But she didn't have time to consider how disappointingly soft it really was, because another stroke landed, coming from the opposite direction. He laid the flanges on her skin, swiping side to side, entering a rhythm that drew not a single moment of anxiety, because the strokes, while warming her skin, also soothed.

Light swats. Targeted swats, she realized when each lash landed in a different place. High on the left buttock, high on the right. Lower, and then lower still, until she wriggled because now, she hoped a flange might touch her sex.

But he passed her sex, stroking the creases between buttocks and thighs, the backs of her thighs, the tender interiors...

Tilly floated, her body warm and open. Her mind releasing all her worries, all her fears. For long moments, she forgot the man behind her, concentrating solely on the friction warming her bottom.

And then the strokes grew harder, a little sharper. She could hear the change in the sounds—no longer a soft whoosh, but a more insistent thwack. The first jarred. The second nearly stung. She held her breath, wondering if she could take this for long. Then the repetition of the motions lulled her again.

Only this time, surprisingly, the soft bites pulled at her core. Liquid filtered down her channel, leaking down one thigh. Her pussy pulsed, just loud enough she heard the juicy sound.

Her own sounds aroused her. With her mouth stuffed, hard plastic muffling her voice, every murmur sounded like a guttural whimper. Slightly animalistic.

Whimpers that came more quickly the hotter her bottom grew.

A soft knock sounded at the door. She heard it but couldn't muster any concern.

That is, not until the slapping leather halted.

Rousing, she lifted her head and heard Boone pad to the door. When the door lock snicked, she jerked. *No, he had not!*

"I brought what you texted, Boone."

The voice was Serge's, and he was stepping inside the room.

Tilly made a squeal behind her gag, but the guys didn't seem to notice.

"Heard from Alejandro," Serge murmured as he drew closer. "The trade's going down in two days."

Boone said something, but she couldn't hear what over the pounding in her ears.

A hand patted her rump.

Was it Boone's? Why wasn't she more shocked at the possibility it wasn't?

Every sense alert, she startled when the mattress dipped.

"Boone asked me here, Tilly," Serge said from right next to her. A hand smoothed over her back, down to the small dip and over her rump. "He thinks it's better to acclimate you with his best friends now than to just thrust you into the life at a more public outing. He thinks you're ready." He tucked her hair behind her ear and tugged her lobe. "Remember the welcome dinner? Remember how you spread your legs and let us all watch you come apart? That didn't feel dirty, did it? And we haven't embarrassed you with reminders since. This is for you. Not Boone. Whatever he said. When one of us is here, we'll watch out for your well-being and satisfaction. Do you understand?"

She didn't, not really, but she nodded anyway. Questions screamed in her mind. Her throat tightened. Was Boone going to let Serge do something intimate? Would he let him fuck her?

For just a moment, she worried she was just a toy to be passed among his men, and the thought made her tense.

"Relax, sweetheart. We won't fuck, Tilly," he whispered near her ear. "You're Boone's. That's something special between you and him. I won't even stay that long. But I have a gift for you. A set of anal plugs in graduated sizes. Something that helps prepare your pretty ass for use. I'll start with the smallest. We'll work our way up. Start slow. Keep one in for an hour a couple of times a day. And there's a cleanser under the sink for washing them when they're removed. Understand?"

Understand? Sweet fuck. Tilly's mind filled with images.

Although she'd felt the scratch of his shirt when he'd leaned near, she imagined him nude, from his burly, muscular chest to his toes. Of Boone hovering nearby, his gaze raking her body, spread for his enjoyment, her bottom red, her sex engorged. Why didn't that picture send her into paroxysms of humiliation?

The answer was simple. Boone wanted this. He believed she'd derive pleasure from it. If only she'd allow herself to. However foreign this was from anything she'd ever dreamed might happen to her, she had to trust he knew her better than she did herself. He'd been right about so much already.

Serge moved, and the bed rose. Then his hands, a little cooler than Boone's, smoothed over her bottom. He parted her cheeks. A finger glided through her crease, rubbing even cooler gel into her asshole. A moment later, something pressed against her puckered hole.

Behind her blindfold, she clenched her eyes tight and moaned with embarrassment.

A hand petted her hair. Boone's. "Breathe, baby. Serge will be gentle."

With her breaths coming noisily through her nostrils, she

inhaled, slowing her breaths, deepening them until at last she released a little tension.

Serge slid the lubed plug inside. It was narrow, nothing to worry about, not even as large as the circumference of Boone's finger, but as it sank deeper the gadget swelled.

"It widens and then narrows again," Serge said.

Maybe because she'd tightened in rejection.

"You don't have to clench around it to hold it inside."

She rolled her closed eyes. That wasn't why she'd clenched. Having Boone prod her ass was one thing. Having another man do the same, someone she had no intentions of being intimate with, was a little too much to bear without puckering up.

"Easy there," he said, patting her ass like he might a horse's.

But the pats against her fiery skin worked, reminding her of the lassitude Boone had created with his gentle strokes.

The plug eased inside, at last narrowing, and lodged. His hand drew away.

"I'll put the box of plugs under your sink. Later, Boone."

She heard him leave, and then sank against the bed, groaning again. Her shoulders ached because she'd been unconsciously fighting the ropes while Serge had been there. Her thighs throbbed from pressing inward against the bar spreading her thighs.

Tilly's mind was awash with everything that had happened. She hoped with all her might there would be no more "surprises." She thought maybe she'd had enough. Her mind drifted for a moment, thinking ahead to the pleasures Boone would introduce her to.

Barataria. That would be her word. The name of the bay that held the bayou captive in a storm.

Not something she'd ever think accidentally during one of

Boone's sexy sessions. She whimpered and pressed her forehead into the mattress.

The ropes tightening her arms eased. Hands turned her shoulders and the clamps were released from her breasts.

As blood rushed into the tips, she cried out. A mouth covered one breast and a hand massaged the other. The sting lessened, soothed away by Boone's tender actions. Then he walked around the bed, loosening the straps above her knees.

The moment she was freed, she pressed her thighs together, but her pussy felt too puffy, and she opened them again, just not as wide.

Hands gripped her waist and pushed her to the center of the bed, following her there. Fingers slid under her head and unlatched the strap holding the gag in place.

She widened her jaw and spat it out, and then reached up and shoved away the blindfold. Blinking against the light, she swung her gaze to Boone, who knelt beside her.

His expression was neutral, but his ice-blue eyes glittered darkly.

She couldn't read his expression, but she knew he waited for her response.

"You let him touch me," she whispered. A complaint, but she'd earned the right to utter it.

His head canted, his gaze studying her. "Did it revolt or please you?"

Tilly lowered her brows. "Can I put a check beside both?"

"What put you off?"

Swallowing hard, she glanced away, afraid to reveal her insecurity. "I know I'm just a novelty, but—"

"Wait right there," he said, his tone lowering. "Do you think I don't respect you, that I was passing you around to a friend for kicks?"

Her chin jutted. "What am I supposed to think?" she said, her eyes tearing up, because the answer was important—would determine how much more of her heart she'd invest in this curious relationship.

A fingertip slid along the side of her cheek. "Tilly, it's true. We've shared women. Women who like to play. But that wasn't what this was about."

Even though she felt painfully exposed, she turned her face toward him and let him see her emotions. "Please explain it to me, because right now, I'm feeling…I don't know….naked." She paused to swallow and wet her dry mouth. "He saw me like that. Hell, they all saw me come. I spread my legs at dinner, wet a chair, and they all saw me do it. And I was all right with that. And I accepted what Serge did, even felt a little…" She clamped her mouth shut.

"Pleasure? And now you're on overload?" The gleam in his eyes darkened, and he reached up for a pillow, which he put beneath his head, and then he signaled for her to come to him by opening his arms.

Not for a second did she consider refusing. After everything, she needed reassurance she meant enough to him that he'd want to comfort her. When she was snuggled against his warm skin, his hand stroking her back, her confidence seeped back.

Reflecting, she realized that Boone had soothed her every step of the way. He'd guided her, reading her body and looking past the things she'd said to find what she really needed.

There'd been pleasure, so much she was truly on sensory overload, but there'd also been something awakening inside her. Some secret part of her, deep inside, that reveled in the feelings he'd drawn from her and betrayed by every embarrassed whimper, every shocked gasp.

For Boone to have the patience to draw those feelings to the surface had to mean something.

Soft glides of his hand soothed up and down her back. Boone blew out a breath. "I don't know why I am the way I am. I was raised pretty much like you. Mom and Dad pretended to be faithful while they both chased their pleasure elsewhere. Dad took me to a whore for my twelfth birthday so I could become a man."

Tilly snorted. "I wasn't raised anything like you."

Boone grunted. "No, I guess not. Your dad didn't bother keeping up the appearance. He ran off with his whore and left your mother to raise his kids."

The truth stung, but he'd nailed it. She didn't bother arguing. Instead, she rubbed her cheek over his heart, liking the way the beat thudded in her ear. Strong and steady.

"We're a pair, Tilly. Given how we were both raised, you'll understand if I didn't see a whole lot of value in doing things the expected way." His hand smoothed down her back and cupped her bottom. "I also discovered pretty early on that I like to control my partner. Celie taught me that."

She lifted her head, afraid to hear more, but needing to. Letting him know by her silence that she was ready.

His expression was bleak. "She liked me to tie her up and tease her 'til she came. She also liked a heavy hand on her bottom."

His hand rubbed her bottom in soft caresses. Tilly wondered whether he was even aware, because the motion was slow, and his hand paused now and then.

"I liked giving it to her that way." He swallowed, his gaze flicked to her face and then focused on the far wall. "Once she was gone, I drifted into the BDSM scene. Tried the clubs. Every one of my guys, by their own preference, is in that lifestyle too.

But we have rules we abide by. We never infringe on another's woman. Never play where we're not invited."

His hand left her bottom. Fingers combed through her hair then tugged to center her face over his.

Escaping his steady gaze was impossible. His face was more open than she'd ever seen it. Somehow younger. Maybe it was opening to her, letting her see the turmoil inside him.

She touched his cheek, encouraging him to continue.

He turned his head and gave her palm a kiss, then cupped her hand against his cheek. "The dinner party was a revelation, Tilly. If you'd shied even the littlest bit, I wouldn't have taken it so far. But you blossomed. Everyone could see you're meant for me. For this."

A thrill ran through her at his praise. Tilly met his somber gaze. "I don't want to be a plaything, Boone. A toy you set aside when you get bored."

He gave a short, sharp shake of his head. "Won't ever happen," he said, his voice gruff.

"But what if I don't like everything you do?"

His mouth curved slightly. "We'll find things that give us both pleasure, and that's the point. Not everyone shares the same tastes. But just because we're different doesn't mean I'll go looking for someone else who'll give me that one thing you won't. You'll give me everything I *need*. I promise I'll be more than satisfied."

She warmed to his promise. Something inside her gave way. She'd stop worrying about where they were going, and let him take the lead. Because he needed that from her. But for now, she'd had enough of deep conversation. While her chest was still knotted from everything she'd said, she pouted her lips, wanting to make him smile. "I can't believe you let him see me that way."

Boone arched a brow. "Do you know what it does to me? And

how much he enjoyed that? You spread and tied, your sweet ass pink and hot? It's a glorious thing for men like us."

She shook her head. "I don't understand you. You turn propriety on its head and make it sound so natural." And *feel* as natural as breathing.

"Because it is." His hand sifted through her hair, then curved to cup the back of her head. "And you feel it too. You haven't gone running. You're right here in my arms. Letting me comfort you after I pushed. This is how it works."

She let her gaze drop, watched the steady rise and fall of his chest as he waited again for her response. From under her eyelashes, she glanced at him. "Was that the whole lesson?"

A smile stretched across his face. "Lessons are over for now. Do you need to come?"

The knot loosened. She spread her legs over his hips and bore down on the thick ridge trapped between their bodies. "Feel how wet I am? How hot?" She pointed a finger and tapped his chest accusingly. "You left me like that."

"Is this you complaining to your Dom?"

"I'm complaining to the man who owns my pleasure."

Boone sucked in a deep breath, his eyelids dipping as he scanned her face, gaze settling on her mouth. The hands surrounding her head pulled, bringing her down.

She tilted her head a second before their lips touched, loving the soft pressure of his firm lips, the slight suction that pulled her closer still.

"Take me, Tilly," he whispered against her mouth. "Take your pleasure. However you want. Your reward."

"I don't want to take you, Boone." She pressed a kiss against his bristly cheek. "I don't want to be in control. I want to be completely in your thrall."

A growl rumbled from his throat and he let go of her head. Arms encircled her body and he rolled, taking her underneath him.

Tilly let her hands fall beside her head on the pillow, staring upward, telling him silently she was his. However he wished.

He came up on an elbow and leaned away to rake her body with a hot gaze. "How's your ass feel?"

She wrinkled her nose. "It burns."

"Mind leaving the plug in a little longer?"

"You're the expert here. If you think I should…"

"You'll like the sensation. The extra pressure. But don't come—"

"Until you say so. Got it." She grinned.

Boone shook his head, the corners of his mouth beginning to curl. "I like you, Tilly Floret."

Warmth spread through her chest. "I like you too, Boone Benoit," she said, her voice as smooth as honey.

He pushed up on his arms, then crawled down her body. The moment his lips latched onto a nipple, she closed her eyes, expressing her joy in a soft sigh as he gently sucked the turgid tip. Fully engorged, they were sensitive to every pull and curl of his tongue. Her legs moved restlessly, trapped beneath his body. But he took his time, treating each nipple with lavish affection.

And then he moved lower.

Tilly cupped her breasts and warmed them with her hands while he settled between her legs. Fingers traced the length of her slit. Hands slipped beneath her and cupped her bottom, raising her to his mouth.

When his tongue slid between her folds, she moaned and closed her thighs around his head, holding him there.

With every swipe of his tongue along her smooth labia, she lifted her hips higher, tilting to give him access to her depths.

Fingers pushed inside, twisting inward, rubbing toward the front of her channel until he found the sensitive place that made her body tremble.

He rubbed and swirled while his mouth closed around her hooded clit.

Tilly mewled, then reached down to twine her fingers in his short hair. She dug into his scalp and rolled her hips, the movements instinctive. Her pleasure rose; her sighs deepened.

Boone drew away and knelt between her thighs. "Turn around, baby. I want you on your knees. Your ass in my face."

For once, she didn't mind his crude words, rolling, then getting onto her hands and knees, letting him guide her into position with her chest lowered and her rump high.

Again, fingers traced her slit, parted her, and then the round, wide knob of his cock pushed against her entrance.

On her elbows, she clutched the bedding, her body growing tense as he eased inside her. So much of him, so thick and hot. He crowded her walls, but pulled back, then pushed again. His girth stretched her tender tissues, making her ass tighten around the plug lodged inside. The burning was more intense now, but not intolerable.

Moisture flooded her channel as he eased his way inside. He churned his hips in short, measured bursts, taking her an inch at a time until he was seated deep inside. Holding still, he shifted behind her, his body folding over hers, his hand reaching around, sliding between her legs.

She loved the heat of him pressing against her back and bottom, the thickness lodged inside her. She was surrounded, connected. His.

Forking his fingers, he pulled up her stretched labia, exposing her clit to the cooler air.

Tilly hissed between her teeth, but widened her knees and tilted her ass higher. The first wet swirl atop her engorged knot set her belly and thighs quivering.

"Can you feel the plug?" he asked, his voice a deep, soothing rumble.

"Yes, I'm on fire, Boone." But she rolled her hips to let him know her discomfort wasn't something she wanted to end.

"It's going to get a little rough. You'll feel the jolts against the plug. Can you take that?"

Tilly moaned. "Please, Boone. Stop talking."

A graveled chuckle sounded. His fingers left her clit. "Play with your clit, baby. I'm going to be busy."

She lowered her chest to the mattress and reached between her legs to swirl her fingers on her clit.

Boone straightened behind her, his fingers digging into the hot, tender skin of her ass. The first thrust was smooth and gliding, pushing all the way inside before he withdrew, the slick sound he made lewd and exciting. But then he moved faster. His motions churning in her creamy depths, building friction with his movements.

Tilly's breaths chopped apart. When he withdrew, she pulled air into her lungs only to feel it leave in harsh gasps as he shoved deep again. Faster and faster...deeper...harder.

He parted her cheeks, and the next flurry of thrusts were so deep his groin touched the base of the plug, jarring it inside her.

Taken in two places now, her mind was set free, overwhelmed by sensation—sharp slaps skin-to-tender-skin, deep thrusts that overfilled her hot, slick inner walls, blunt raps against the plug that excited the nerves of that sensitive orifice.

"It's too much," she moaned, letting her fingers fall away from her clit.

Boone pulled free, turned her body and eased down over her. "Wrap yourself around me, baby."

Limbs and torso trembling, she slipped her hands around his back, digging her nails into the deep indention of his spine and lifted her legs to ride the hard edges of his hips. When he began to move, she kept her eyes open, watching his face, excited all over again by the feral heat, the tightness of his jaw, the way his lips pulled away from his teeth.

Boone was relentless, pistoning quickly, each thrust a deep targeted lunge that caused her breath to gust. She grunted inelegantly, but dug her fingers deeper, her heart beating wildly inside her chest. Desire coiled deep in her belly, building that familiar tension she knew was poised to explode. "Please, Boone. God, please."

"Now, Tilly. Come for me now," he growled. He leaned closer, his body forcing her hips to tilt higher.

She raised her legs, letting them fall wider, opening herself to his powerful strokes until at last, her breath caught, her back arched, and she splintered apart.

The room darkened around her; her breaths were harsh, but distant. Sweat melted between them, letting their bodies rub and glide with ease, their opposing motions a wild dance.

When his head jerked back and he gave a guttural roar, she smoothed her palms over the tense muscles rippling in his back until he fell against her, his face nuzzling into the corner of her neck while he dragged in ragged breaths.

She rubbed her cheek against his hair, cupped his head, and soothed him with nonsensical murmurs until his breaths evened out and his body relaxed. Below, she felt the last pulses of his cock releasing semen inside her.

Neither of them had thought about protection for a while,

something that surprised her, because she'd always been cautious about unprotected sex. But Tilly wasn't worried. She trusted that since he knew everything about her, he knew he needn't worry she had anything to be concerned about. She trusted he had shown the same care for her. Boone wasn't a careless man. And if their coupling resulted in a child… Tilly smiled at the thought.

A groan sounded in her ear, and her smile widened. "I can't move. I have this large immovable object anchorin' me to this bed."

"Can you breathe?"

She nodded against his hair.

"Then it's all good. Not moving. I like where my dick is," he muttered.

She snickered softly, pressed a kiss against his shoulder, and then closed her eyes.

As she drifted off to sleep, the niggling worry in the back of her mind resurfaced.

Denny. What would Boone do with what he'd learned about her brother? Boone wasn't a monster, wasn't without compassion. He'd shown her plenty when he'd had cause to hate her.

And yet, here she lay, content and sated. Happier than she'd ever been.

Was she selfish not to be more concerned? Tilly took as deep a breath as she could manage, then let it go.

Tomorrow. She'd worry tomorrow.

Chapter Nineteen

The next morning, Boone slipped from bed, careful not to waken Tilly. He dressed in the bathroom, and then walked quietly across the room, letting himself into the hallway and carefully closing the door.

The house was deceptively quiet, but he knew his night crew was still on duty, watching the security monitors, patrolling the grounds.

He was halfway to the stairs when he heard a door open and close, and glanced back to find Jonesy, dressed in sweatpants and flip-flops, following him. "There's nothing happening. You can go back to bed."

Jonesy rubbed the back of his head with a hand and squinted his eyes. "You can't sleep. Neither can I. I'll keep you company."

Boone narrowed his gaze. "I don't want to talk." What had passed with Tilly was no one's business but his own now.

Jonesy flashed a quick smile. "Not much of a talker myself."

"I'm just going for a walk." Boone shook his head, then cupped his hand to invite the other man. "Might be good to have you along in case a gator crosses our path."

"But you can outrun me."

Boone flashed a smile. "Precisely. Slower target."

Jonesy chuckled and followed him down the stairs.

Once outside, Boone walked to the edge of the back porch, glancing up at the gray twilight peeking between the leaves of a giant, moss-draped oak. Here, deep in the bayou, the outdoors was much noisier than inside. Birds tweeted and cawed, the occasional raspy bark of a squirrel echoed above the distant sound of water lapping against riverbanks.

"I hated living here," he said, more to himself than his friend. "Growing up, the place felt small, close, like I was suffocating from the humid air and my father's expectations. All I wanted was to graduate and get the hell out."

Jonesy leaned his hips against the porch rail, his arms crossed over his broad, naked chest.

Boone shook his head. Jonesy didn't say a word, simply gave Boone a steady stare, telling him in his quiet way he was there for him. So he sighed and began, needing to talk through what was really on his mind.

"The night Celie died, the sheriff ripped me from my bed and marched me to that cabin to see what I had done. Told me there was no escaping punishment, that my father couldn't save me. Didn't matter how many times I said I didn't do it. I knelt at the cabin door, staring at her bloody body, and suddenly, I didn't want it to be over. Not her life. Not mine. I didn't want to leave Bayou Vert."

Boone shut his eyes and gripped the rail with his hands, pressing hard enough he drove splinters into his palms. He remembered shivering in his pajama bottoms, his knees bloody from being shoved to the dirt as he'd stared at the carnage—at Celie's ravaged belly and face—feeling weak-kneed with horror, his belly ready to erupt. He hadn't been able to wrap his mind around what had happened, but imagined the horror of her ordeal. He'd barely breathed, his chest had constricted so tightly.

"Even my father wouldn't listen. Last time I saw him was in the middle of that night. The sheriff stood over my cot and kicked it to wake me up. Said I had a reprieve. That he'd better never see me in these parts again, or he'd string me up himself. I was hustled to a limo, past my father, who averted his face, and then I was driven all the way to South Carolina and dropped at the steps of a military prep school, still in prison stripes." He'd been cut adrift from everything familiar, and even though he knew he was innocent, he'd felt pounded into the dirt with guilt.

He raised his head and stared at the sunlight, gleaming brighter now. "I never saw my mother or my father again. They turned their backs on me. Assumed I'd done it. A couple of years later, Mom died in a car wreck. Drunk. My father got into some trouble, something to do with taking money for votes, and he killed himself while I was on my first tour in Afghanistan. I inherited this wreck of an old plantation, along with all of their debts." Boone swallowed to ease the ache in the back of his throat. "I didn't have any place to go. No matter how many medals I earned, I couldn't escape the stain it left inside me. Didn't matter that no one knew what I was accused of outside of this place. So I stayed in the navy."

"All of us have our stories, Boone. Not one of us is lily white."

"I'm not saying I was ever a Boy Scout, Jonesy, but I didn't do this. I would never..." He slammed his hand against the rail. "Guilt over what happened fueled me to excel. And once I got my head on straight, I decided I had to find a way to build enough wealth so I could return on my terms and find the truth. I couldn't let things rest. I owed Celie that much. And I can't let it hang over my head for the rest of my life. I want more than this, Jonesy. More than revenge or justice. I feel like I can't start the rest of my life until this is over."

"And now you're closer to the truth. What are you going to do?"

What Jonesy really meant was what was he going to do with Tilly? If he pursued her brother, she might not ever forgive him. Boone thought about the woman he'd left sleeping in his bed. How she'd comforted him when it should have been the other way around. His growing affection for her hadn't been part of his plan. "I don't know. I just don't know."

"She's different."

He nodded. "I knew one day I'd marry. I assumed I'd find someone I could tolerate and go about my way."

"I don't think Tilly would accept you just tolerating her, Boone." He waggled his eyebrows but kept his voice dead even.

"She made me want more. I can see a future that's about something other than just…amassing wealth or demolishing bad guys."

"So what do you want to do?" he asked again.

This time Jonesy's words were softer, like an echo of Boone's conscience.

"I have to follow this, Jonesy. I can't let it go. But I don't…" He shook his head again, feeling a knot lodge in his gut. "I can't lose her."

"Whatever you choose, we're with you. You want to let the investigation go, we'll call off the dogs. Leave little brother alone."

"I'm already in too deep." Boone's shoulders fell. "If I don't find my answers, this matter will always be between us. I have to know. So does she."

"Even if learning the truth destroys her?"

Boone shook his head, his jaw tightening. "I won't let that happen."

"She's not like us, Boone. She's got a tender heart. Anything happens to that brother of hers, when she had a chance to keep him safe, she won't ever forgive herself."

"I know." He glanced back toward the door, wondering if she'd awoken, and knowing that the moment she found herself alone, she'd be weighed down with worry over his intentions. He straightened his shoulders. "I want the psychologist I sent to check on Denny at the group home on the phone now."

Jonesy dropped his arms and gave him a nod. "On it, boss. And we did as you asked, dropped a hint in town with that gossip, Mrs. Nolan, that we were searching for the bracelet. That it might have DNA evidence. If someone else gets nervous about it…" He arched a brow and then began to move away.

"Jonesy."

His friend glanced over his shoulder. "Don't get all sentimental or I'll have to kick your ass."

Boone flashed a smile and stepped off the porch. He didn't know how he'd managed it, but he'd made good friends. The kind who would risk their own lives for him, or step in to tell him he was being an idiot. They were an odd, mismatched bunch. All from different parts of the country and different upbringings, but bound by blood and honor.

Needing to think, he headed down the path toward the cabins in the back to the one reduced to ashes around a scorched foundation. He'd follow the investigation no matter where it led. He owed it to Celie. But he'd do his best to shield Tilly from hurt. He hoped being there for her, making things right for her brother, would be enough to restore her faith in him.

* * *

Tilly awoke feeling refreshed despite soreness in some intimate places. She was glad Boone was gone from the room. Although she wasn't gripped by fear as she had been the previous night when she'd revealed the things she'd kept from Boone, she was far from feeling comfortable, having given him some pretty damning truths.

Still, she was relaxed. Maybe it was the aftermath of great sex, but she suspected the feeling was rooted in something much deeper than that. She was hopeful for the future in a way she'd never been before despite everything she'd revealed. She had confidence Boone would find a way to get to the truth while keeping her brother safe.

After gathering lingerie and a change of clothing, she entered Boone's bathroom, exploring the feminine toiletries that were lined up beside his inside the cabinet under the sink, and selected a floral bath gel and her favorite shampoo and conditioner. Unscrewing the cap of the gel, she sniffed then turned on the water to heat.

She could get used to having everything she needed provided without ever giving a thought of who did the shopping or how they knew exactly what she'd like. However, if she did think about it, she doubted Beatrice had been so considerate, which meant one of his buddies had shopped for her. Were they responsible for the tampons under the sink?

While her cheeks warmed to the thought, she smiled. She'd changed. Her boundaries were expanding. In more ways than simply sexual. All thanks to Boone. The world was becoming a bigger place. And maybe that was what had her feeling lighter at heart than circumstances warranted.

After showering, Tilly dressed and applied her makeup. Glancing in the mirror, she wondered how much more she would change, and whether she would recognize herself in the coming months.

Exiting the bathroom, she realized with a pang that she hadn't checked her phone for messages, so she left the house via the servants' stairs. Once inside the foreman's cottage, she plucked her phone from where it had been left to charge atop the counter. Someone, not her, had plugged it in.

A press of a button and the screen illuminated. She dragged down her finger and her heart thudded. She'd missed a call from Denny's group home.

Guilt dampened her mood, and she quickly dialed the number, waiting impatiently for the supervisor to answer.

"Oh, thank the Lord," Ms. Parham said the moment she answered.

Tilly's heart dropped to her toes. "What's wrong?"

"Denny's gone missing. Wasn't in his bed this mornin'."

She drew in a deep breath. "It's still early. Did he take a walk?"

"He wasn't in his bed at all last night. The boy never makes his bed without me standin' over him, but his room was neat as a pin. It's how I know he snuck out last night."

Where would he be? Tilly swallowed to wet her dry throat. "Have you called the police?"

"Already done. They're lookin' for him everywhere, but knowin' Denny, he's tryin' to go home."

Tilly closed her eyes. Denny had been so adamant about coming home. She guessed he'd grown impatient waiting for her to come. With her fingers tightened on the sides of the phone, she forced herself to remain calm. "I'll be on the lookout. It's an awful long way for him to come. He'd have to hitch a ride."

"God looks out for innocents," Ms. Parham said, although her voice was filled with worry.

"Keep me informed," Tilly said, then ended the call. Dread weighted her movements. She raised the phone again, preparing to call the sheriff's office, but hesitated. Denny was heading home. She didn't doubt that for a minute. He'd sounded so lonely the other day, so lost. She should have dropped everything to go see him; instead she'd gallivanted off to Mexico.

If something happened to him because she'd been selfishly living her life, she'd never forgive herself. But still, she hesitated to call the sheriff. What tangent of conversation might Denny follow? What secret might he inadvertently spill?

She gathered her phone and purse and headed to the garage, glancing around as she moved.

The thought crossed her mind to ask for Boone's help, but he'd know soon enough something was going on. As soon as the Thibodaux police called the sheriff's office, the APB would be on the police band. She wanted to be ahead of Boone and his men. Wanted to be the one to find Denny. He was her brother. He deserved to have family holding his hand when Boone dragged out that damn bracelet and dangled it in front of his nose.

Knowing Boone's people would know the moment she left, she pretended nonchalance as she headed to her car. Maybe they'd think she had an errand. No doubt someone would follow, but she wouldn't give them any cause for alarm.

The garage was empty when she climbed into her car. She met no one, saw no one as she unwound the wire holding together the iron gate and drove toward town.

The phone on the seat beside her hummed.

She picked it up, tapped the screen, and tucked it into the crook of her neck.

"Tilly?"

"Denny? That you?" she asked, the relief nearly overwhelming.

"Tilly, I'm home."

Tilly gunned the gas pedal, her fingers tightening around the steering wheel. "Denny, are you at our old house?"

"I'm home. No one's here. She said she'd bring me, but she doesn't have a key."

Tilly's brows drew together. "Denny, who's with you? Put them on the phone."

But the call ended. She glanced at the face of the phone, hit the recent calls, and saw the readout. Mae Baillio.

Mae? Tilly frowned, wondering how the crotchety woman had become involved, but then remembered Denny would have had to pass Mae's on his way to the house. No doubt the older woman picked him up when he came into town. She hit REDIAL but the phone rang and rang.

"Dammit." At least she knew he was safe, but she wasn't very happy about seeing Mae again so soon. She'd had enough of her censure the other day in the cafe.

Glancing in the rearview mirror, she saw a dark sedan in the distance and bit back a curse. Since she wanted a little time alone with her brother before the cavalry arrived, she passed Belle Tierre, turned on the next street, and made another sharp turn, gunning it. Whoever was following was far enough behind her that he couldn't be sure which road she'd taken.

She turned again, onto Belle Tierre, and noted with relief Mae's car was parked near the culvert. Tilly pulled in behind Mae's older-model sedan, turned off the ignition, and got out of her car.

On the edge of the road she stood listening. The sound of footsteps tromping on pine needles drew her to the riverbank. In the daylight, she wasn't nearly as nervous as she'd been last night when she'd led Boone and his men through the brush. She followed the side of the bank to her and Denny's tree, then glanced around the small clearing. "Denny?" she called out softly, not wanting to alert anyone living in the houses near the edge of the woods. "Denny?"

"Tilly!" Denny came crashing through the underbrush, a large grin splitting his face. "I couldn't get into the house, so I came to see our tree."

"It's our spot. Nothing will ever change that." Tilly opened her arms, relief making her weak. His hug was hard and familiar.

"Make her go away," Denny whispered in her ear.

Tilly jerked back, about to ask him what he meant, when she spotted Mae standing beside the large oak. "Mae, thank you for finding him," she said, although something about the older woman's expression rang alarm bells.

Mae's tall frame seemed larger, more ominous. Maybe because she wore dark trousers and a loose dark blouse rather than her usual server's dress.

"Denny said you had his treasure."

Her eyes widened before she could caution herself to pretend she didn't know what the woman was talking about. "His treasure?" she asked, suddenly breathless.

Mae's expression remained eerily blank. "His pirate's hoard."

"I have it," Tilly said, giving her a stiff smile. "I've kept it safe for you, Denny," she said, pushing at his chest and moving to his side. "Don't you worry."

Denny gripped her arm with his large hand, his forehead wrinkled in a frown. "Gotta have it, Tilly. Need my treasure. A pirate ain't a pirate 'thout treasure."

"You're exactly right," she said, unable to look away from Mae, who slowly moved closer.

"Told Mae sometimes we bury treasure here." He shook his head. "But someone done dug it up. Found the hole."

Mae's dark eyes narrowed. "Where's Denny's treasure, Tilly?"

Tilly shook her head. Mae's strange insistence caused a slow shiver of apprehension to snake down her spine. "I gave it to Boone," she whispered, dread stealing her voice. "For his safekeeping."

Mae shook her head. "Shouldn't o' done that."

Suddenly, Tilly wished she hadn't been so keen to lose the dark sedan. She knew only moments would pass before he found her vehicle, but she had the sinking feeling he might not radio for backup soon enough to make a difference. "Why shouldn't I have done that, Mae?"

But she thought she knew. Everything clicked into place.

Mae had been Celie's nanny. Boone and Leon weren't the only ones who'd loved her cousin. And since Tilly knew Boone wasn't crazy, she knew he hadn't been crazy jealous enough to kill Celie because she'd been stepping out on him.

Leon had been a fleeting possibility, but even though Tilly had acknowledged him as a suspect, he just didn't seem the type. Leon was a flirt, but not possessive. Although she really didn't know what type it took to slash a young girl to death.

Except the unholy light gleaming in Mae's eyes made the hairs on the back of her neck and her arms rise. "What do you want with Denny's treasure, Mae?" she asked, keeping her voice even.

The woman's mouth tightened. "Denny's a dirty little thief. Always findin' buttons and change on the floor. Didn't realize he searched drawers too. He's got somethin' o' mine."

"Don't mean to steal, Tilly," Denny said, whining a bit because even he understood something was terribly wrong.

"Why don't you go up to the road, Denny?" She wrapped an

arm around his waist. "My car's there. You can sit in the back while I talk to Mae."

Mae shook her head. "We'll go together." She pulled a small handgun from her trouser pocket that looked like a toy and pointed it straight at Tilly.

Denny dragged on her arm. "Tilly? I wanna go home."

"So do I, Denny," she whispered, and patted his arm. "Mae. It's already too late. Boone has it. If there's anything, any blood, that might point to...the killer...he's gonna know."

Mae's upper lip curled. "Maybe so, but I can make him sorry. Just like I did all those years ago."

Tilly's body froze. "Why would you want him sorry, Mae? What did Boone ever do to you?"

"He got my girl pregnant. She didn't think I knew. But I took care o' her so long, I knew her cycles. She didn't know it, but I sure did!" Her chin jutted out. "Damn slut was havin' his baby, and her daddy would o' fired me."

"But you killed her," she said softly over the lump in her throat. "You lost your job anyway."

Mae waved her free hand. "That was an accident. I followed her. She went back to that cabin, waited for Leon."

Stalling for time, Tilly lifted a hand to interrupt. "If you knew about Leon, why did you assume the baby was Boone's?"

Mae's expression screwed up. Hatred blazed from her eyes. "Baby was his. I watched her with Leon. She insisted he wear a condom. They did it on the same dirty mattress as her and Boone. All tied up like a Christmas present. When Leon left, I called her back. She pleaded with me not to tell. Said she loved Boone, but couldn't help herself. Said she'd been careful."

Mae shook her head. "Girl was spoiled. Wanted the rich boy. But she wanted to flirt with trouble too. I lost my head." Her lips pressed together and she sniffed. "Didn't mean to kill my baby."

Denny muttered under his breath, "Pretty bells. Pretty bells."

Tilly's stomach roiled. Fear made her start to sweat. "You took the bracelet."

"Don't know why I did. It was so pretty, so delicate. She was my baby. Why shouldn't I have something from her 'sides all that worry? But your brother found it in my desk at the restaurant. I thought I'd lost it 'til that Mrs. Nolan said they'd been lookin' for a bracelet. That they tore apart that cabin 'fore they burned it." Her eyes glittered with hatred. "I knew why he wanted it. Couldn't let that happen."

Tilly cleared her throat to speak past the lump lodged there. "But it's too late. He has it now. You can't kill us both, can't kill Boone and his men too. They'll figure it out. Your blood will be inside those pretty bells."

"Pretty bells. Pretty bells," Denny chanted, wringing his hands beside her.

Mae's eyes narrowed. "I can't kill 'em all, but you're a whore just like your cousin. Playin' nasty games with that man." She jabbed the gun forward. "I may be done, but he'll never have any satisfaction."

Fear shivered through her, but she held Mae's cold gaze. "Let my brother go, Mae, and you can take me. Okay?"

Mae hesitated, but then gave a nod.

Tilly turned to Denny and reached up, cupping the sides of his face. "I remember what a fast runner you always were," she said, fighting the burning at the backs of her eyes. "Think you can run to LeRoy's bait shop? I'll be there in a bit. After I find your treasure for Mae."

Denny glanced at Mae, his eyes narrowing. "You come too, Tilly."

"I will. Tell you what, we'll race. But I'll give you a head start. You go now, Denny."

His smile brightened. "I'll be first."

"You'll be first," she whispered to his back as he raced away.

Tilly held still as Mae approached. Waiting for the right moment, but not finding an opening. If she turned away, she had no doubt Mae would shoot her in the back. She'd have to fight her, and Tilly wasn't sure she could win. Mae had a solid fifty pounds on her and a much longer reach. "Thank you for that," she said, stalling again. "Denny isn't any part of this."

A twig snapped in the underbrush. Mae's face jerked toward the sound.

Tilly darted forward and shoved Mae's arm upward, barreling into her and pushing her to the ground, and then dashed toward the large tree.

A shot rang out behind her, accompanied by the whistle of a bullet and the dull thud of metal striking wood. She darted behind the tree and ran smack into the middle of a hard chest.

Jonesy pushed her against the trunk, his hand clamping over her mouth.

Her wide eyes teared as she heard other sounds: several sets of footsteps running toward the canal, the crackle of underbrush. And then a loud explosion.

Until he stepped away, she didn't realize she was crying. Rough hands drew her against another solid chest, enfolding her as her body shook.

"Shhh, baby. Shhh…"

Tilly balled her fist and struck Boone's chest. "I'll cry if I want to."

Hushed voices sounded all around them. A siren chirped.

More movement. A herd of crunching footsteps. But she leaned against Boone, fisted her hand in his shirt, and cried.

Boone rocked her forward and back, his head tucked beside hers, his hands running up and down her back, soothing her.

When Tilly had herself somewhat under control, she leaned away and looked up. "My brother?"

Boone's arms remained around her. His hands gripped her shoulders. "Safe with Serge at the road."

"How'd you know?"

"Jonesy followed you. Then the police band went nuts. Your brother was missing. Figured you knew where he was headed. I didn't want to take any chances, so I rousted the boys."

She gave him a tremulous smile. "I'm so glad you're a control freak."

Boone's mouth quirked up at the sides, but then his gaze lifted beyond her.

Tilly moved to his side, grateful for the arm he kept around her back when Linc and Bear trudged toward them, blood staining their hands.

Linc's gaze skipped over her, and he gave Boone a shake of his head.

"What the hell's goin' on here, Boone?"

Leon pushed aside brush and entered the clearing, his gun drawn and a deputy behind him, holding a shotgun.

"Mae held Denny and Tilly at gunpoint. When Tilly charged her, we moved in."

Leon's eyes narrowed. "And you just happened to be here."

"I didn't set it up, if that's what you're intimating."

Tilly gripped Boone's hand hard and stepped away from his side. "I gave his men the slip. Wanted to find Denny first. I thought...maybe..." She shook her head. "I thought maybe he'd killed Celie. Thought you might have too." She shrugged before giving him an apologetic stare. "For about a minute."

Leon blinked and then gave Boone a measured stare.

Boone shrugged. "Yeah, she knows about you and Celie."

"I couldn't have hurt her," Leon said, his mouth thinning as his eyes narrowed. "I loved her, but she loved what you could buy her more." His gaze fell to Tilly. "Sorry. Don't mean to speak ill of your kin."

Tilly forced a faint smile. "Mae killed her, Leon. She thought Celie was pregnant. That she'd lose her job. She was furious and lashed out."

Boone jerked beside her. She reached out a hand to clasp his. She hadn't meant to blurt that news.

Leon's face turned gray. "Never knew. If she was, might have been mine. But evidence went missing. And I'm sure our daddies had the coroner keep any news about a baby quiet." Leon's gaze swept the clearing. "And Mae's where?"

Serge stepped forward. "At the river's edge. She shot herself. Gun's beside her body. Check it for ballistics."

"Dammit." Leon reached for his radio, called for the coroner, and told dispatch to contact the county to muster a forensics team.

Tilly swayed. It was all too much. Mae had killed Celeste. Her cousin might have died with a baby inside her. It was all so sad. Tilly had nearly been killed by Mae...Suddenly, her knees felt like Jell-O.

Boone bolstered her up, pulling her closer to his side. "Can you save the questions for later? I need to get Tilly somewhere she can sit."

Leon took one look at Tilly's face and must have read her

shock, because he gave Boone a swift nod, and then walked toward the river.

With tears beginning to track down her cheeks, Tilly didn't offer a word of protest as Boone picked her up and trudged through the brush toward the road.

Chapter Twenty

Fifteen minutes later, Boone swept Tilly into his arms and carried her up the front steps of Maison Plaisir. Without a word being spoken, help was mustered, a pot of warm tea set on a side table, and Denny was led away to the kitchen to find a meal.

Boone closed the door and then strode back to Tilly, who lay on a chaise in the sunshine spilling through a window, her eyes closed, her head turned toward the warmth.

He sat beside her, worried because she hadn't said a word since they'd left the river. He didn't know what to say, was afraid she might still blame him for the danger she and her brother had found themselves in. So he remained silent, his hands pressed together, waiting.

"Boone?"

She sounded fragile, her voice thin. It worried him all the more. "Yes, Tilly?"

"What would you have done if the killer had been Denny?"

"I bought your old house." Boone released a deep breath. "I'd have followed through getting it fixed up to look like it did when you still lived there. I already hired a caregiver to help him."

Her head turned, a crease forming between her pale brows. "You'd have done that, even if he'd been the one responsible for Celie's death?"

Boone nodded. "Denny's important to you. If he'd been the one, I would have kept that news to myself to make sure he didn't suffer. I'd have kept him safe and supervised."

Her gaze lowered to his chest. "So it's over."

"Yeah." Boone looked down at his folded hands. "Funny, I thought I'd feel something."

"Maybe you'll finally sleep easier." Tilly struggled to sit up.

Boone reached out a hand to help her, but she stared at it, so he let it drop.

"I should head back to my place."

Boone stomach tightened. "This is your place."

Her eyes filled and her head rolled on the chaise back. "I'll understand if you want to walk away. From everything here, from me. You accomplished what you came for—Celeste's murder is solved. You cleared your name once and for all and you saved my life...and my brother's. You don't owe me a thing."

Boone reached out and glided a hand up her leg, letting it rest on her thigh. "I don't owe you anything..." He snorted, then shifted, coming closer to Tilly. As he pulled near, he spotted her wet, cornflower-blue eyes shining like mirrors.

The tremble of her lower lip was what hurt him most. His gut twisted, and he framed her jaw and cheek with a hand and bent to kiss her.

She sniffed, her mouth opening around a soft sob.

Relief poured through him as he smothered the sound, taking her breaths, raking her tongue with his, laying claim to her lush mouth. When he drew back, he pressed his forehead against hers.

"I don't know what this is between us, Tilly. But I'm not letting it go. I'm not letting *you* go."

Tilly's wide, wet eyes studied him. Then her eyelids dipped. Her mouth pouted.

Despite the turmoil swirling inside him, arousal stirred in his groin. He knew her. Knew that look.

Her gaze fell away. "I should be doing something. Making some sort of arrangements. Mae didn't have anyone."

"You'd do that for the woman who killed your cousin?"

Tilly locked her glance with his. "She was damaged, somehow. She was sorry about hurting her."

Boone gave a rough shake of his head. "I'll see to arrangements. It's not your worry."

Again, her lips plumped. The tip of her tongue sneaked out and wet the bottom.

Boone felt that furtive swipe right against his balls.

From beneath the fringe of her dark lashes, her eyes slowly smiled. "I need you, Boone. Please, sir?"

* * *

Tilly should have been exhausted. After making love with Boone, she'd spent the rest of the day at Leon's office, writing out her statement, answering an endless round of questions, before she'd been released with an admonishment not to leave town any time soon.

She sniffed. Leon sure liked to throw his weight around. Right now, he was the big man in town with a cold case all wrapped up in a tidy bow. No matter that he had only caught the tail end of the excitement. His investigation would provide Bayou Vert the closure the town had needed for so many years.

After she'd returned to the Big House, she'd dined with Boone's team, this time left to eat her meal in comfortable silence. The easy conversation that surrounded her soothed her nerves. She liked his friends, gruff and rough around the edges, aggressively masculine, but she trusted every one of them because Boone did. Denny had joined them with an endless line of questions about the estate. Linc and Jonesy didn't show any irritation with his childish curiosity.

Her brother had been led away to bed, the new caregiver sleeping in the room next to his. Until Tilly's family home in town was ready, they'd both remain on the estate. Then Denny would be returned to familiar surroundings. Something Tilly would be forever in Boone's debt for, because right after dinner, he handed her the deed to the house on Belle Tierre.

"I can't take that," she said, the deed quivering in her grasp.

"Sure you can," he said, pushing it back. "It's a gift. I certainly don't need it."

"I haven't earned it."

His eyebrows quirked. "Will you feel better about accepting it if I attach some strings?"

Holding still, Tilly pressed her lips together to hide a smile she felt growing inside. "You really should expect more in return. I don't know how you ever got to be such a big-shot CEO when you don't know how to strike a proper bargain."

A growl rumbled deep in Boone's chest and he strode toward her, his hands reaching out.

Tilly gave a yelp and darted away, running past the bed to the French doors and throwing them open. Once outside, she sped down the balcony, passing Serge's door, running for the wrought-iron stairs that led to ground level.

Before she reached the stairs, an arm snaked around her

middle, and she was turned, lifted, and draped over a rock-hard shoulder.

She gasped. Laughter followed. A hand smacked her backside, but she only laughed harder.

Back at his bedroom doors, he set her on her feet, then crowded her against the porch rail, his hands landing on the iron at either side of her hips, bracketing her in.

Moonlight filtering through the big oaks gleamed on the side of his face, skipped the dark sockets of his eyes, and shone bluish in his dark hair. "You look like a pirate," she whispered.

"You make me feel like one." Strong hands slid up her sides.

She lifted her chin. "Pirates take what they want."

Boone's eyebrows gave a single waggle, and he leered downward. "In that case, I want your clothes."

"Here?" she asked, glancing around.

"Your brother's on the opposite side of the house."

"But your men are crawling all over the estate. Don't you care what they might see?" She widened her eyes, feigning concern, but she liked this Boone—free of worry, hunger burning in his eyes.

"Let them see what I'm bargaining for…sweet little sub."

Her breath caught as she understood a direct challenge had been issued.

With her thighs clamping tight from excitement, Tilly leaned away and pulled off her tee, tossing it to the lawn behind her. Then she unsnapped her bra and dangled it off a finger before letting it fall to the ground as well.

Boone swallowed loudly. His gaze dropped from her face to her tightly beaded nipples. His stance widened, and she wondered if he needed the extra room because he was growing aroused.

Tilly heard footsteps crunch below her, but lifted her chin, determined not to betray any embarrassment. Boone deserved courage. She needed to show him she trusted him implicitly. She unsnapped her shorts and pushed them and her undies off her hips, stepping out of them and then giving them a backward kick.

Boone stood still, his nostrils flaring, his gaze raking her body.

Tilly stood proudly on the balcony, knowing her hair was silver in the moonlight, and that her body was softly gilded. She read approval in Boone's eyes, and that was all she needed to remain strong while she waited for his response.

"Turn around and grip the rail," he said, his tone firm, but the edges smoothed by his honeyed drawl. "Then bend over, your arms stretched, your legs spread."

Delight rather than shock rippled through her at his softly worded command. He'd take her standing. Pleasure swept like a wave over her skin, pricking up goose bumps and wetting her folds. Lord, she'd come a long way.

He stepped back, his hands on his hips, waiting.

On a heel, she turned silently, looking out over the balcony and knowing any of the men combing the estate could see her pale skin perfectly illuminated in moonlight. She wasn't so inured she didn't blush, but joy surpassed any misgivings.

Bending at the waist, she reached out and gripped the porch rail, and then slowly shifted her feet apart on the plank floor. Her breasts were stretched, the nipples tingling. Her pussy and cheeks parted.

The rustle of clothing behind her made her shiver with delight. She jerked slightly when a hand smoothed over her ass, then beneath her, rubbing over her stomach, her ribs, and then closing around one ripened breast. "Oh, Boone." She sighed, letting her back sink to tilt her ass toward him.

Another hand slipped between her legs to fondle her pussy, cupping her smooth sex, warming it with his hand, before sliding two fingers inside her.

Beyond caring what anyone saw or heard, she welcomed the lush, wet sound her body made as he fondled her, the intrusion of his skillful fingers as he prodded both holes. She was his. To pleasure or hurt. To love or set aside. She'd decided to open her heart. Live without expectations. Trust he'd take care of her. For now.

Their attraction was powerful. Inevitable. Like the storms rumbling in from the Gulf. Devastation was something one prepared for, but didn't live in fear of. One accepted change. Cherished good times, and soldiered through the bad.

"You're thinking too much." A kiss landed on one hip. "Am I boring you?"

Tilly tossed back her hair. "I'm not bored, Boone. I'm happy."

Another kiss landed, this one followed by a lick through the crease dividing her buttocks. She shied from the intimacy but didn't voice her concern. Now she knew better.

"I'll be traveling soon," he murmured. "We still have the Tex-Oil trouble in Mexico to resolve."

Warm air wafted along her lower back. She held her breath and raised her head. "I'll miss you."

Fingers dug into her soft bottom. "You'll be with me. First I'm taking you to my club. Then we'll head back to Mexico. We have that hostage situation to resolve."

Happiness unfurled inside her. She'd be with him. "I haven't proven to be much help. I think I'm a lousy personal assistant."

"This time I'll bring you into the meetings. Let you see the inner workings of my operations." His hand smoothed over an ass cheek.

Her heart kicked up another notch. "You have some very capable men helping you. You have Beatrice."

"Beatrice has been reassigned."

At this statement, a thrill ran through her. "So I will be your secretary."

"Baby, you'll be so much more. Trust me, Tilly. The work will be rewarding. The perks... Well, they start now..."

He thrust his fingers deep and gave her a swirl that had her rising on her toes, her tummy sucking inward. "Good Lord, Boone. Do that again."

The bristly hairs on his thighs tickled the backs of hers as he lowered himself behind her to the wood floor. His fingers pulled away, but he didn't leave her wanting. With his hands clutching the globes of her ass, his mouth opened to suck her folds inside.

A finger toggled her clit while he feasted, and Tilly had no doubts every one of his team watched. A gust of laughter caught her by surprise. She hoped someday to rerun the footage, because she knew for sure the sight of Boone Benoit, naked and kneeling behind her, was an image that would take any woman's breath away.

Boone pulled back.

She dragged in deep breaths, still clenching her fingers around the edge of the porch rail. The moment his cockhead butted against her swollen pussy, she groaned. Opening her stance, she waited while he shifted. Glancing to the side, she noted the wide placement of his feet as he lowered to match the height of her hips. Then he leaned over her, his hands bracketing hers, and began to pump, slowly working his way deeper and deeper inside her body.

Before long, his lunges jarred her body, forced out her breaths in deep, labored grunts. But she didn't care, didn't want it to end. His powerful body buffeted hers from behind and she embraced the power, reveled in the fact that for right now, Boone was staking his claim in front of everyone who mattered to him.

She had no doubt that was what this was about. As she writhed and moaned, her body shuddering as desire curled tighter and tighter around her core, she stared at the length of the long graveled drive, down the long, dark tunnel where oak branches above interwove, draped with thick moss. Where a dark, painful past was slowly undergoing a glorious resurrection. It wasn't just sex.

Their bodies connected in the most intimate way. She felt as though he marked her, branded her with his sweat and seed. She widened her stance and stepped atop his feet, heard his soft grunting laughter, but couldn't smile herself, because she was close. So close.

Her skin tingled, her pussy burned, her hard clit throbbed. "Boone," she gasped as the first wave of pleasure rolled across her body.

"Come, baby. Make some noise."

Freed, she bucked against him, letting loose a long wail as she orgasmed. Her pussy clenched around his cock, spasms rippling up her channel, massaging his cock, pulling him deeper.

He slammed against her bottom, grinding deep, pounding her in shallow bursts that rocked her whole body. She tightened her grip on the porch rail, afraid she'd be shaken off.

Then Boone moved his arms, encircling her body while he remained curled over her back and rutting wildly inside her, until at last, he gave a muffled shout.

When he slowed, he reached up and leaned on the rail for support, dragging deep ragged breaths into his lungs.

Tilly curved a hand around his upper arm, holding herself steady as she tried to remember how to breathe too.

They clung together, bodies still in motion, swaying forward and back.

Lord, she wanted more nights like these. A thousand wouldn't be enough.

Boone hugged her and then pulled free. Liquid flowed in a gush down her inner thighs. He turned her in his arms, and encircled her body, pulling her chest flush with his. They stared into each other's eyes for a long moment, until a grin quirked up one side of his mouth.

"What's so funny?" she whispered, gliding her hands up his damp chest, then behind his neck to cling tightly.

He shook his head. "How will you like receiving guests?"

"Here at Maison Plaisir?"

The grin widening, he nodded.

"I suppose I'll let you guide me." She squinted, studying his expression. "So far, you've eased my modesty, my embarrassment. I suppose you were right about me all along."

"Only close friends and associates. Only those I trust not to alarm you or make you uncomfortable."

"You can't promise I won't be uncomfortable," she said, arching a brow.

"Right." He tilted his head. "I'll make sure you're never truly afraid. That you'll be introduced slowly to new pleasures."

Her fingers tangled in the hair at his nape. "I'd like that, Boone. But only with you." And that fact was true. She couldn't imagine ever making a journey like this with any other man.

Only in the tenderness he'd shown her could he prove the love underlying all his actions. That was the new secret she harbored. One she'd cherish for as long as love endured.

Please turn the page for a preview of
Delilah Devlin's next book

His Every Fantasy

Chapter One

He'd been here before. A makeshift tent city on a lonely stretch of desert with a *shamal* wind kicking up fine wheat-flour sand into a blinding storm. Tar-paper shacks nestled in a rock-strewn valley in the Hindu Kush mountains with fat snowflakes whipping into a blizzard.

This ramshackle camp hidden in the middle of a Yucatan jungle was surrounded. About to be destroyed. The men guarding the perimeter, smoking cigarettes and bragging about their latest sexual conquests, were already dead. They just didn't know it.

Sergei Gun drew a deep breath, inhaling the scents of rotting vegetation and the diesel fueling the site's generator. Dim lights burned in huts close to the entrance of the encampment. He'd chosen the far side of the camp, illuminated only by slivers of moonlight peeking through the forest canopy, for their attack. Checking the lit dial of his watch, he noted the time. Although he couldn't see them and they'd maintained radio silence throughout their trek from the rutted road to the camp, he knew his team was in place.

He raised his arm and motioned twice with sharp pumps of

his fist to the men beside him. Five seconds later, the soft muffled thuds of silenced rounds took each guard down. Seconds after that, his men, their faces blackened, bits of vines stuck into their helmets and the straps of their web gear to break up the outlines of their tall frames, crept into the encampment, the crunch of their footsteps on the jungle floor masked by the howling wind from a tropical storm.

One by one, the camp security force drug money had bought fell beneath swift and brutal knifes and brawny, suffocating headlocks.

Serge slipped past his men, making his way to the hut where their intel said the kidnapped Tex-Oil men were kept—one of a line of shacks with slatted wood sides that did little to keep out the elements. Tin roofs clapped as the wind picked up.

Through his night-vision goggles, he noted the man sitting beside the door of the hut, his head slumped toward his chest in sleep.

Serge snorted softly. The guards were poorly trained, likely recruited from the local village, given guns and more money than they'd ever see farming or leading tourists into the jungle to do the cartel's bidding. One or two actual cartel members were somewhere in the camp, and they'd be harder to take down than this one slumbering idiot.

With only a moment's regret for the man's poor judgment, Serge slipped beside him, encircled his neck, his arm cinching to cut off his oxygen, and waited as the man's heels drummed the dirt and his hands clawed at his arms, until he hung limply inside Serge's embrace. Setting the body to the side, Serge motioned to Bear to follow him while another of his team kept watch.

Inside, they found the two Tex-Oil men sleeping on the dirt. Serge reached down, placed a hand over one man's mouth, and waited for his eyes to spring open.

"Shhh," he said softly. "Your name?" He lifted his hand up an inch.

"Frank West," the man gasped, the ragged texture to his voice a testament to the ordeal he'd endured the past weeks.

"Mr. West, we're here to get you out. We're Black Spear."

The man's relief, even in the green glow of the night-vision goggles, was written on his face. He gave a quick nod, and Serge backed away, holding his arm to guide him upward in the pitch dark. "Hold on to my shirt and follow me. Don't let go."

As Serge turned, Frank tugged on his jacket.

"Wait," Frank whispered. "There's a girl."

Serge stiffened. "We're here for you. We've only got minutes before the whole camp knows we're here."

"She's in the shack next to ours. They brought her in yesterday. She's the only other hostage. You can't leave her."

Serge hesitated. Their mission was to extract the two executives who'd been kidnapped. Ransom demands had been met, but the cartel had decided to squeeze the oil company for more. Serge's plan called for a swift extraction, and to destroy the guards' ability to escape or tip off the cartel that they'd been raided just long enough to get the two men out of the country.

Still, the thought of another hostage, this one a woman, rankled. Breaking protocol, Serge tapped his headset. "We've got another lamb. Need two on West and Campion."

Stepping outside, he kept close to the side of the hut as two more of his team peeled away from the trees and sped quietly toward them. He and Bear handed off the men, then peered around the side of the hut at the other isolated shack. This one was guarded by two men, rifles slung over their shoulders, standing on either side of the door of the hut and peering up into the swaying canopy above them as limbs creaked ominously.

Signaling to Bear that he'd lay down cover fire if needed, Serge raised his weapon, sighting on the man nearest to him. Bear crouched, then ran past him, but neither guard noticed his movement between the huts. Once safe, Bear knelt at the corner of the building, his weapon trained on the men as Serge darted across.

Leaning against the hut, Serge signaled *thirty seconds*, holstered his weapon, and drew his knife from his sheath on his web belt before circling behind the hut, coming to a halt at the corner of the building. At the end of the thirty count, he slipped around the corner, rushing the man nearest as Bear launched toward the other.

The struggle was brief. Neither guard had time to draw a breath, much less shout. Serge wiped off his bloody hand on his jacket, then opened the latch of the hut and stepped inside.

A scuffing sound from his right had him whirling. Liquid spilled over his head, the scent acrid. *Urine.* A bucket clanked next, shifting his goggles and blinding him, but he was already on his opponent, clamping an arm around a slim body that he backed into the rickety wooden wall. Sheathing his knife because he didn't want to inadvertently hurt her, he slipped his hand over the woman's mouth.

Her jaw opened.

"*Don't. Bite,*" he gritted out. "Ma'am, we're here to rescue you."

Her body quivered inside his embrace, her curves pressed so close she could barely draw a deep breath, but he considered that a good thing. She'd be less likely to scream.

"I don't believe you," she said in a harsh whisper. "No one knows I'm here."

"I came for the two men in the cabin next to yours. They wouldn't leave without you."

When her wriggling ceased, and she appeared ready to cooperate, he righted his goggles and stared down at her. Even bathed in a blurry neon glow she was beautiful. And terribly young. Dark-haired, slender, and wearing shorts and a very thin tee that hugged her upper torso. Braless. That fact bothered him even more than her youth. "I'm your way out. Or do you want to stay here?"

Her lips pursed. Her gaze darted to the side. When her chin shot up, he knew her answer even before she whispered, "No."

"Then do exactly as I say. Hold on to my jacket when we leave here. I'll guide you out. But, lady, I'm warning you, I won't allow any antics out of you. If you try to make a run for it, you'll put me and my team at risk."

"You have a team?"

Serge pressed a finger over her lips. "Not another word. Follow me."

He turned, felt her fist gather a bundle of his camouflaged jacket, then stepped outside. She followed on his heels, her steps soft. A quick glance behind him confirmed she was barefoot. But better she suffer bruised and cut feet than remain trapped here. There wasn't a thing he could do about it now. Not that she was complaining. Her expression was tense, her mouth a tight, determined line.

From the periphery of his goggles, he noted his team, slipping into the forest, melting away. Serge hurried toward the trees then pulled his compass from a pack on his web belt, checked the tritium-lit direction lines to orient, and took off at a swift pace in the direction of the rutted logging trail they'd used as their assembly area.

Serge trudged quickly forward, not speaking, impressed despite himself when the barefoot girl behind him kept quiet, her breaths even as he set a swift pace. Fifteen minutes later, he stopped at the edge of a road, checking up and down the line as members of his team slid into their vehicles.

He turned and put an arm around the girl to guide her toward the second vehicle in the line, although here in the clearing moonlight provided plenty of illumination. When she stiffened against his touch, he kept his arm around her, telling himself he didn't want to risk her falling and injuring herself, but the truth was, he wanted her near. Wanted her close enough to grab in case they came under attack or she tried to run. His hand glided from her shoulder to the small of her back. All nicely fleshed, firm muscle beneath. Not relevant, but interesting.

At the SUV, he opened the rear door. "Get in." Tapping his headset, he asked for a quick head count, and each of the team members chimed in using hushed tones.

They'd made it out without setting off alarms. And without a single casualty. Another tap of headset. "You set the charges, Linc?"

"Yes, sir. Countin' down now. Eight, seven, six…"

Serge swung into his vehicle, tore off his goggles, and gave a quick glance at Bear, who tapped the ignition button. At *one*, explosions ripped through the air, light bursting above the trees. Satisfied the cartel camp would be busy for a while, Serge said, "Now let's get the fuck out of here."

Engines fired, wheels bit into the muddy trail, and they careened down the rutted track. Bear's smile gleamed in the moonlight.

"Don't say it," Serge said, not wanting to hear a celebratory whoop. "Don't jinx it."

Bear glanced into the rearview mirror at their unexpected passenger. "Get a name?"

Serge aimed a stare at the young woman huddled in the center of the seat, moonlight filtering over her features. She wasn't just beautiful, she was exquisite, even despite the frown marring her dark brow. "Not yet. Time for introductions once we get to the helos. We're not out of Omega territory yet."

The vehicle hit a deep rut, then bumped over it, unseating him. He reached for the strap above his window. "Better grab the oh-shit handle, sweetheart. It's gonna be a bumpy ride." And then he grinned, because for the first time since his feet had hit the tarmac in Cancun, tension lifted. It was still too soon to announce the all-clear, but this operation had just gotten a little more interesting.

* * *

Kara Nichols wrapped her fist around the plastic strap and slid toward the door, jamming her shoulder against it and gripping the top of her rescuer's seat to keep from flopping around the backseat like a rag doll. Her stomach lurched as they sped along the rugged trail. How "the team" managed to drive at breakneck speed in near darkness without headlights was a testament to their skill.

Who they were didn't matter as much as what their intentions were. Not that she'd really had any choice but to come with them. Not since the moment the burly man in front of her had crept like a thief into her hut had she had a moment to think. She'd reacted on pure instinct. First tossing her pee into his face and then braining him with the bucket it had been stored in. She'd intended to scamper past him, but he'd been faster, knocking the breath out of her as he'd pinned her to the wall.

At that moment, her worst fears had risen up, like the scream she hadn't been able to emit because he'd taken her breath.

Convinced he was one of the men who'd kidnapped her, there to rape her or worse, she'd been ready to fight him to the death.

But the struggle had revealed a couple of things. First, he was heavily armed and armored. A big man. Obviously not one of the dirty, ragged bunch who'd been guarding her. And his first words had been in English. He was an American. Relief had poured through her, leaving her shaking, even though there was no good reason to trust he meant her no harm.

Everything after that moment had happened so quickly, she hadn't had time to think whether she was jumping from the frying pan into the fire. He was from home. A way out of the hell she'd found herself in just days earlier, when one really bad decision had landed her in this mess.

The fact her "rescuers" were well organized, well armed, and appeared to have military training by their gear and the precision of their raid left her hopeful for the first time in days.

"What the fuck's that smell?" the driver asked, his glance going to his companion. "Man, you reek."

Kara suppressed a smile, although plenty of the bucket's contents had splashed back on her. Better to smell like a cesspool than to smell like something they might want to jump. She'd read stories about female prisoners who'd covered themselves in feces rather than suffer rape, and that scenario had definitely looped in her mind since her capture.

"Just shut up and drive," her new captor bit out. Then he cast another glance her way.

She wished she could see his face, but the helmet he wore deepened the shadow obscuring his expression. "Sorry about that," she muttered, not really meaning it, but she didn't want him pissed off too.

"Don't be. It was gutsy." A flash of white gleamed.

His smile tugged an answering grin from her own mouth. Somehow, his humor at her action humanized him. And shouldn't she be trying to get on his good side, anyway? If he really was rescuing her, she owed him big-time. If he was only preparing to hand her off to another captor, she needed his guard down to try another dash for freedom.

His free hand reached around to touch the mic wire poised in front of his mouth. Then he aimed a glance at the driver. "The pilots are firing up the helos," he said. "We'll be in the air in a few minutes."

In the air. But what was their destination?

They left the dirt track, bumping over the edge of a paved road, the rear of the vehicle fishtailing, but not losing any speed, as their convoy headed north. Kara held tight to the strap, a mixture of hope and dread building up bile in her empty belly. At least the road was smoother now. If they didn't take too many turns she might not vomit. Although he hadn't been fazed by her throwing pee at him, she didn't want to test his temper if she messed up his vehicle too.

The forest receded. They passed houses crammed together with dark narrow alleys separating them. The men in front grew more tense, their bodies tightening, their jaws honing to sharp edges.

Another turn, and they were passing dilapidated industrial buildings and shops with boarded-up windows. They pulled into a parking lot, the entrance guarded by a gate topped with rolled-up barbed wire. The chain-link gate slid back, and they barreled past a long row of shipping docks to a wider lot lit by security lamps on long poles, where three large helicopters awaited, blades chopping the air.

The man in the front passenger seat flashed her a smile. "Ever flown in one?"

She shook her head.

"Stick with me. You'll be okay."

The door locks clicked open, and she stepped barefoot onto crumbling pavement. Again, his arm went around her back, and this time she didn't stiffen against it, accepting his support as he ushered her to the smallest of the three waiting aircraft. Metal steps were lowered by a crew member. Hands gripped her elbow to help her inside. The interior was not what she'd expected. Plush, leather-upholstered seats, a row of three facing the front of the helicopter, two facing backward. Her captor indicated with a hand that she should take one of the two backward-facing seats.

He pulled a blanket from the console compartment separating the two seats. "Here, you'll need this. It gets cool in the upper elevations."

Reminded she was wearing only a very short pair of pajama shorts and a tight tee, she reached for it, only to hesitate when the interior lights blinked on. She stared at his hands.

Dried blood streaked his palms and dirtied his sleeve.

His gaze dropped and he pushed the blanket toward her again, letting go the second she accepted it. A glance at his face told her she'd made a mistake. His expression was carefully neutral, no trace of a smile left. Not a hint of warmth.

Kara sank into the seat and pulled the blanket around her body, looking away from him. Oddly upset with herself for showing him even a hint of revulsion.

Hadn't she known the rescue had come at a price? Just because she hadn't witnessed the attack that removed the guards before she stepped out her door didn't absolve her from any guilt over the fact men had died during the rescue. Intellectually, she knew it made no sense to feel ashamed, as though the violence were her fault, but good sense had nothing to do with why she'd been in that camp in the first place.

Three more men climbed into the cabin and took seats across from her and her rescuer. They sat, unstrapping belts and packs, and dropping their gear to the floor of the helicopter. Then helmets came off.

"You'll need to buckle up," came a gruff voice from beside her.

Because she'd screwed up before, she pasted on a smile before she looked his way. Her breath caught.

He'd removed his helmet, his armor, and the bloody jacket. Seated next to her on the edge of his seat, every thick muscle of his broad chest was defined by the T-shirt stuck to his sweaty skin. Her heartbeat thudded. He wasn't her usual type. Too muscled, too burly, but good Lord, that physique didn't intimidate her. He was built for protection. Something she desperately needed. That had to be why she was reacting this way, her body warming. And then she glanced up into his face.

Again, so not her type. And yet, her type, lean and sophisticated, wickedly handsome, instantly lost its appeal. This man's face was shuttered, still, but radiated a quiet calm. The strength of his firm jaw, his firm mouth, the intensity of his dark gaze tugged at something inside her. His hair was dark and long, restrained by a thick rubber band. His brows were dark, but not so heavy they looked foreboding.

His gaze rested on hers, waiting for something. Oh yeah, he'd wanted her to buckle herself into the seat. Reaching beneath the blanket, she caught the two ends of the seat belt and buckled herself in.

Although the cabin was insulated, the sound of the blades beating the air and the drone of the powerful engine were overwhelming as the aircraft slowly lifted into the air. She glanced toward the parking lot. The other two craft were rising as well. The lot beneath them was empty, the security lights blinking out and leaving it dark.

Kara swallowed hard, wanting to relax, not trusting the situation she now found herself in. The men opposite her had their gazes trained away. Had he done that? Asked them not stare? Then she glanced at him again. He was leaning back against his seat, his body relaxed, but his head turned her way.

Across the short distance, their gazes locked. He gave her a small smile, then reached into the compartment again and pulled out a box of wet wipes and carefully cleaned his hands, streaks of red-brown grime soiling the white cloths. Then he reached under his seat, opened yet another compartment, and pulled out water bottles. He handed three to the men across the way, then another to her. It was cool, and she quickly twisted the cap and drank it down, groaning because the water tasted sweet after the warm, metallic-tasting stuff she'd been drinking from canteens in the camp.

When she lowered the bottle, she looked at him, wanting another, but he shook his head, mouthing, *Two-hour flight.*

And no bathroom. She nodded her understanding and sat back, pulling the blanket high around her shoulders. If she wouldn't have looked foolish, she would have pulled it over her head to hide. She wanted to be alone. To think. But sleep was another kind of escape. She closed her eyes.

Chapter Two

*K*ara gazed at the handsome man sitting across from her. His large brown eyes crinkled at the corners, a smile not reflected in the curve of his full, sensuous lips. With his deep brown eyes and thick, curling hair, he was easily the most beautifully made man she'd ever met. The fact she was sitting across from him, seemingly the center of his attention, thrilled her to her toes.

How had she gotten so lucky? Working as a lowly intern at Kemp & Young, she escaped notice most of the time. High-powered clients strode past reception without sparing a glance toward the row of desks where paralegals and secretarial support sat.

Lucio Marroquin had arrived with an entourage of his own assistants, sweeping past the desks, setting all the women atwitter because of his movie-star appearance and great wealth. He's visiting his American holdings, *Mr. Kemp's executive assistant had whispered, although she ought to have known better. But she was a gossip without an audience, so she confided too much in Kara, because Kara was safe, the niece of Robert Young, therefore family, even if she was just an intern.*

Dressed in the practice's "uniform" of dark-skirted suit, pale *blouse, and neat black heels, with her heavy hair neatly twisted into a French braid, Kara had been shocked when Lucio's gaze clung to her as he passed, sweeping her from head to toe. The wink he gave her set her belly fluttering.*

Just a month out of college, she had been pouring herself into her work, wanting to impress because she wanted her uncle's endorsement when she applied for law school. Plus she needed the salary—her own parents were gone, and there was no one footing the bill for her education but her.

The fact she was now seated in a restaurant, a very public setting, was a huge risk. Her uncle wouldn't tolerate her dating an important client.

Tonight's venue had surprised her. Lucio had seemed to understand the need for secrecy from the start. He'd kept his glances so discreet when he happened upon her at the office that she hadn't a clue he was interested. Not until he'd caught her leaving for the day, heading toward a VIA bus stand in downtown San Antonio.

His Lexus had been parked, and he was leaning against it as she strode by, giving him a polite nod, her cheeks flushed with pleasure at seeing him. He'd offered her a lift, and then invited her to dinner before he'd deposited her at her door.

And although she knew she was risking her job, she'd agreed. The days since had run together in a happy whirl of intimate dinners and dancing. And yet he'd kissed her only once.

Tonight, she hoped for more.

* * *

A hand touched her arm, and she jerked awake. The man beside her pointed toward the windows. Lights shined below them. A carpet of city lights. They were descending toward an airport.

She straightened in her seat and combed her hair with her fingers, out of habit, until she realized the men were watching her. How long had that been going on?

Cheeks heating, she kept her gaze averted, watching as they touched down near a hangar, a man with glowing torches waving them in.

And then she unbuckled, her stomach drawing inward, her breaths shortening. Tense because she was preparing to run, if she had to, even though she knew the man beside her would be impossible to escape. Still, she refused to be a victim. Not again.

She stood, dropping the blanket.

"Put it over your head," he said, his voice even.

Kara drew a deep breath. *No, no, no.* She wasn't safe. Covering herself voluntarily was too much to ask when she didn't know what he was going to do.

His breath billowed his cheeks, and he set his hands on his hips. "Look, the hangar is ours, but we can't be sure who might be watching. Do you want to be seen?"

He said it without any inflection in his voice. If he'd softened it, cajoled her, she wouldn't have trusted him. If he'd ordered her to, she would have bolted. How had he known?

Slowly, she reached down and dragged up the blanket, giving him one last look, trying to read into his expression to know what he intended. But her fate couldn't get any worse, could it? She pulled it over her head.

Hands guided her to the doorway. Heat sank into the blanket as she hovered there, listening to his heavy tread as he stepped down. Then arms surrounded her, lifting her. He carried her.

Because she was frightened again, she held still, barely breathing, afraid she'd begin to cry because she was exhausted, nearly at the end of her strength.

A car door opened, and he lowered her, sliding her across a seat. The blanket still over her head, she scooted farther away. He nudged her feet then sat beside her. The door closed.

And then a steady pull removed the blanket. She blinked.

There was warmth in the smile he gave her. "You're going to be okay."

Afraid to believe, she only nodded.

"What's your name?" he asked, studying her face.

Kara swallowed. He really didn't know. Maybe it was best for now that she keep it that way. "Who are you?"

His eyes narrowed. "I work for a company that provides specialized services. The men in the other hut—their company hired us to retrieve them. By any means necessary."

"Your services must be very expensive."

"They are."

He glanced away, and she drew another deep breath, feeling like she had the moment the ropes around her wrists had been cut and she'd been shoved into the dirty hut—glad to put distance between her and her captors, but with a sinking sensation her situation was going to get worse. Only she hadn't landed in another squalid place. With a start, she realized she was sitting in a limousine.

First the plush interior of the helicopter, now this. He wasn't kidding about his services coming at a high price. Not something she found comforting at the moment, because she couldn't be sure money wouldn't become a factor in his rescue of her.

He rapped the window separating their compartment from the driver's. The car pulled away from the hangar, tinted glass hiding the occupants and dulling the harsh glare of the early morning sun rising above a ridge of mountains in the distance. Where the hell were they? The Sierra Madres? Could she be in Monterrey?

"I'm Sergei Gun," he said, his sharp-eyed gaze returning to her.

She opened her mouth, ready to give her name, but something stopped her.

He sighed. "It's okay. You don't know who to trust. I get it. We'll get you to the safe house. Get you showered and fed. Find you some clothes," he said, his glance dropping to her shirt. "Then we'll talk."

He held her with that dark, intelligent stare for a moment longer, and then settled back against the seat, letting out a deep breath and easing his head side to side as though relaxing too-tense muscles.

Kara continued to watch him, although her eyelids were getting heavy again. She'd catnapped in the helo, but she hadn't had a lot of rest since she'd woken after Lucio had drugged her.

Lucio. How she hated him. He'd played her from the start. She'd been so enamored, so sure he'd treated her well out of respect and affection, she hadn't realized she was being vetted. That he'd only wanted to confirm the fact she was a virgin.

Still was, she hoped, although she couldn't be sure. The moment her mind had cleared, she'd been frozen in fear, realizing she'd been stripped and dressed in someone else's clothing. She'd woken groggy in the back of a covered military transport, guarded by men wearing Mexican military uniforms, but felt no different, no soreness where it counted.

The car sped up, zipping past streets that wound higher and higher up the side of a mountain, until at last they approached a walled compound with a set of iron gates and drove through them, one other vehicle in their entourage following them.

They parked in front of a large many-doored garage. A tall, handsome man strode toward them, his long black hair tied back into a ponytail. Her type—urban, lean, moving like a cat. But her type had betrayed her, so she jerked back when he opened her door.

He bent into the doorway, his gaze noting her appearance then darting to the man beside her. A dark brow rose. "Seriously, *amigo?*"

"Didn't know what else to do with her."

"And now she's seen the compound? You couldn't at least have hooded her?"

Her rescuer shrugged. "She's my responsibility."

"Without a doubt," the striking Hispanic man said, raising his hands. "*Dios*, what a fucking mess." Then he turned on his heel and strode away, his black boots striking the cobbled drive like bullets.

"I shouldn't be here," she said, not framed as a question.

The large man beside her didn't say a word, letting himself out of the car, then striding around to her door. He held out his hand. Once she stood beside him, he ducked and whipped her up into his arms.

Gasping, Kara grabbed for his shoulders. "I can walk."

"Well, you shouldn't. Your feet are a mess."

At the mention of their condition, they began to throb. They'd been cut and bruised on the trek through the jungle, but she'd shoved her discomfort aside. She had more important things to be worried about, like where he was taking her now.

She glanced around as they walked beneath an arch into a courtyard, and through tall wooden doors that looked sturdy enough and old enough to have been around in the days of the conquistadors.

Inside, the walls were a soft ivory, the furnishings dark and massively proportioned. Warm-colored Saltillo tiles covered the floors. They walked through the entryway, then down a long, wide hallway to a door near the end. Turning, he bumped her up gently against the door, reached beneath her for the handle, and pushed open the door.

Once inside, he strode to the bed and set her on the edge of a soft comforter.

The urge to bolt upward to keep from soiling the fabric was in her, but he hovered over her, and suddenly her stomach dove to her toes. Was this, after all, what he'd been after?

His gaze raked her face and glanced away, sucking in a deep breath before raking a hand through his hair and aiming a glare her way. "I'm not going to rape you."

"So says every rapist."

"No, they don't." He closed his jaw and shook his head. "Look, we're both tired and cranky. And you need to soak those feet. There's Epsom salts under the sink. Use them. I'll be back for you at dinnertime." He turned on his heels, seemingly all too eager to escape her. "Help yourself to the clothes in the closet."

After the door slammed behind him, she jerked up, striding to it and placing her ear against the door. The sound of his footsteps stomping away, echoed from down the hall. Her shoulders sagged and she turned, leaning against the cool wood for support.

His anger hadn't frightened her one bit. It had reassured her as no amount of spoken assurances would have. He didn't mean her any harm. She was safe. For now. And at last, alone.

Kara glanced down at her body, and her lips drew away from her teeth in a feral snarl. Stepping away from the door, she stripped the shirt over her head, shoved down her skimpy shorts, and then stood still. Her own body was so dirty, her scent made her stomach roil.

She'd been kidnapped, drugged, forced into unbearable conditions without a single explanation as to why, but with one bit of knowledge that left her trembling where she stood. She couldn't go home. Ever.

* * *

Serge headed straight to the security room where he knew Alejandro would be waiting for him. Flinging open the door, he held up a hand. "Don't. Not now." Then he glanced at the monitor with the feed from the camera inside the woman's room. The expression on her face as she tore off her clothes was that of a woman who'd reached the very end of her rope. She snarled, whipping off her clothing and grinding it into the floor with her heels. Then she stood perfectly still, her expression shifting from feral anger to abject dejection, the corners of her mouth turning downward and fat tears slipping down her cheeks. In moments, she was sobbing, her arms wrapped around her middle for comfort.

"You did the right thing," Alejandro said softly. "She needs to be here. With us."

Serge was incapable of answering, he was so struck. His fists curled at his sides. His heart squeezing, his body taut, he continued to watch, listening as she sobbed. The longer he stood there, sharing her pain, his determination grew. Her beauty wasn't the thing that drew him, though he'd never seen a lovelier woman. Her face was a perfect oval, her mouth soft and plump. Her gray eyes were changeable, shifting from cold flint to a deep, moody storm-cloud gray. Her long hair, though tangled, was thick and soft, and curled to hug her shoulders. Her slender curves and neat, round breasts were also attractive, but not the reason he was ensnared.

Instead, he recalled how she'd fought him, how even when she'd been so frightened a pulse drummed at the side her throat, she'd kept her chin high. Her pride, even in the face of an immovable object—him—had been just as palpable. As frightened and vulnerable as she was, her spirit was a glorious thing he wanted to protect.

The realization of just how determined he was to save her, no matter what kind of trouble she might be in, made his skin prickle and his heart thud slowly in his chest. He'd earn her trust, learn her secrets, keep her safe.

His mission, now, was her.

About the Author

Until just a few years ago, *USA Today* bestselling erotica and romance author Delilah Devlin lived in South Texas at the intersection of two dry creeks, surrounded by sexy cowboys in Wranglers. These days, she's missing the wide-open skies and starry nights but loving her dark forest in Central Arkansas, with its eccentric characters and isolation—the better to feed her hungry muse! For Delilah, the greatest sin is driving between the lines, because it's comfortable and safe. Her personal journey has taken her through one war and many countries, cultures, jobs, and relationships to bring her to the place where she is now: writing sexy adventures that hold more than a kernel of autobiography and often share a common thread of self-discovery and transformation.

Learn more at:
DelilahDevlin.com
Twitter, @DelilahDevlin
Facebook.com/DelilahDevlinFanPage

CPSIA information can be obtained at www.ICGtesting.com
Printed in the USA
LVOW13s1421240414

383105LV00001B/32/P

9 781455 546497